the sandman presents

THE FURIES

VERTIGO COMICS
NEW YORK, NEW YORK

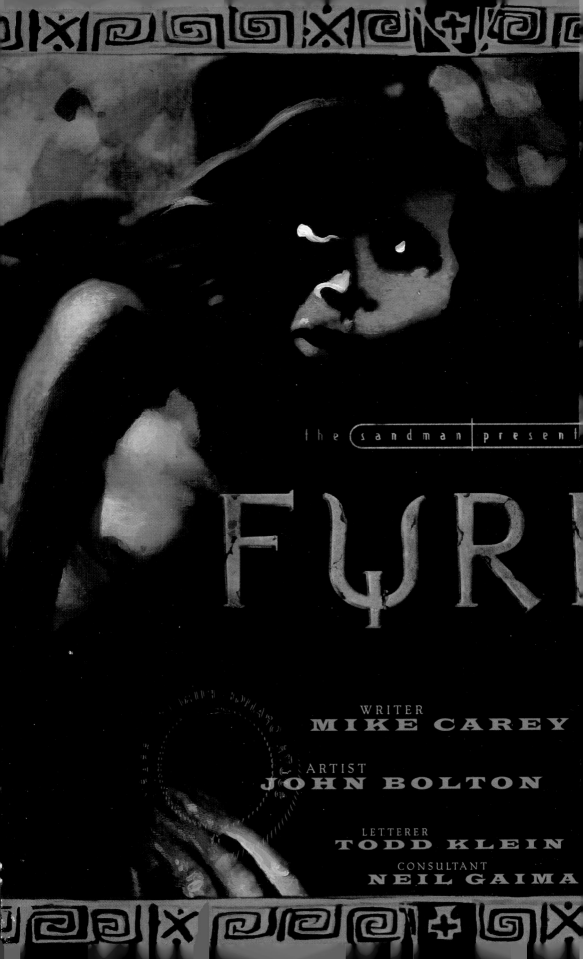

the sandman present

FURI

WRITER
MIKE CAREY

ARTIST
JOHN BOLTON

LETTERER
TODD KLEIN

CONSULTANT
NEIL GAIMA

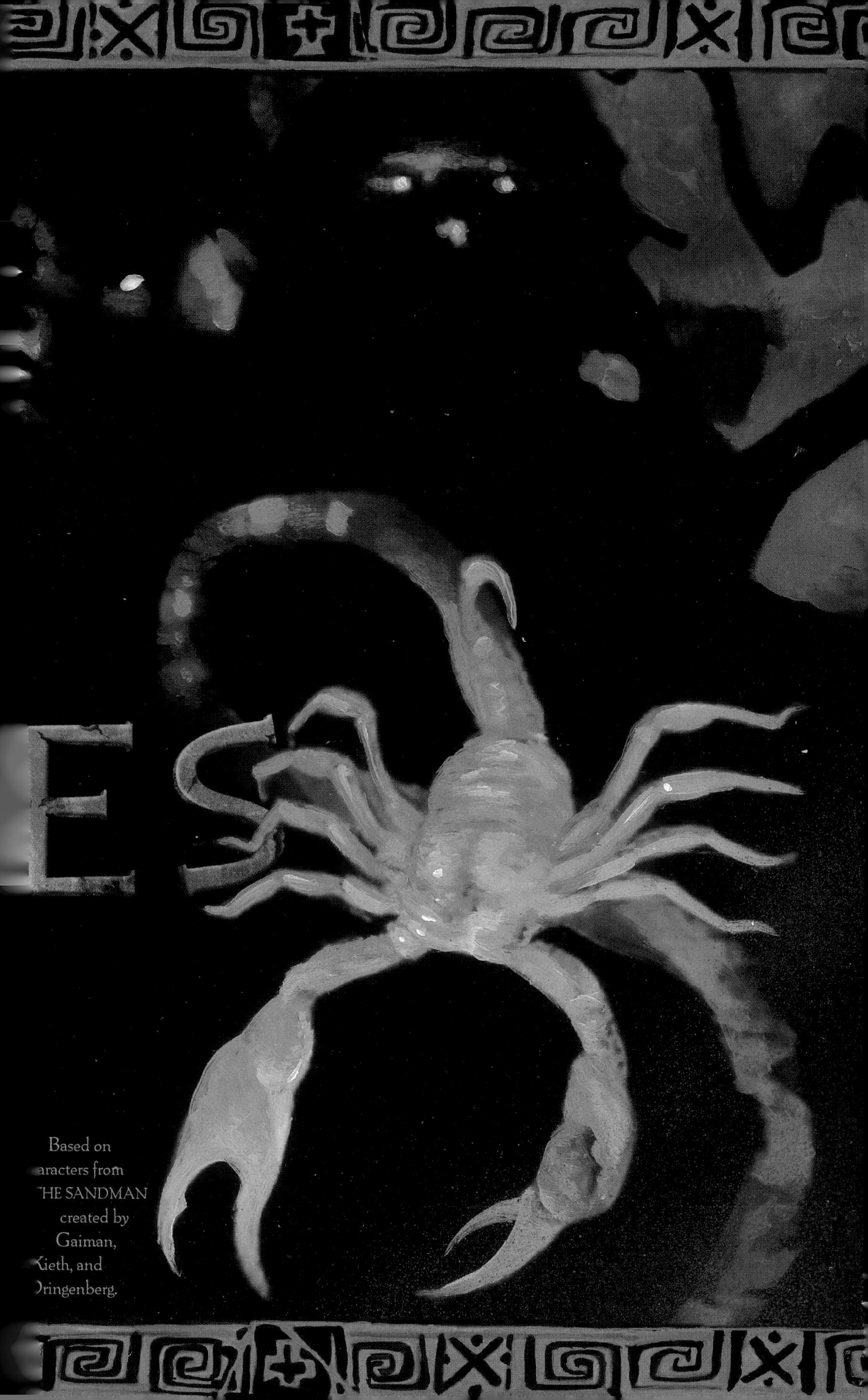
Based on
aracters from
HE SANDMAN
created by
Gaiman,
ieth, and
ringenberg.

for
PAULINE
CAREY

She got what anybody gets;
I can't help thinking
she deserved a little more

—MIKE CAREY

for
HEN

Just for being a good egg

—JOHN BOLTON

DC COMICS

JENETTE KAHN, President & Editor-in-Chief · PAUL LEVITZ, Executive Vice President & Publisher

KAREN BERGER, VP—Executive Editor · SHELLY BOND, Senior Editor · MARIAH HUEHNER, Assistant Editor

AMIE BROCKWAY-METCALF, Art Director · GEORG BREWER, VP—Design & Retail Product Development

RICHARD BRUNING, VP—Creative Director · PATRICK CALDON, Senior VP—Finance & Operations

TERRI CUNNINGHAM, VP—Managing Editor · DAN DIDIO, VP—Editorial · JOEL EHRLICH, Senior VP—Advertising & Promotions

ALISON GILL, VP—Manufacturing · LILLIAN LASERSON, VP & General Counsel · DAVID McKILLIPS, VP—Advertising

JOHN NEE, VP—Business Development · CHERYL RUBIN, VP—Licensing & Merchandising · BOB WAYNE, VP—Sales & Marketing

Cover Artist: JOHN BOLTON · Logo Design: TERRY MARKS

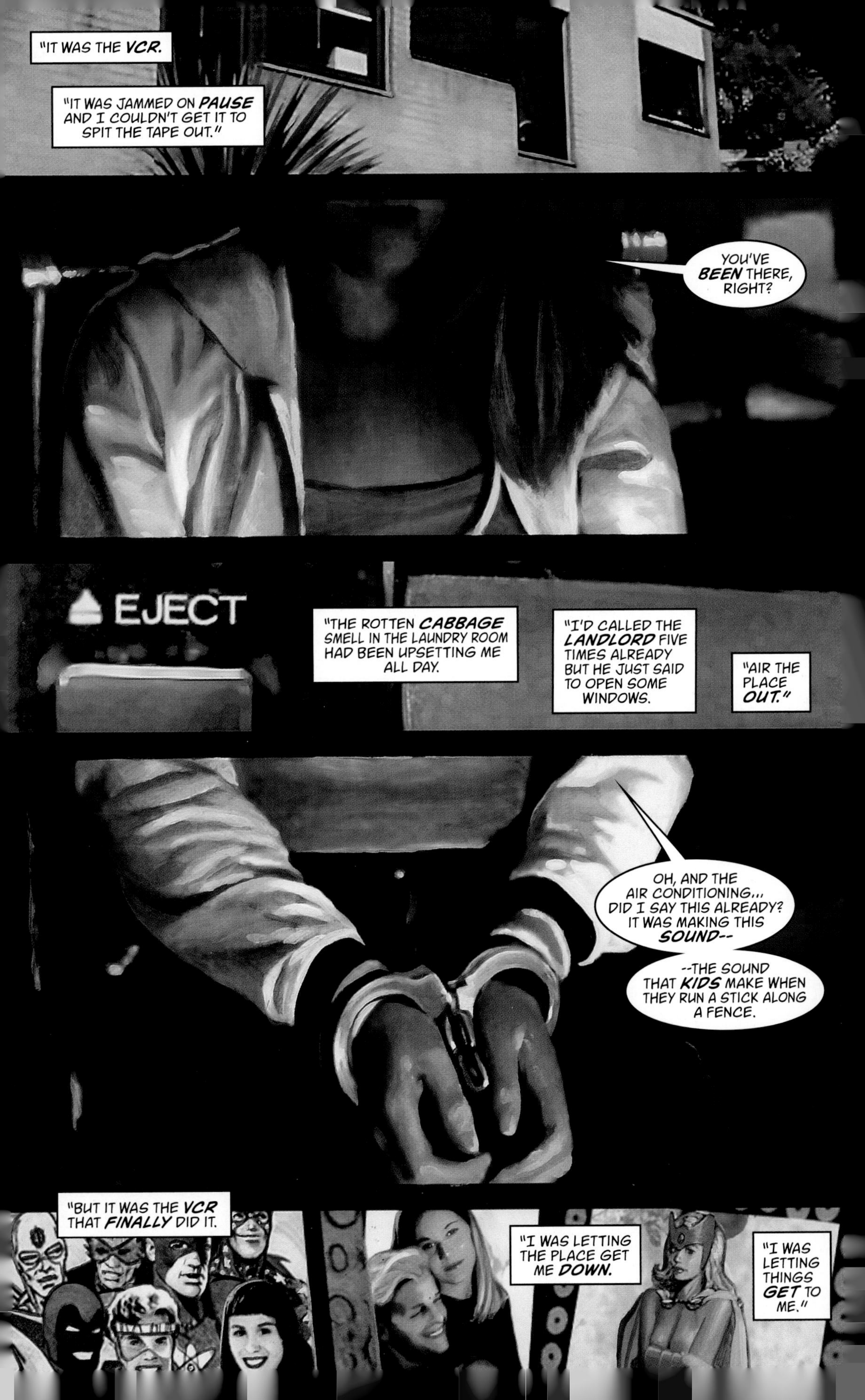
"IT WAS THE VCR.
"IT WAS JAMMED ON PAUSE AND I COULDN'T GET IT TO SPIT THE TAPE OUT."
YOU'VE BEEN THERE, RIGHT?
EJECT
"THE ROTTEN CABBAGE SMELL IN THE LAUNDRY ROOM HAD BEEN UPSETTING ME ALL DAY.
"I'D CALLED THE LANDLORD FIVE TIMES ALREADY BUT HE JUST SAID TO OPEN SOME WINDOWS.
"AIR THE PLACE OUT."
OH, AND THE AIR CONDITIONING... DID I SAY THIS ALREADY? IT WAS MAKING THIS SOUND--
--THE SOUND THAT KIDS MAKE WHEN THEY RUN A STICK ALONG A FENCE.
"BUT IT WAS THE VCR THAT FINALLY DID IT.
"I WAS LETTING THE PLACE GET ME DOWN.
"I WAS LETTING THINGS GET TO ME."

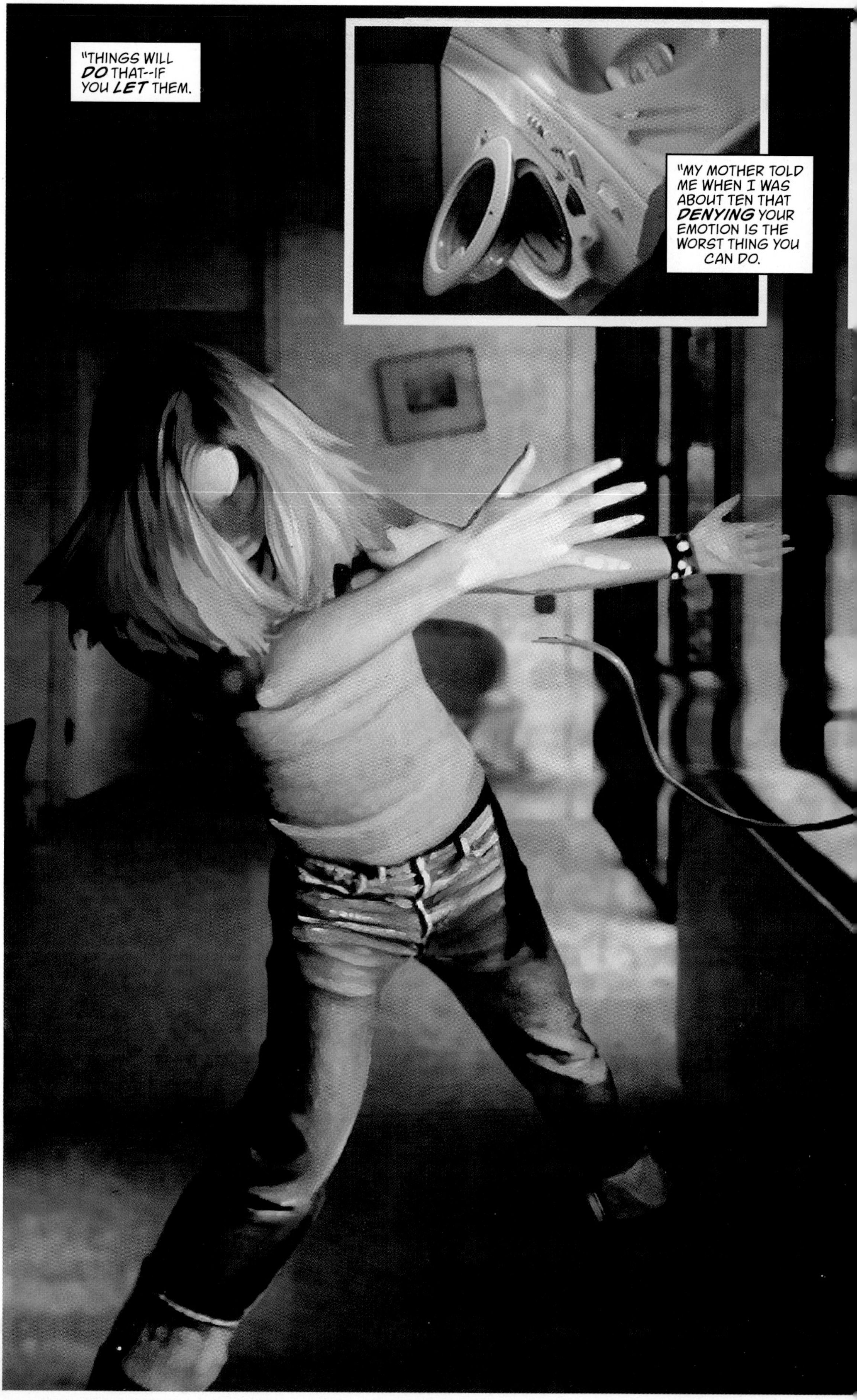
"THINGS WILL *DO* THAT--IF YOU *LET* THEM.
"MY MOTHER TOLD ME WHEN I WAS ABOUT TEN THAT *DENYING* YOUR EMOTION IS THE WORST THING YOU CAN DO.

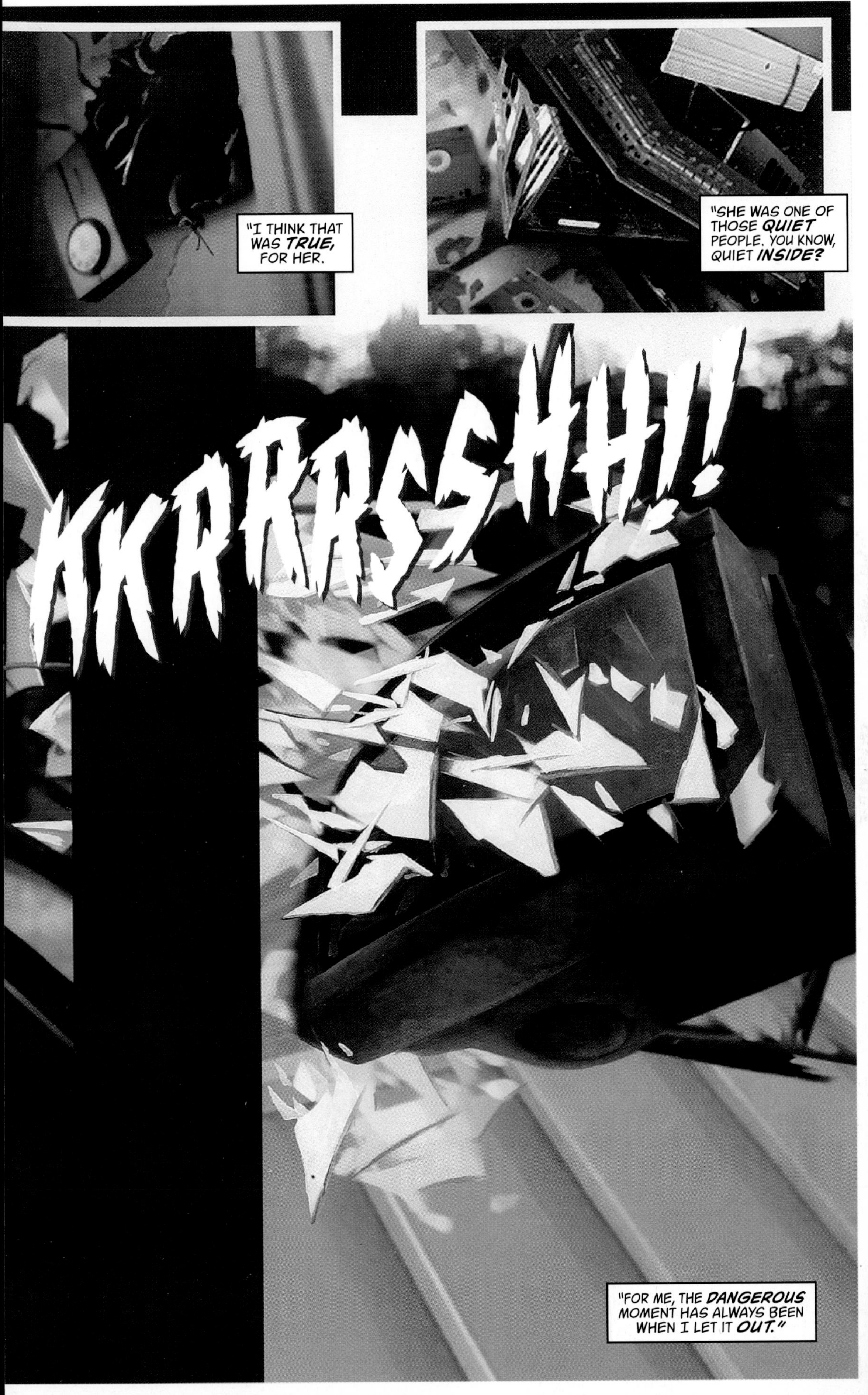
"I THINK THAT
WAS TRUE,
FOR HER.
"SHE WAS ONE OF
THOSE QUIET
PEOPLE. YOU KNOW,
QUIET INSIDE?
KKRRASSHH!!
"FOR ME, THE DANGEROUS
MOMENT HAS ALWAYS BEEN
WHEN I LET IT OUT."

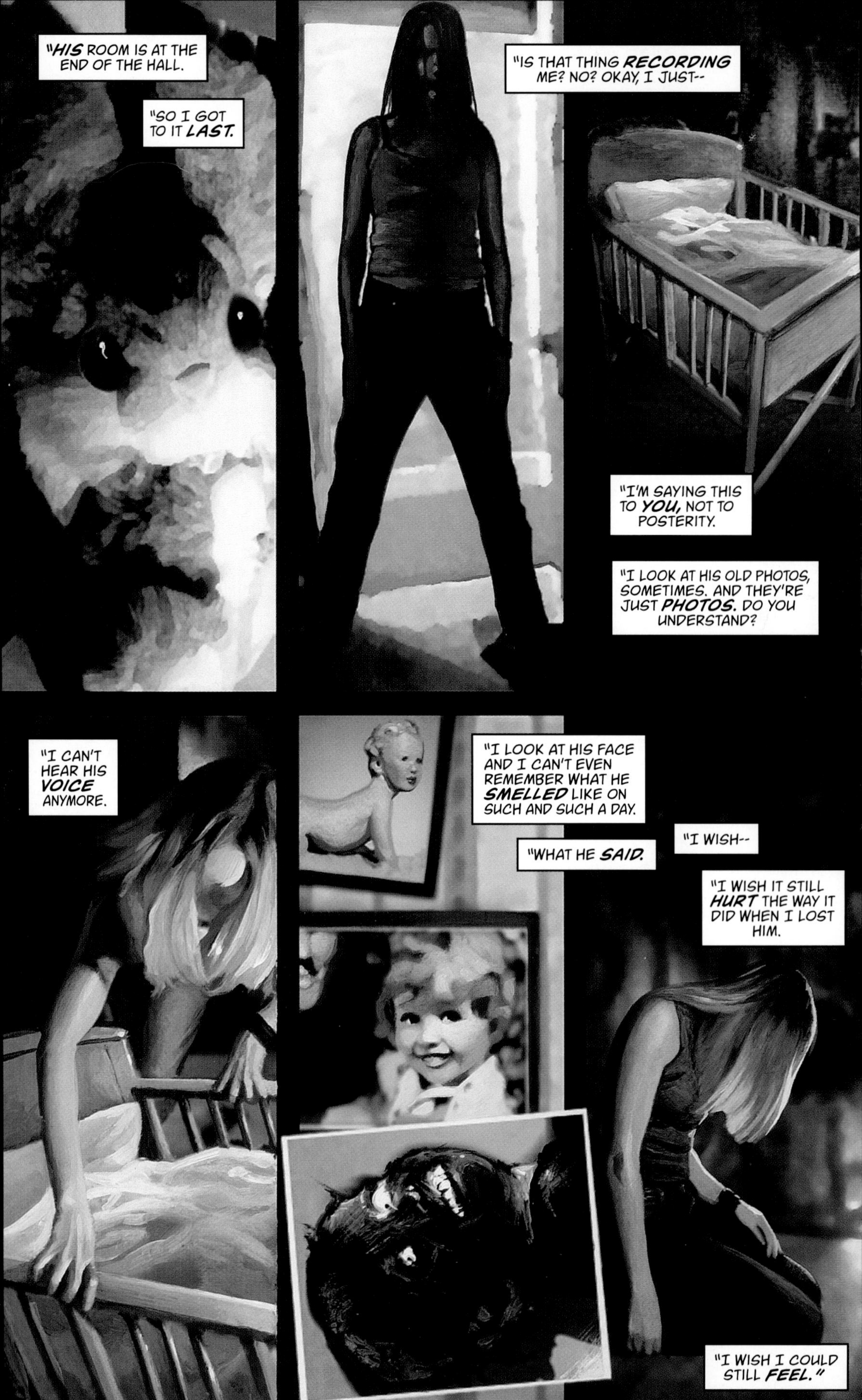
"HIS ROOM IS AT THE END OF THE HALL.
"SO I GOT TO IT LAST.
"IS THAT THING RECORDING ME? NO? OKAY, I JUST--
"I'M SAYING THIS TO YOU, NOT TO POSTERITY.
"I LOOK AT HIS OLD PHOTOS, SOMETIMES. AND THEY'RE JUST PHOTOS. DO YOU UNDERSTAND?
"I CAN'T HEAR HIS VOICE ANYMORE.
"I LOOK AT HIS FACE AND I CAN'T EVEN REMEMBER WHAT HE SMELLED LIKE ON SUCH AND SUCH A DAY.
"WHAT HE SAID.
"I WISH--
"I WISH IT STILL HURT THE WAY IT DID WHEN I LOST HIM.
"I WISH I COULD STILL FEEL."

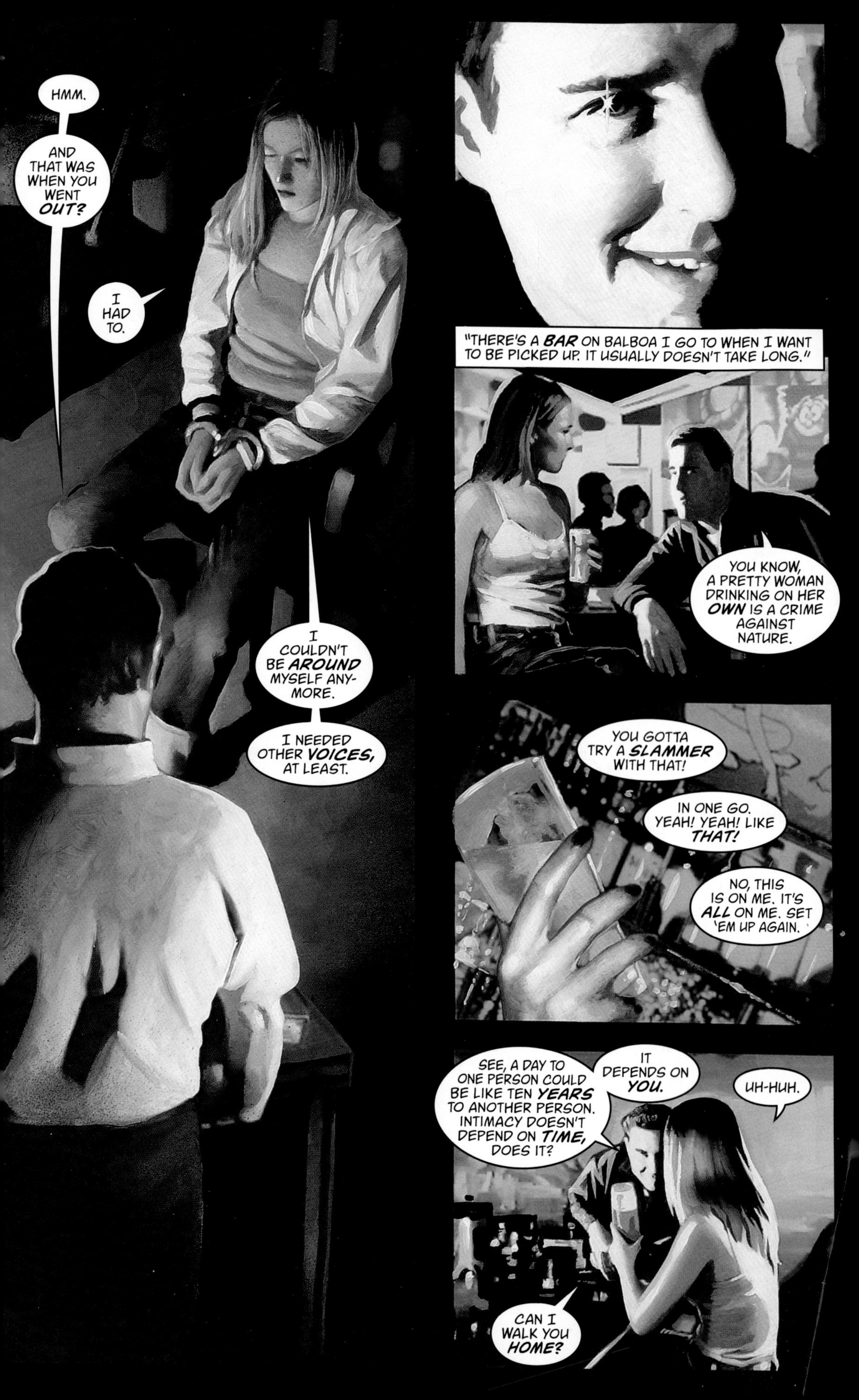
HMM.
AND THAT WAS WHEN YOU WENT OUT?
I HAD TO.
I COULDN'T BE AROUND MYSELF ANY-MORE.
I NEEDED OTHER VOICES, AT LEAST.
"THERE'S A BAR ON BALBOA I GO TO WHEN I WANT TO BE PICKED UP. IT USUALLY DOESN'T TAKE LONG."
YOU KNOW, A PRETTY WOMAN DRINKING ON HER OWN IS A CRIME AGAINST NATURE.
YOU GOTTA TRY A SLAMMER WITH THAT!
IN ONE GO. YEAH! YEAH! LIKE THAT!
NO, THIS IS ON ME. IT'S ALL ON ME. SET 'EM UP AGAIN.
SEE, A DAY TO ONE PERSON COULD BE LIKE TEN YEARS TO ANOTHER PERSON. INTIMACY DOESN'T DEPEND ON TIME, DOES IT?
IT DEPENDS ON YOU.
UH-HUH.
CAN I WALK YOU HOME?

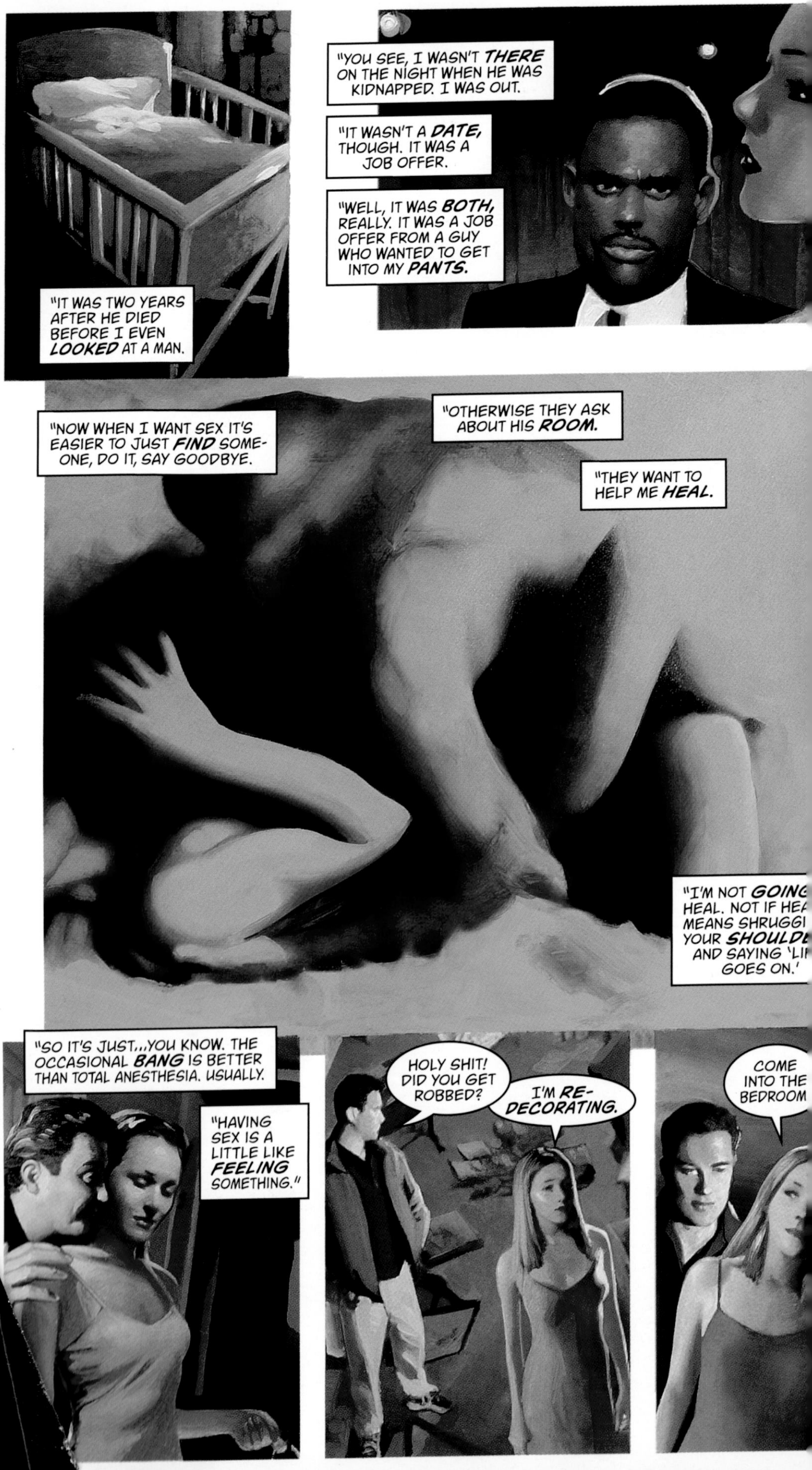
"IT WAS TWO YEARS AFTER HE DIED BEFORE I EVEN LOOKED AT A MAN.
"YOU SEE, I WASN'T THERE ON THE NIGHT WHEN HE WAS KIDNAPPED. I WAS OUT.
"IT WASN'T A DATE, THOUGH. IT WAS A JOB OFFER.
"WELL, IT WAS BOTH, REALLY. IT WAS A JOB OFFER FROM A GUY WHO WANTED TO GET INTO MY PANTS.
"NOW WHEN I WANT SEX IT'S EASIER TO JUST FIND SOME-ONE, DO IT, SAY GOODBYE.
"OTHERWISE THEY ASK ABOUT HIS ROOM.
"THEY WANT TO HELP ME HEAL.
"I'M NOT GOIN HEAL. NOT IF HEA MEANS SHRUGGI YOUR SHOULDE AND SAYING 'LI GOES ON.'
"SO IT'S JUST...YOU KNOW. THE OCCASIONAL BANG IS BETTER THAN TOTAL ANESTHESIA. USUALLY.
"HAVING SEX IS A LITTLE LIKE FEELING SOMETHING."
HOLY SHIT! DID YOU GET ROBBED?
I'M RE-DECORATING.
COME INTO THE BEDROOM

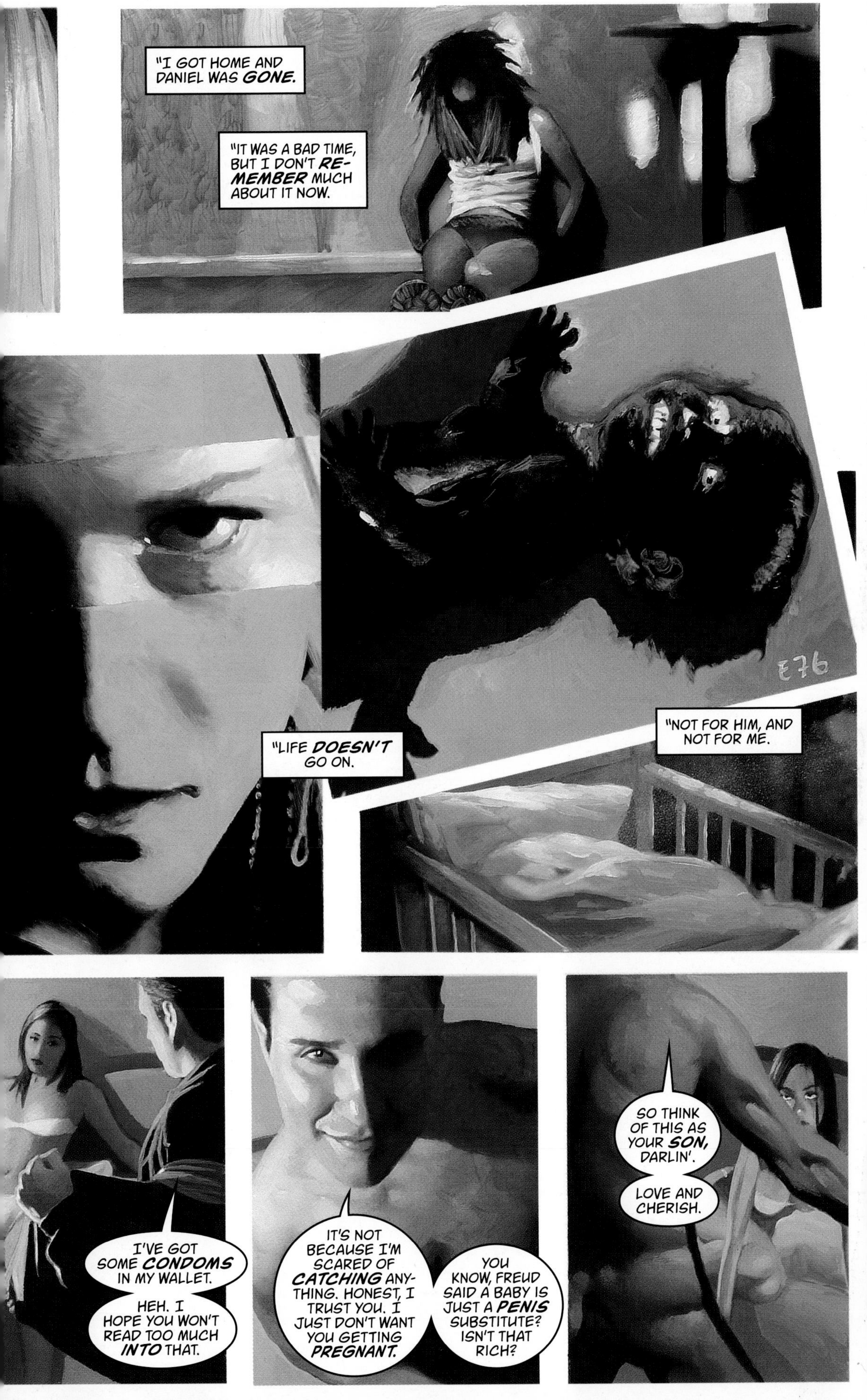
"I GOT HOME AND DANIEL WAS GONE.
"IT WAS A BAD TIME, BUT I DON'T RE-MEMBER MUCH ABOUT IT NOW.
"LIFE DOESN'T GO ON.
"NOT FOR HIM, AND NOT FOR ME.
I'VE GOT SOME CONDOMS IN MY WALLET.
HEH. I HOPE YOU WON'T READ TOO MUCH INTO THAT.
IT'S NOT BECAUSE I'M SCARED OF CATCHING ANY-THING. HONEST, I TRUST YOU. I JUST DON'T WANT YOU GETTING PREGNANT.
YOU KNOW, FREUD SAID A BABY IS JUST A PENIS SUBSTITUTE? ISN'T THAT RICH?
SO THINK OF THIS AS YOUR SON, DARLIN'.
LOVE AND CHERISH.

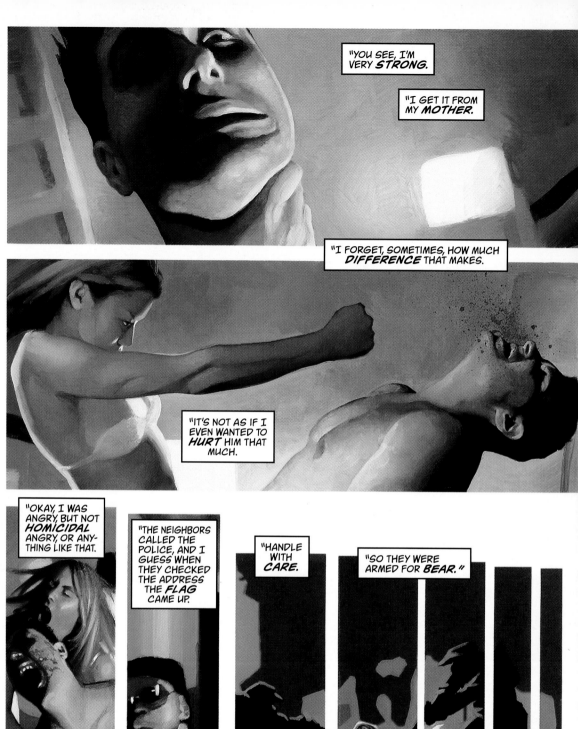

"YOU SEE, I'M VERY *STRONG.*

"I GET IT FROM MY *MOTHER.*

"I FORGET, SOMETIMES, HOW MUCH *DIFFERENCE* THAT MAKES.

"IT'S NOT AS IF I EVEN WANTED TO *HURT* HIM THAT MUCH.

"OKAY, I WAS ANGRY, BUT NOT *HOMICIDAL* ANGRY, OR ANY-THING LIKE THAT.

"THE NEIGHBORS CALLED THE POLICE, AND I GUESS WHEN THEY CHECKED THE ADDRESS THE *FLAG* CAME UP.

"HANDLE WITH *CARE.*

"SO THEY WERE ARMED FOR *BEAR.*"

"THAT'S NOT ME.

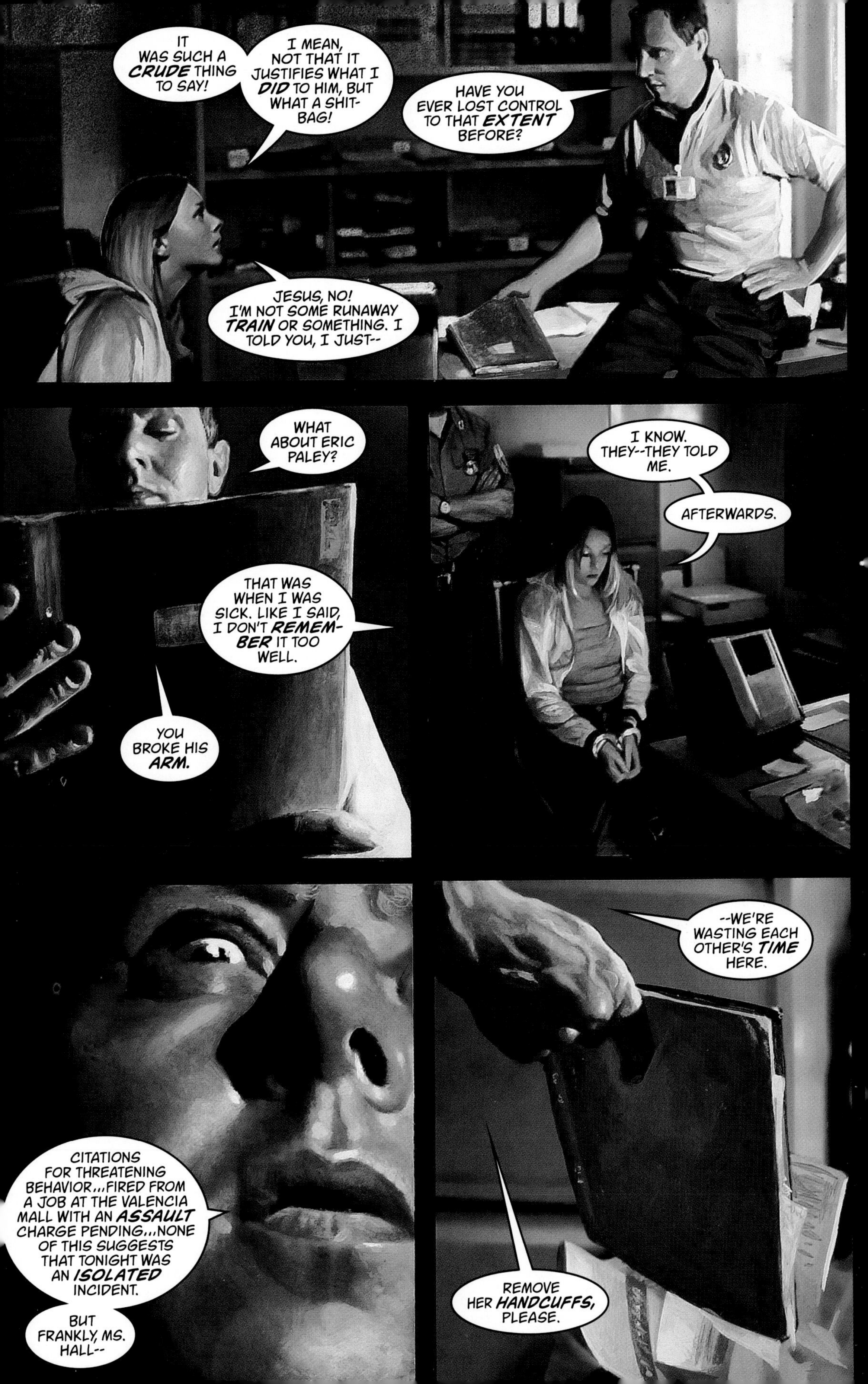
IT WAS SUCH A CRUDE THING TO SAY!
I MEAN, NOT THAT IT JUSTIFIES WHAT I DID TO HIM, BUT WHAT A SHIT-BAG!
HAVE YOU EVER LOST CONTROL TO THAT EXTENT BEFORE?
JESUS, NO! I'M NOT SOME RUNAWAY TRAIN OR SOMETHING. I TOLD YOU, I JUST--
WHAT ABOUT ERIC PALEY?
THAT WAS WHEN I WAS SICK. LIKE I SAID, I DON'T REMEMBER IT TOO WELL.
YOU BROKE HIS ARM.
I KNOW. THEY--THEY TOLD ME.
AFTERWARDS.
CITATIONS FOR THREATENING BEHAVIOR...FIRED FROM A JOB AT THE VALENCIA MALL WITH AN ASSAULT CHARGE PENDING...NONE OF THIS SUGGESTS THAT TONIGHT WAS AN ISOLATED INCIDENT.
BUT FRANKLY, MS. HALL--
--WE'RE WASTING EACH OTHER'S TIME HERE.
REMOVE HER HANDCUFFS, PLEASE.

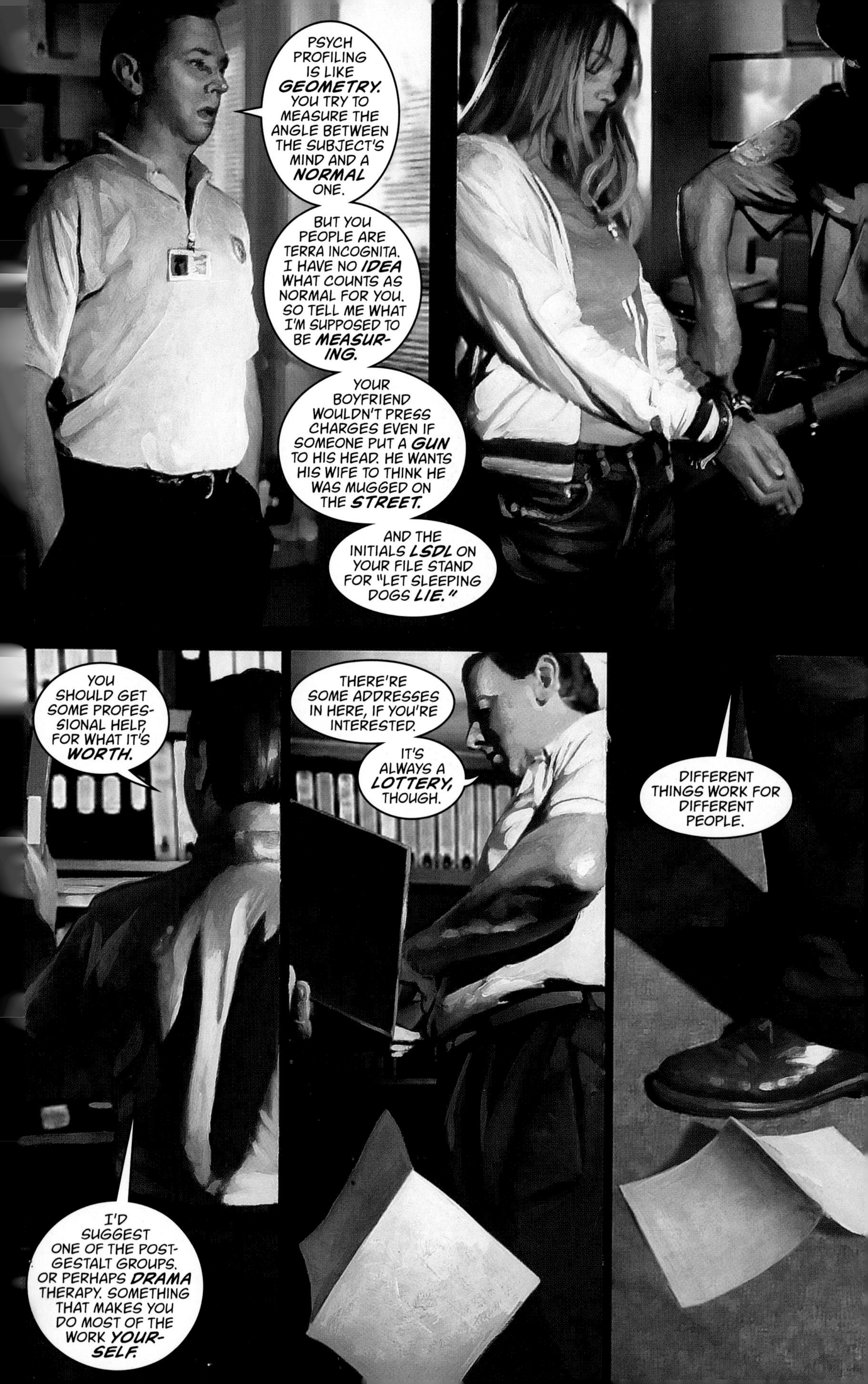
PSYCH PROFILING IS LIKE GEOMETRY. YOU TRY TO MEASURE THE ANGLE BETWEEN THE SUBJECT'S MIND AND A NORMAL ONE.
BUT YOU PEOPLE ARE TERRA INCOGNITA. I HAVE NO IDEA WHAT COUNTS AS NORMAL FOR YOU. SO TELL ME WHAT I'M SUPPOSED TO BE MEASURING.
YOUR BOYFRIEND WOULDN'T PRESS CHARGES EVEN IF SOMEONE PUT A GUN TO HIS HEAD. HE WANTS HIS WIFE TO THINK HE WAS MUGGED ON THE STREET.
AND THE INITIALS LSDL ON YOUR FILE STAND FOR "LET SLEEPING DOGS LIE."
YOU SHOULD GET SOME PROFESSIONAL HELP, FOR WHAT IT'S WORTH.
I'D SUGGEST ONE OF THE POST-GESTALT GROUPS, OR PERHAPS DRAMA THERAPY. SOMETHING THAT MAKES YOU DO MOST OF THE WORK YOURSELF.
THERE'RE SOME ADDRESSES IN HERE, IF YOU'RE INTERESTED.
IT'S ALWAYS A LOTTERY, THOUGH.
DIFFERENT THINGS WORK FOR DIFFERENT PEOPLE.

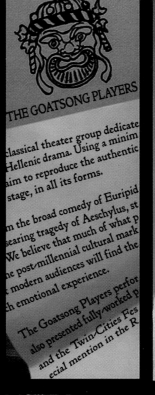

THE GOATSONG PLAYERS

classical theater group dedicate
Hellenic drama. Using a minim
aim to reproduce the authentic
stage, in all its forms,

m the broad comedy of Euripid
searing tragedy of Aeschylus, st
We believe that much of what p
ne post-millennial cultural mark
t modern audiences will find the
ch emotional experience,

The Goatsong Players perfor
also presented fully-worked p
and the Twin-Cities Fes
ecial mention in the R

TRAGEDY.

I'M SORRY?

GOATSONG. IT'S WHAT THE WORD "TRAGEDY" ORIGINALLY MEANT. COULD I **KEEP** THIS?

PLEASE, GO AHEAD.

I DON'T KNOW HOW IT GOT IN THERE IN THE FIRST PLACE. I WISH YOU **LUCK**, MS. HALL. I REALLY DO.

AND WHILE YOU'RE OUT THERE **FINDING** YOURSELF--

"--TRY NOT TO **KILL** ANYONE."

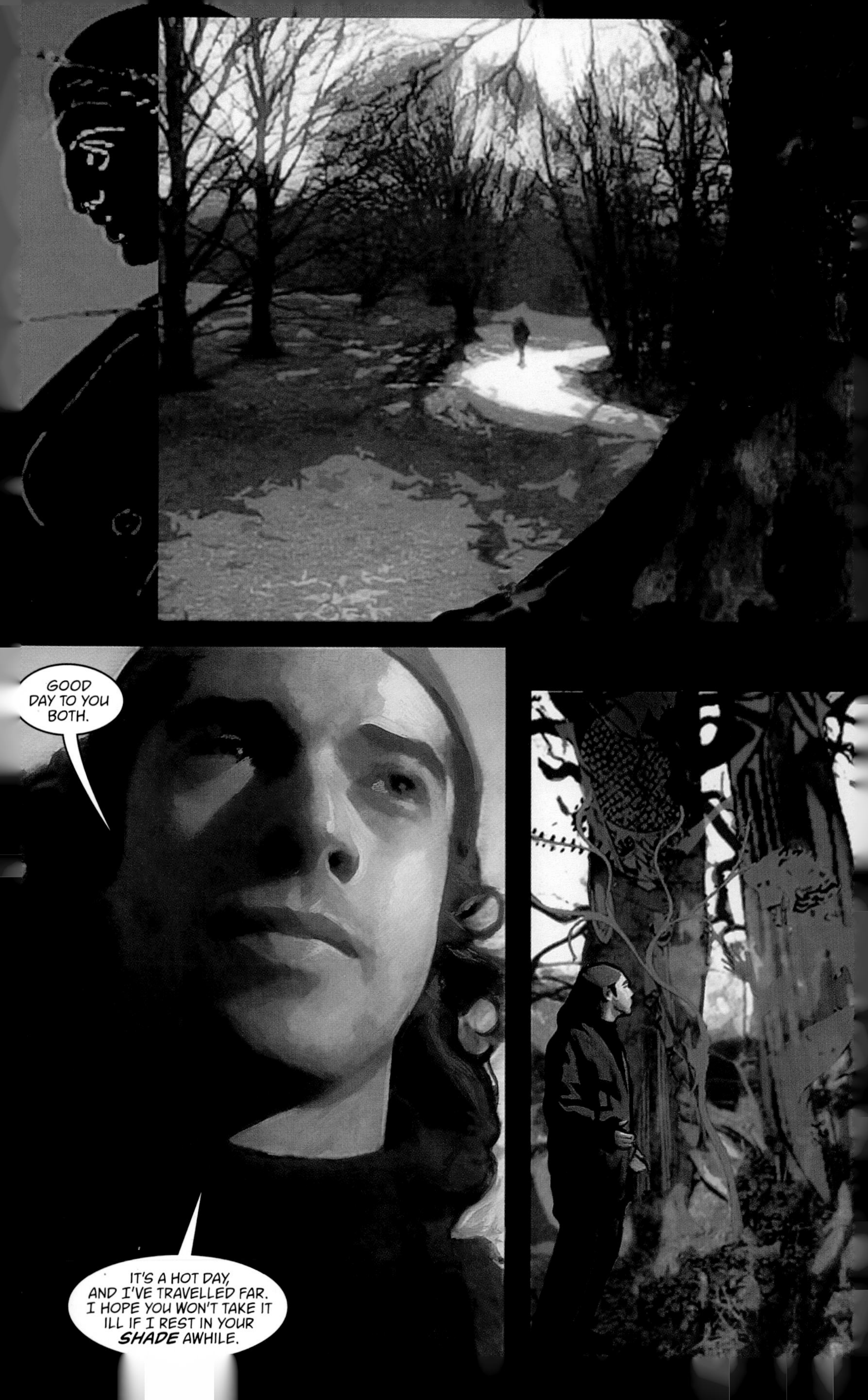
GOOD DAY TO YOU BOTH.
IT'S A HOT DAY, AND I'VE TRAVELLED FAR. I HOPE YOU WON'T TAKE IT ILL IF I REST IN YOUR SHADE AWHILE.

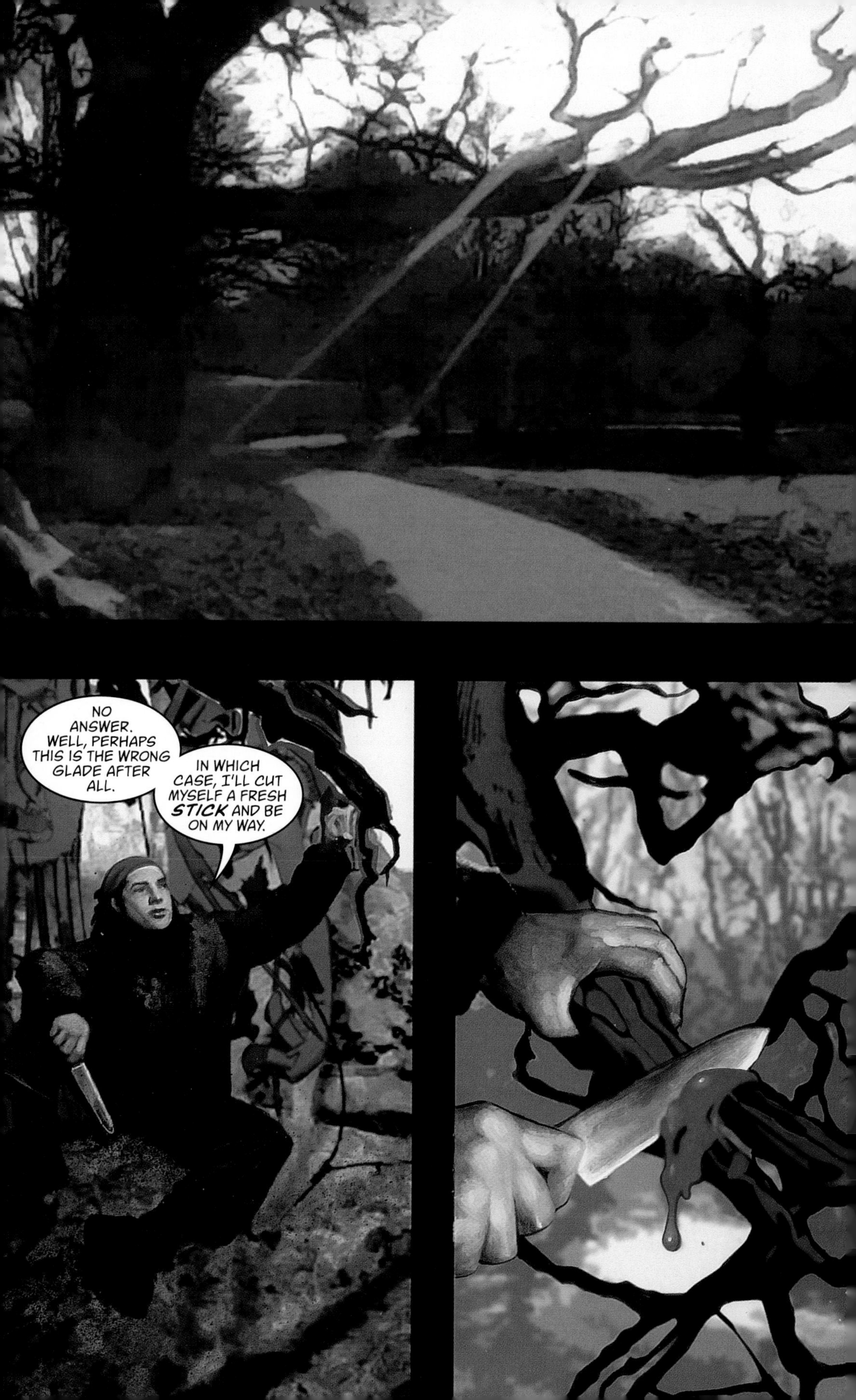
NO ANSWER. WELL, PERHAPS THIS IS THE WRONG GLADE AFTER ALL.
IN WHICH CASE, I'LL CUT MYSELF A FRESH STICK AND BE ON MY WAY.

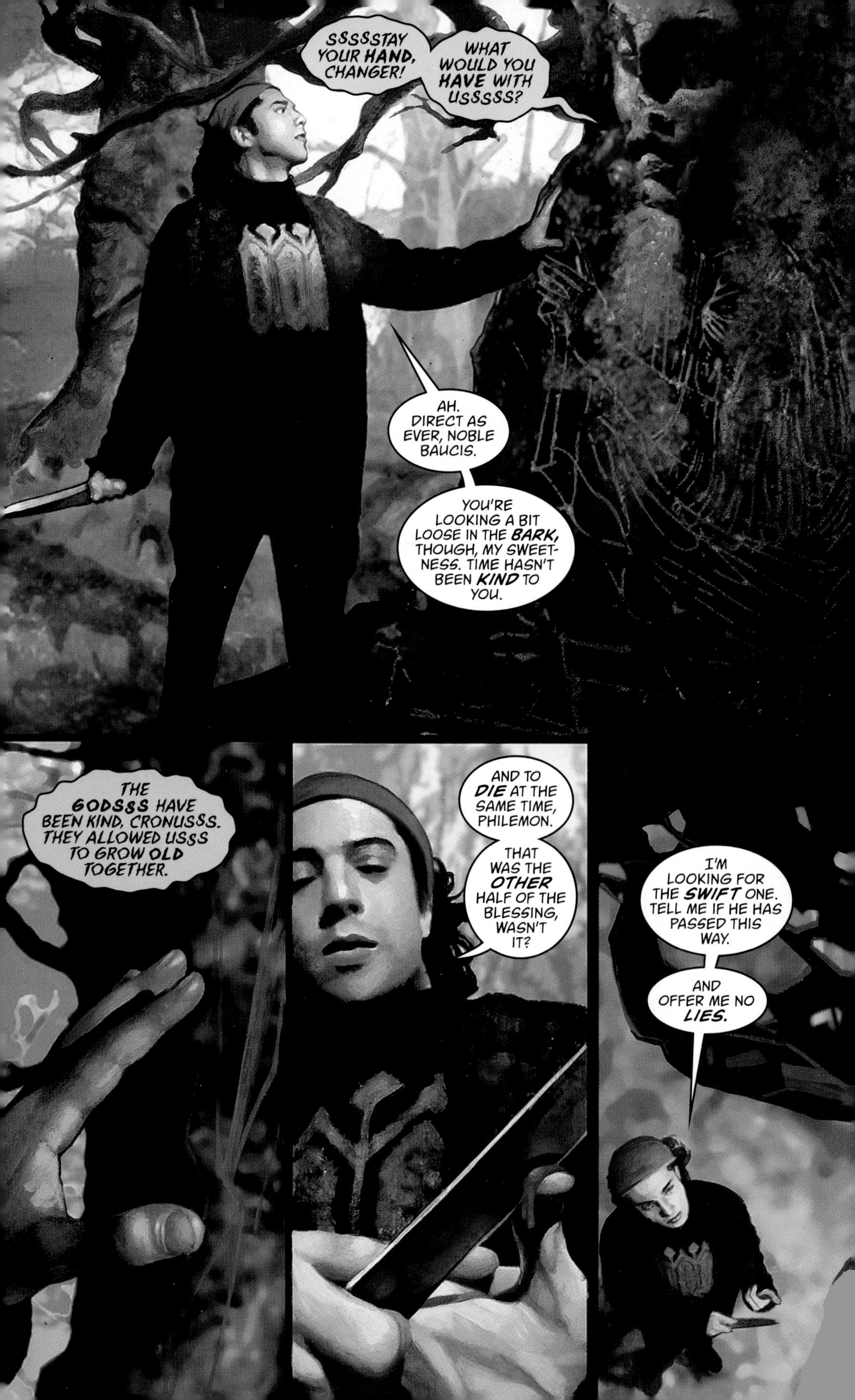
SSSSSTAY YOUR HAND, CHANGER!
WHAT WOULD YOU HAVE WITH USSSSS?
AH. DIRECT AS EVER, NOBLE BAUCIS.
YOU'RE LOOKING A BIT LOOSE IN THE BARK, THOUGH, MY SWEET-NESS. TIME HASN'T BEEN KIND TO YOU.
THE GODSSS HAVE BEEN KIND, CRONUSSS. THEY ALLOWED USSS TO GROW OLD TOGETHER.
AND TO DIE AT THE SAME TIME, PHILEMON.
THAT WAS THE OTHER HALF OF THE BLESSING, WASN'T IT?
I'M LOOKING FOR THE SWIFT ONE. TELL ME IF HE HAS PASSED THIS WAY.
AND OFFER ME NO LIES.

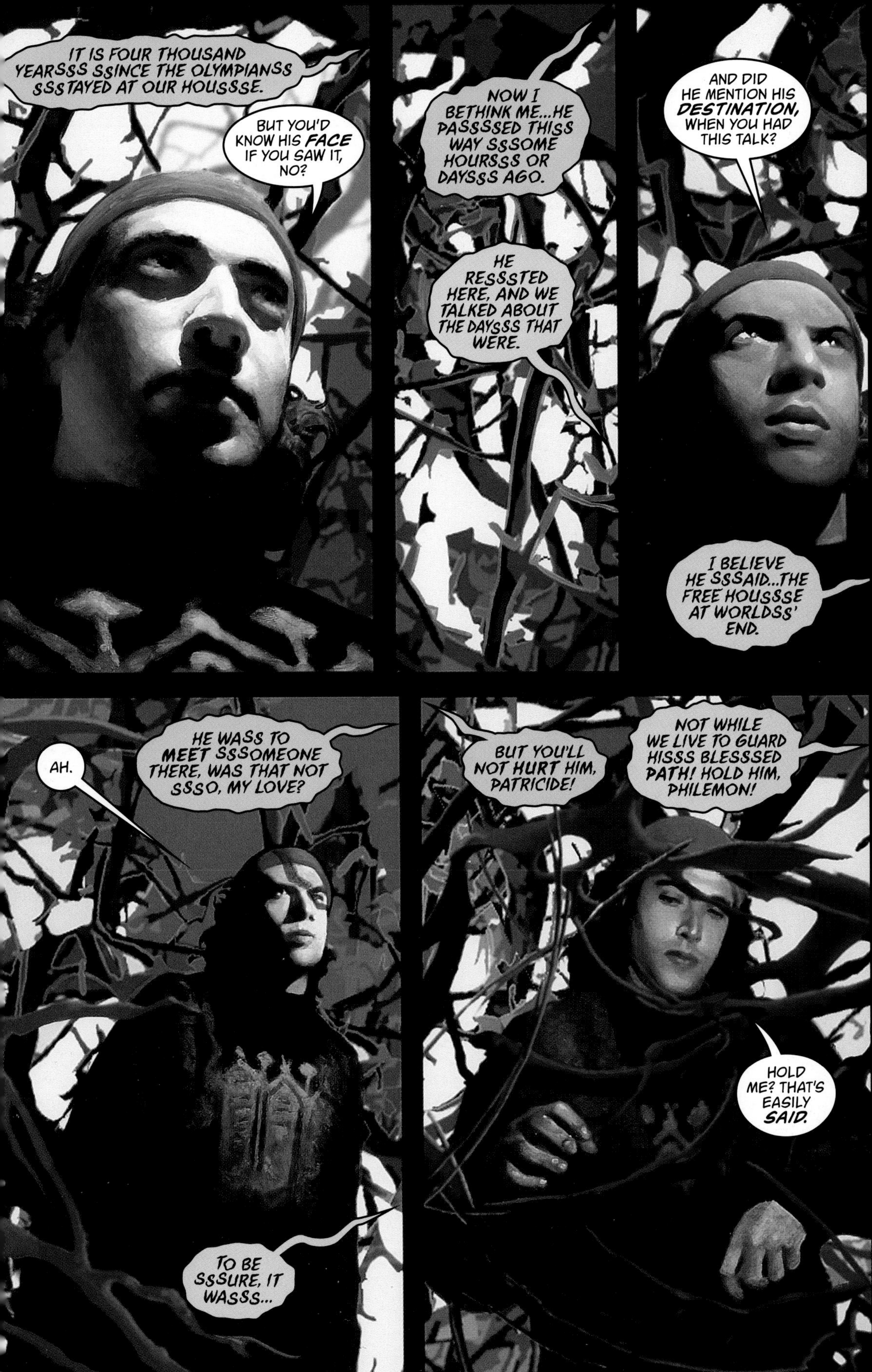
IT IS FOUR THOUSAND YEARSSS SSINCE THE OLYMPIANSS SSSTAYED AT OUR HOUSSSE.
BUT YOU'D KNOW HIS FACE IF YOU SAW IT, NO?
NOW I BETHINK ME...HE PASSSSED THISS WAY SSSOME HOURSSS OR DAYSSS AGO.
HE RESSSTED HERE, AND WE TALKED ABOUT THE DAYSSS THAT WERE.
AND DID HE MENTION HIS DESTINATION, WHEN YOU HAD THIS TALK?
I BELIEVE HE SSSAID...THE FREE HOUSSSE AT WORLDSS' END.
HE WASS TO MEET SSSOMEONE THERE, WAS THAT NOT SSSO, MY LOVE?
AH.
TO BE SSSURE, IT WASSS...
BUT YOU'LL NOT HURT HIM, PATRICIDE!
NOT WHILE WE LIVE TO GUARD HISSS BLESSSED PATH! HOLD HIM, PHILEMON!
HOLD ME? THAT'S EASILY SAID.

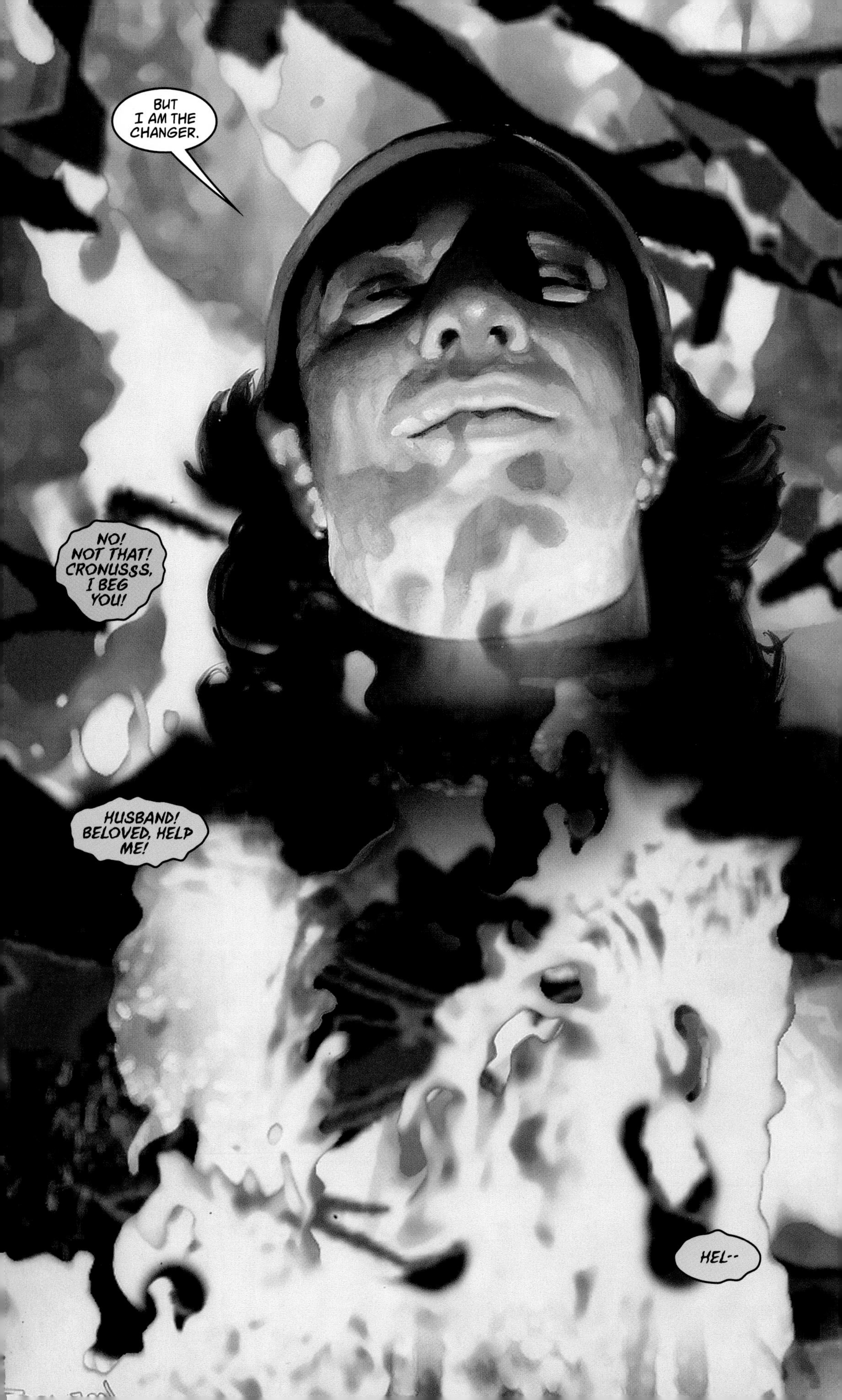
BUT I AM THE CHANGER.
NO! NOT THAT! CRONUSSS, I BEG YOU!
HUSBAND! BELOVED, HELP ME!
HEL--

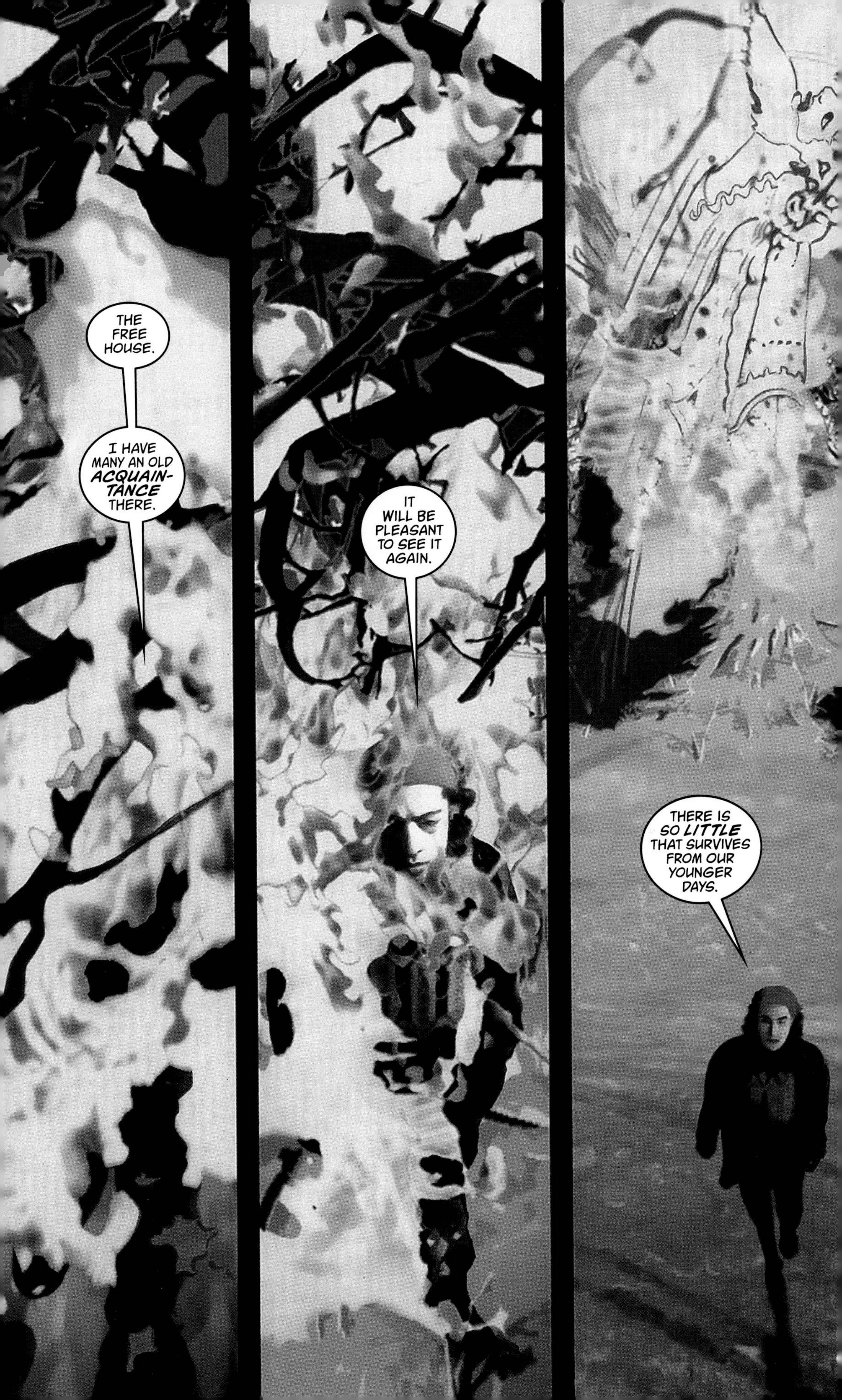
THE FREE HOUSE.
I HAVE MANY AN OLD ACQUAINTANCE THERE.
IT WILL BE PLEASANT TO SEE IT AGAIN.
THERE IS SO LITTLE THAT SURVIVES FROM OUR YOUNGER DAYS.

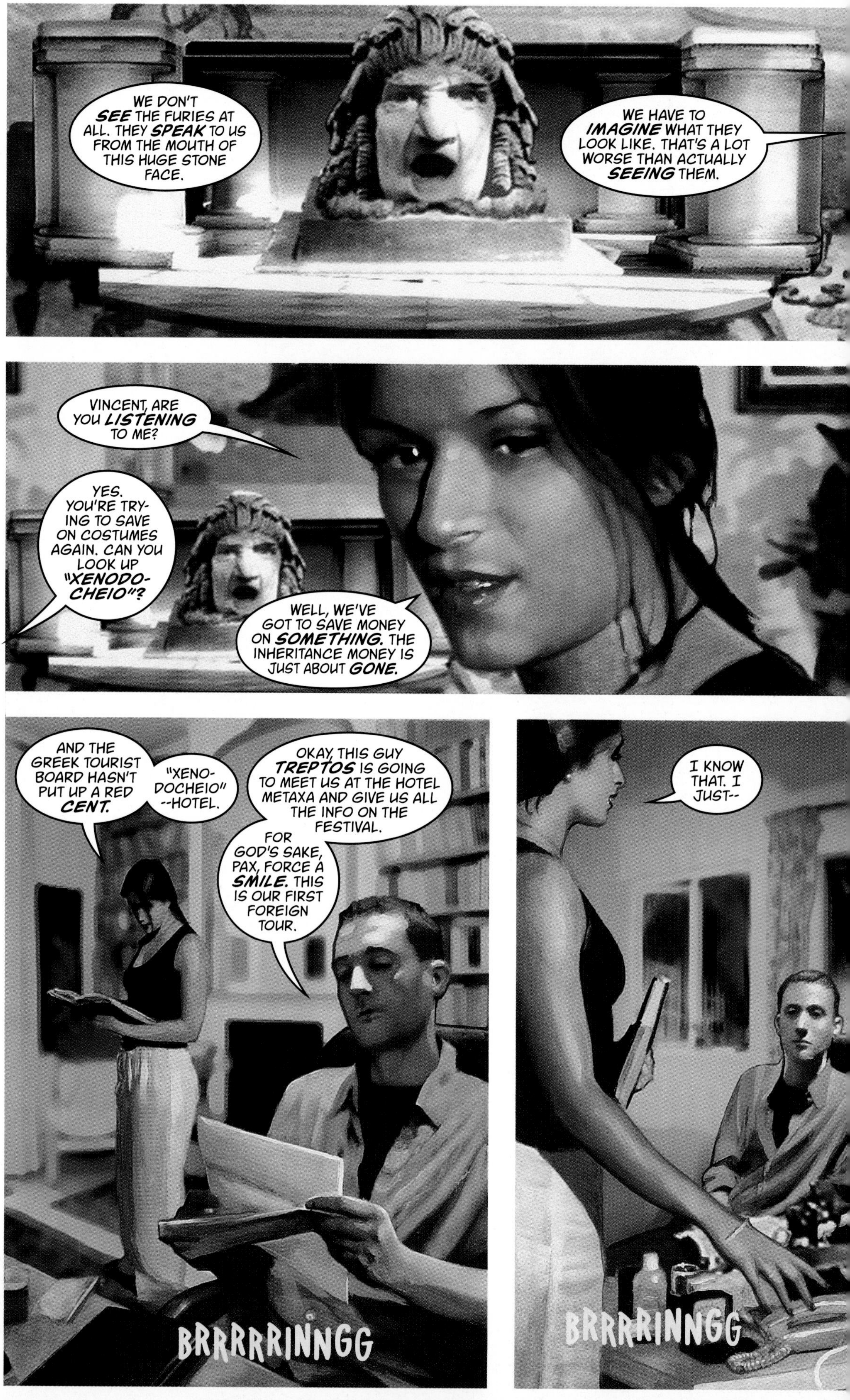
WE DON'T SEE THE FURIES AT ALL. THEY SPEAK TO US FROM THE MOUTH OF THIS HUGE STONE FACE.
WE HAVE TO IMAGINE WHAT THEY LOOK LIKE. THAT'S A LOT WORSE THAN ACTUALLY SEEING THEM.
VINCENT, ARE YOU LISTENING TO ME?
YES. YOU'RE TRYING TO SAVE ON COSTUMES AGAIN. CAN YOU LOOK UP "XENODOCHEIO"?
WELL, WE'VE GOT TO SAVE MONEY ON SOMETHING. THE INHERITANCE MONEY IS JUST ABOUT GONE.
AND THE GREEK TOURIST BOARD HASN'T PUT UP A RED CENT.
"XENODOCHEIO" --HOTEL.
OKAY, THIS GUY TREPTOS IS GOING TO MEET US AT THE HOTEL METAXA AND GIVE US ALL THE INFO ON THE FESTIVAL.
FOR GOD'S SAKE, PAX, FORCE A SMILE. THIS IS OUR FIRST FOREIGN TOUR.
BRRRRRINNGG
I KNOW THAT. I JUST--
BRRRRINNGG

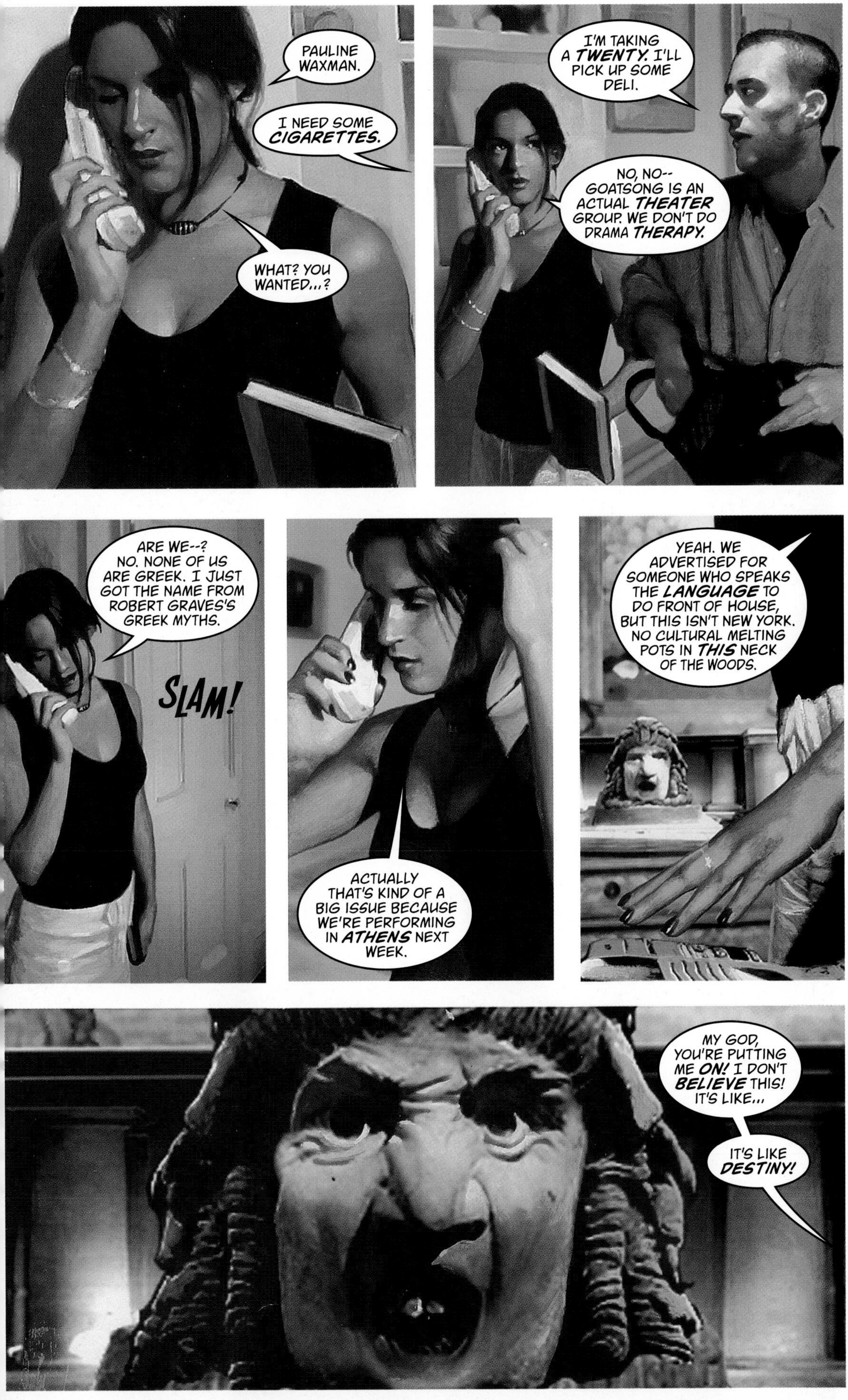
PAULINE WAXMAN.
I NEED SOME CIGARETTES.
WHAT? YOU WANTED...?
I'M TAKING A TWENTY. I'LL PICK UP SOME DELI.
NO, NO-- GOATSONG IS AN ACTUAL THEATER GROUP. WE DON'T DO DRAMA THERAPY.
ARE WE--? NO. NONE OF US ARE GREEK. I JUST GOT THE NAME FROM ROBERT GRAVES'S GREEK MYTHS.
SLAM!
ACTUALLY THAT'S KIND OF A BIG ISSUE BECAUSE WE'RE PERFORMING IN ATHENS NEXT WEEK.
YEAH. WE ADVERTISED FOR SOMEONE WHO SPEAKS THE LANGUAGE TO DO FRONT OF HOUSE, BUT THIS ISN'T NEW YORK. NO CULTURAL MELTING POTS IN THIS NECK OF THE WOODS.
MY GOD, YOU'RE PUTTING ME ON! I DON'T BELIEVE THIS! IT'S LIKE...
IT'S LIKE DESTINY!

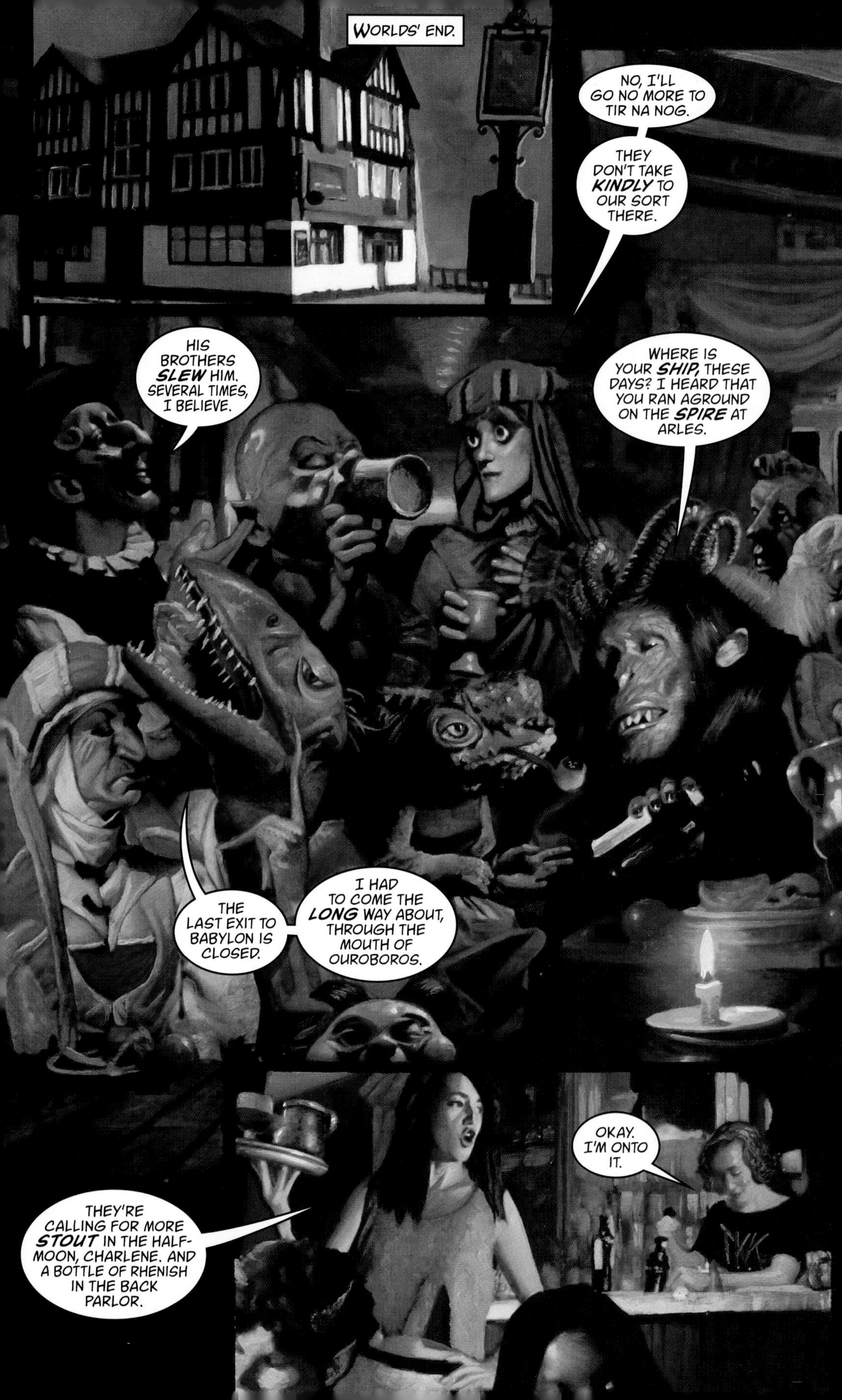
WORLDS' END.
NO, I'LL GO NO MORE TO TIR NA NOG.
THEY DON'T TAKE KINDLY TO OUR SORT THERE.
HIS BROTHERS SLEW HIM. SEVERAL TIMES, I BELIEVE.
WHERE IS YOUR SHIP, THESE DAYS? I HEARD THAT YOU RAN AGROUND ON THE SPIRE AT ARLES.
THE LAST EXIT TO BABYLON IS CLOSED.
I HAD TO COME THE LONG WAY ABOUT, THROUGH THE MOUTH OF OUROBOROS.
OKAY. I'M ONTO IT.
THEY'RE CALLING FOR MORE STOUT IN THE HALF-MOON, CHARLENE. AND A BOTTLE OF RHENISH IN THE BACK PARLOR.

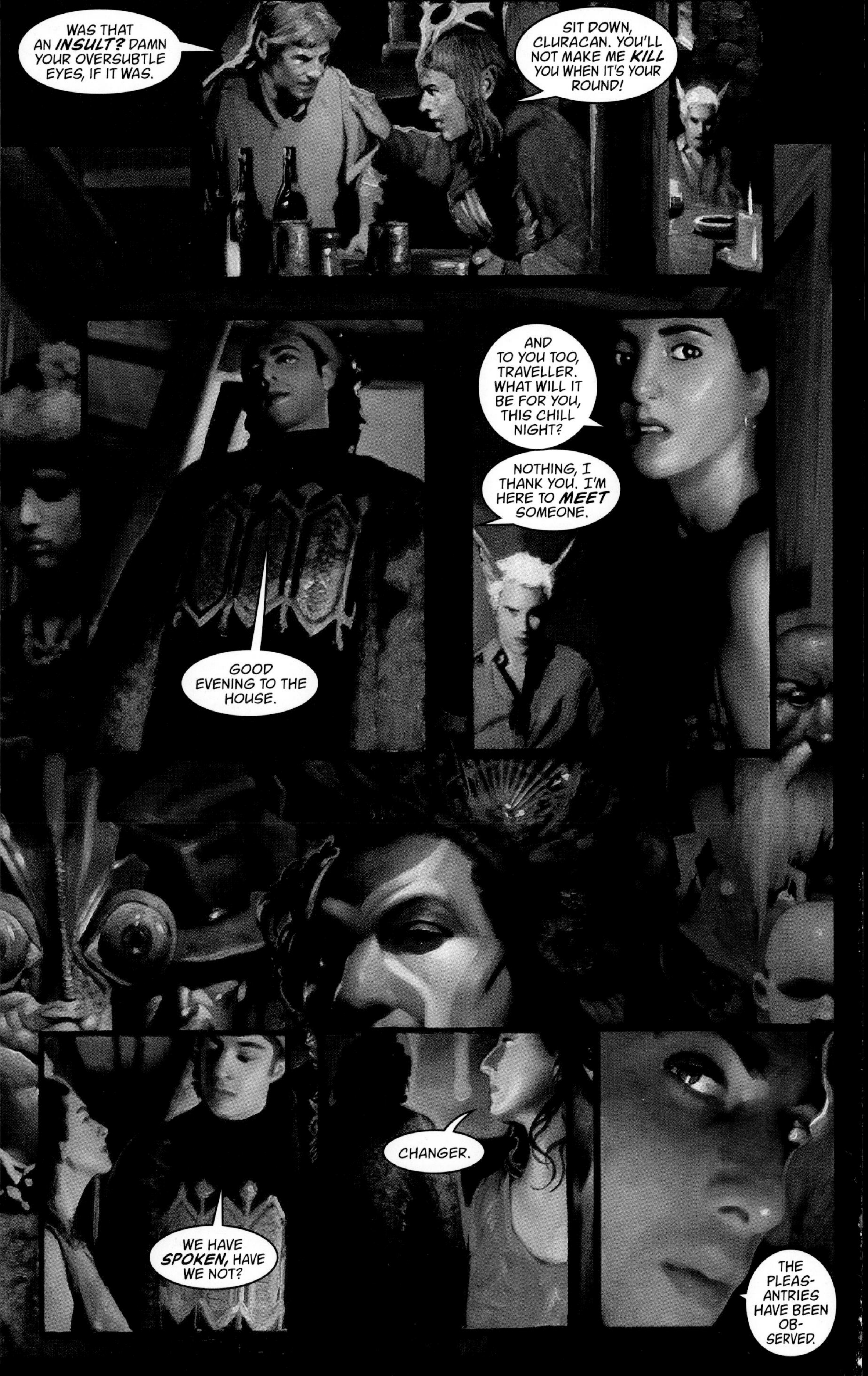
WAS THAT AN *INSULT?* DAMN YOUR OVERSUBTLE EYES, IF IT WAS.
SIT DOWN, CLURACAN. YOU'LL NOT MAKE ME *KILL* YOU WHEN IT'S YOUR ROUND!
GOOD EVENING TO THE HOUSE.
AND TO YOU TOO, TRAVELLER. WHAT WILL IT BE FOR YOU, THIS CHILL NIGHT?
NOTHING, I THANK YOU. I'M HERE TO *MEET* SOMEONE.
WE HAVE *SPOKEN,* HAVE WE NOT?
CHANGER.
THE PLEAS-ANTRIES HAVE BEEN OB-SERVED.

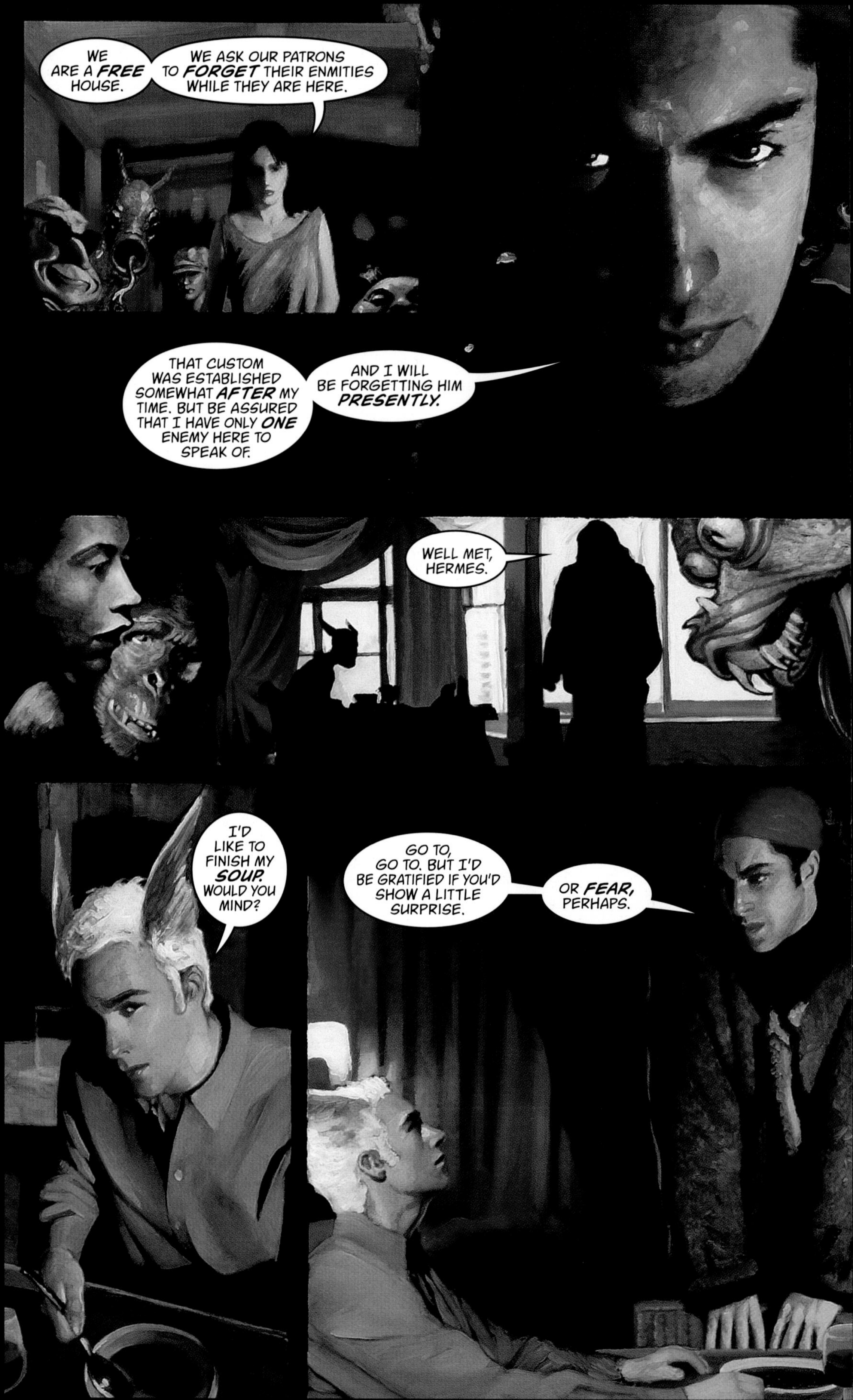
WE ARE A FREE HOUSE.
WE ASK OUR PATRONS TO FORGET THEIR ENMITIES WHILE THEY ARE HERE.
THAT CUSTOM WAS ESTABLISHED SOMEWHAT AFTER MY TIME. BUT BE ASSURED THAT I HAVE ONLY ONE ENEMY HERE TO SPEAK OF.
AND I WILL BE FORGETTING HIM PRESENTLY.
WELL MET, HERMES.
I'D LIKE TO FINISH MY SOUP. WOULD YOU MIND?
GO TO, GO TO. BUT I'D BE GRATIFIED IF YOU'D SHOW A LITTLE SURPRISE.
OR FEAR, PERHAPS.

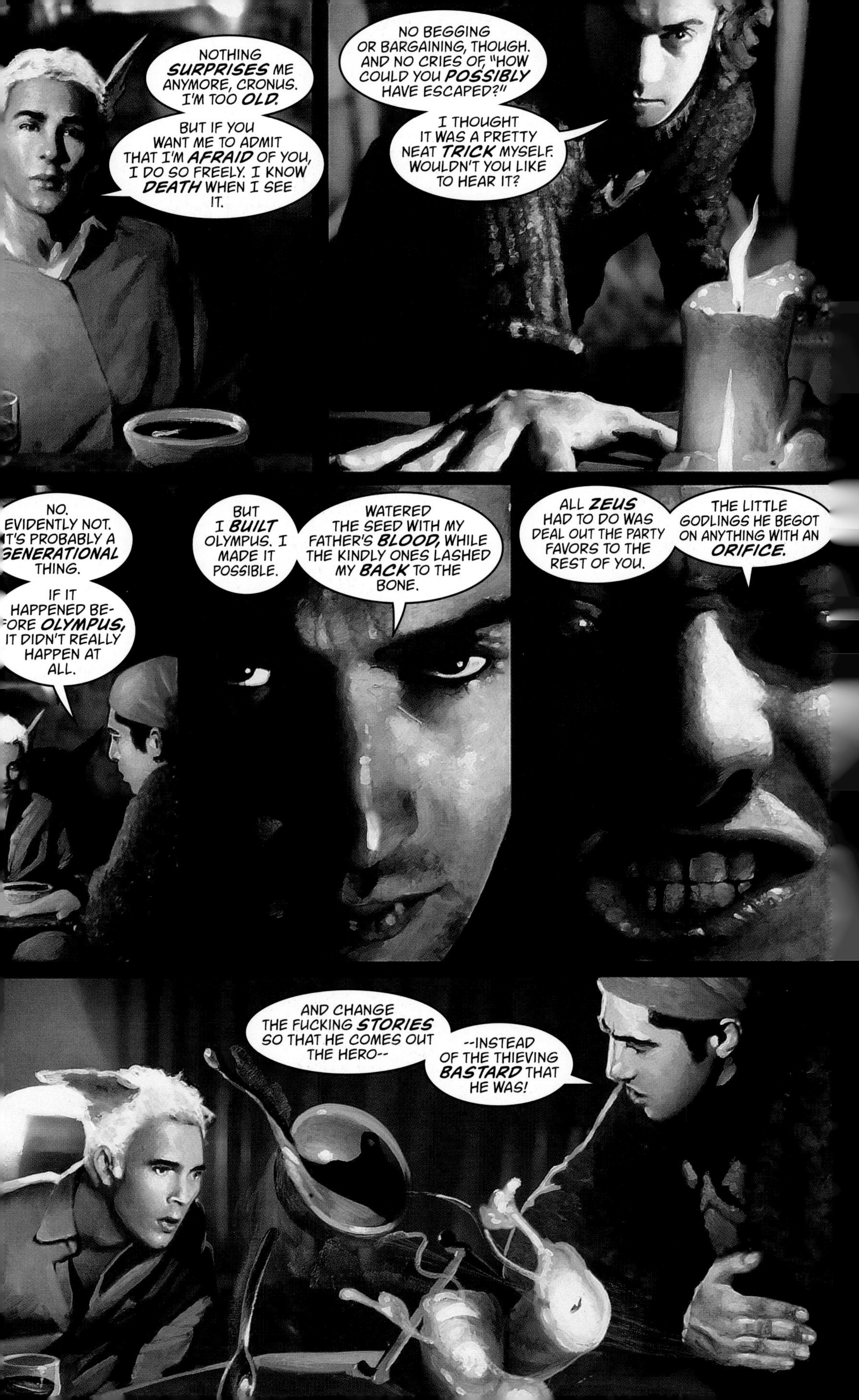
NOTHING SURPRISES ME ANYMORE, CRONUS. I'M TOO OLD.
BUT IF YOU WANT ME TO ADMIT THAT I'M AFRAID OF YOU, I DO SO FREELY. I KNOW DEATH WHEN I SEE IT.
NO BEGGING OR BARGAINING, THOUGH. AND NO CRIES OF, "HOW COULD YOU POSSIBLY HAVE ESCAPED?"
I THOUGHT IT WAS A PRETTY NEAT TRICK MYSELF. WOULDN'T YOU LIKE TO HEAR IT?
NO. EVIDENTLY NOT. IT'S PROBABLY A GENERATIONAL THING.
IF IT HAPPENED BEFORE OLYMPUS, IT DIDN'T REALLY HAPPEN AT ALL.
BUT I BUILT OLYMPUS. I MADE IT POSSIBLE.
WATERED THE SEED WITH MY FATHER'S BLOOD, WHILE THE KINDLY ONES LASHED MY BACK TO THE BONE.
ALL ZEUS HAD TO DO WAS DEAL OUT THE PARTY FAVORS TO THE REST OF YOU.
THE LITTLE GODLINGS HE BEGOT ON ANYTHING WITH AN ORIFICE.
AND CHANGE THE FUCKING STORIES SO THAT HE COMES OUT THE HERO--
--INSTEAD OF THE THIEVING BASTARD THAT HE WAS!

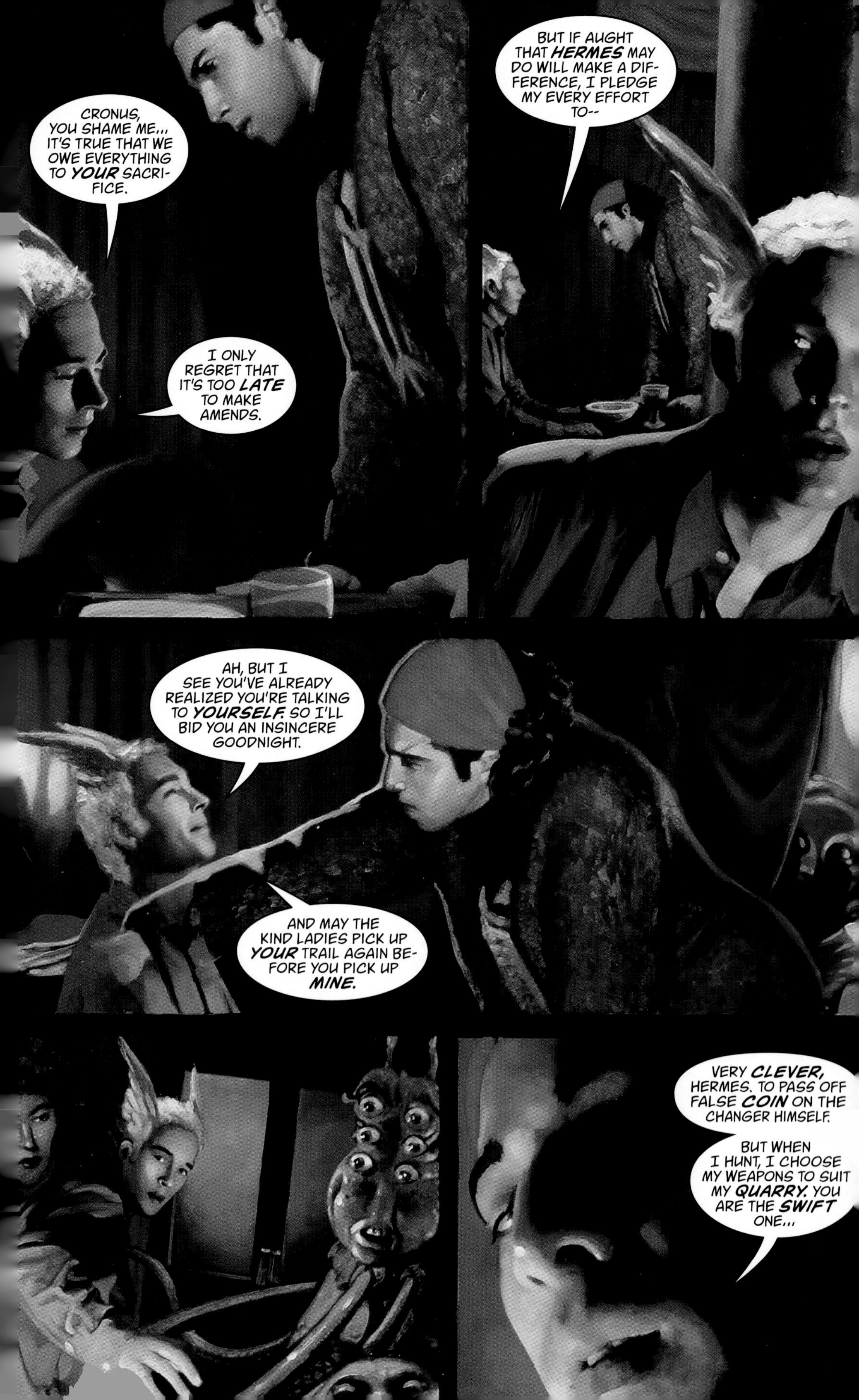
CRONUS, YOU SHAME ME... IT'S TRUE THAT WE OWE EVERYTHING TO YOUR SACRIFICE.
I ONLY REGRET THAT IT'S TOO LATE TO MAKE AMENDS.
BUT IF AUGHT THAT HERMES MAY DO WILL MAKE A DIFFERENCE, I PLEDGE MY EVERY EFFORT TO--
AH, BUT I SEE YOU'VE ALREADY REALIZED YOU'RE TALKING TO YOURSELF. SO I'LL BID YOU AN INSINCERE GOODNIGHT.
AND MAY THE KIND LADIES PICK UP YOUR TRAIL AGAIN BEFORE YOU PICK UP MINE.
VERY CLEVER, HERMES. TO PASS OFF FALSE COIN ON THE CHANGER HIMSELF.
BUT WHEN I HUNT, I CHOOSE MY WEAPONS TO SUIT MY QUARRY. YOU ARE THE SWIFT ONE...

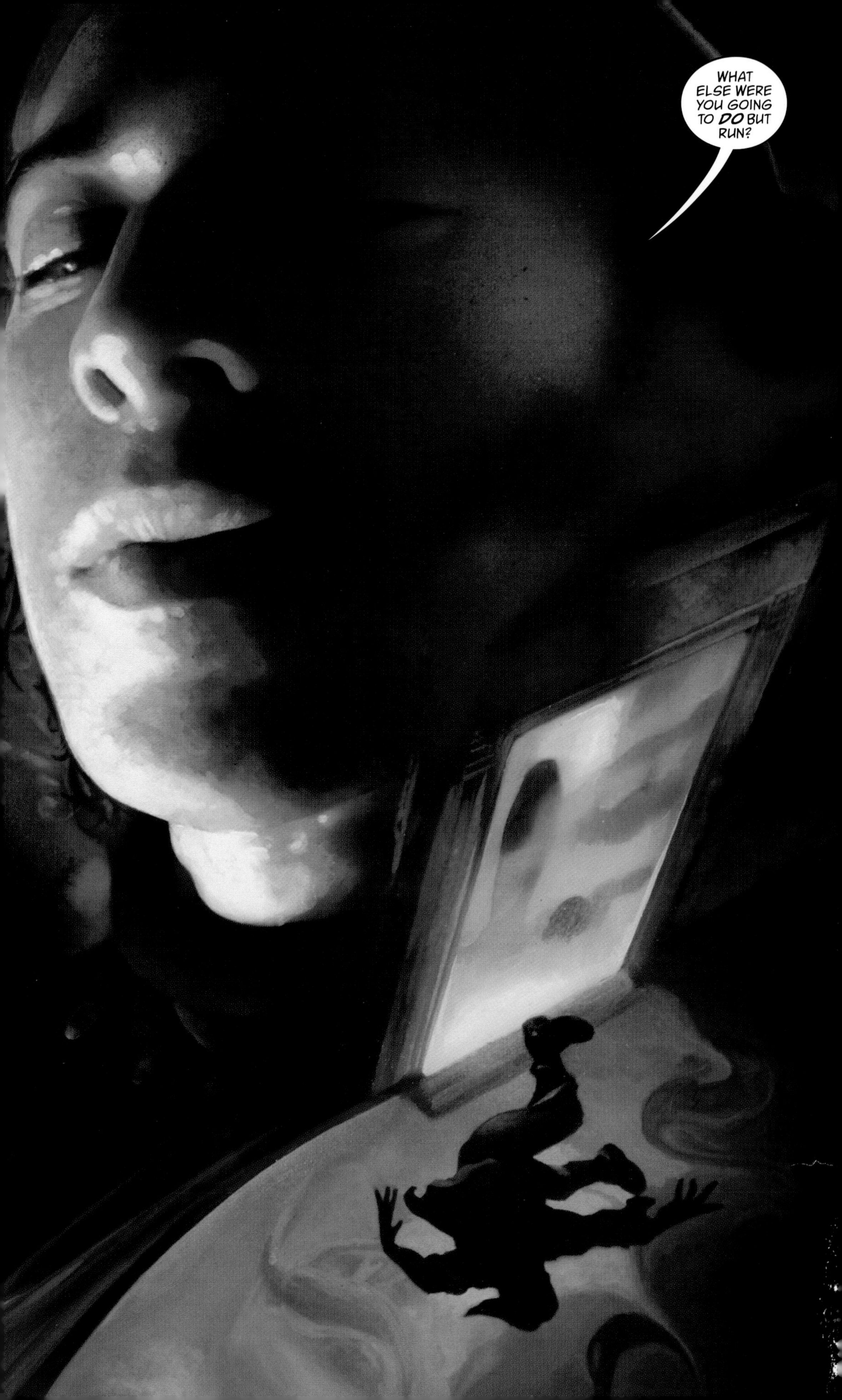
WHAT ELSE WERE YOU GOING TO *DO* BUT RUN?

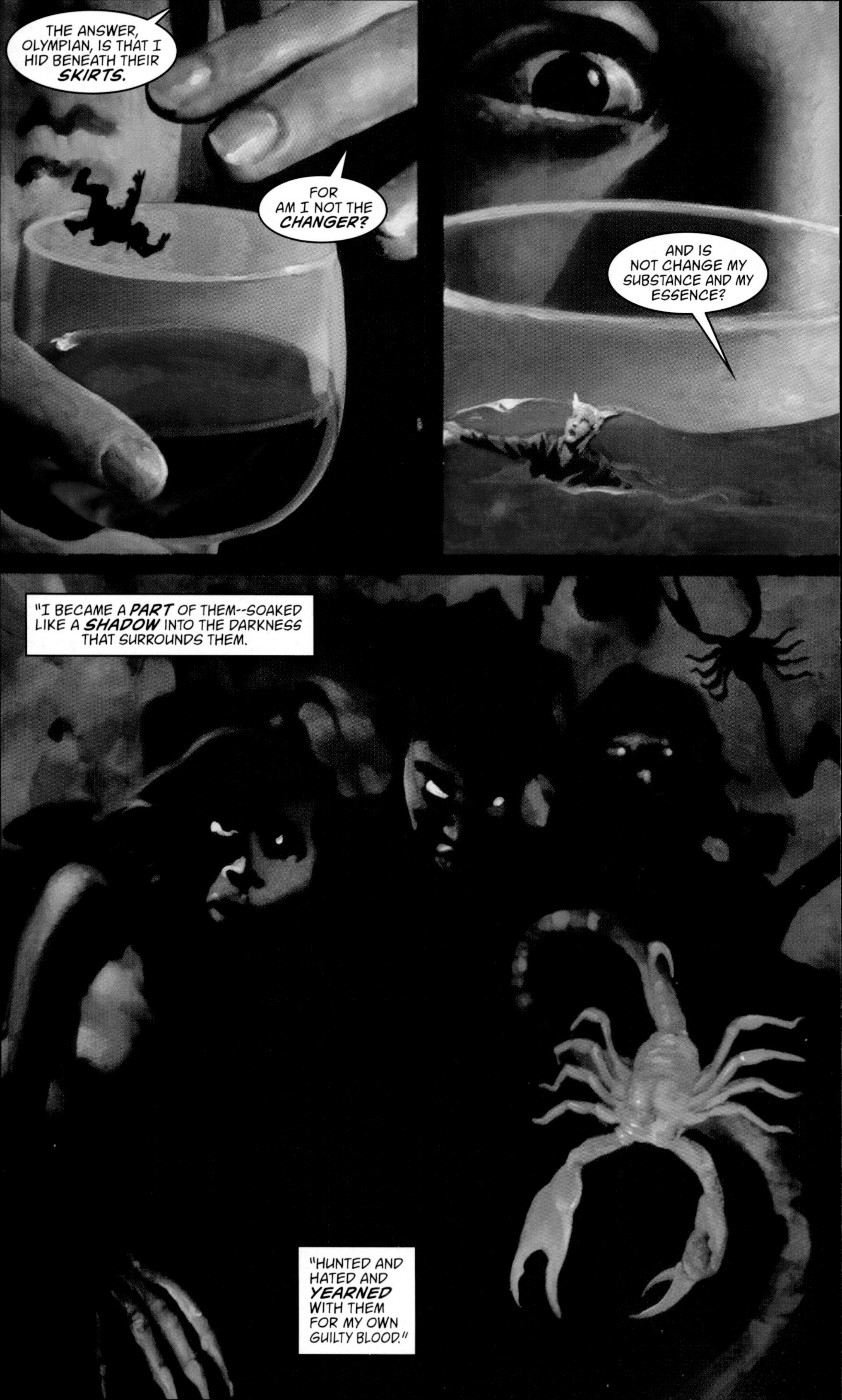

THE ANSWER, OLYMPIAN, IS THAT I HID BENEATH THEIR SKIRTS.
FOR AM I NOT THE CHANGER?
AND IS NOT CHANGE MY SUBSTANCE AND MY ESSENCE?
"I BECAME A PART OF THEM--SOAKED LIKE A SHADOW INTO THE DARKNESS THAT SURROUNDS THEM.
"HUNTED AND HATED AND YEARNED WITH THEM FOR MY OWN GUILTY BLOOD."

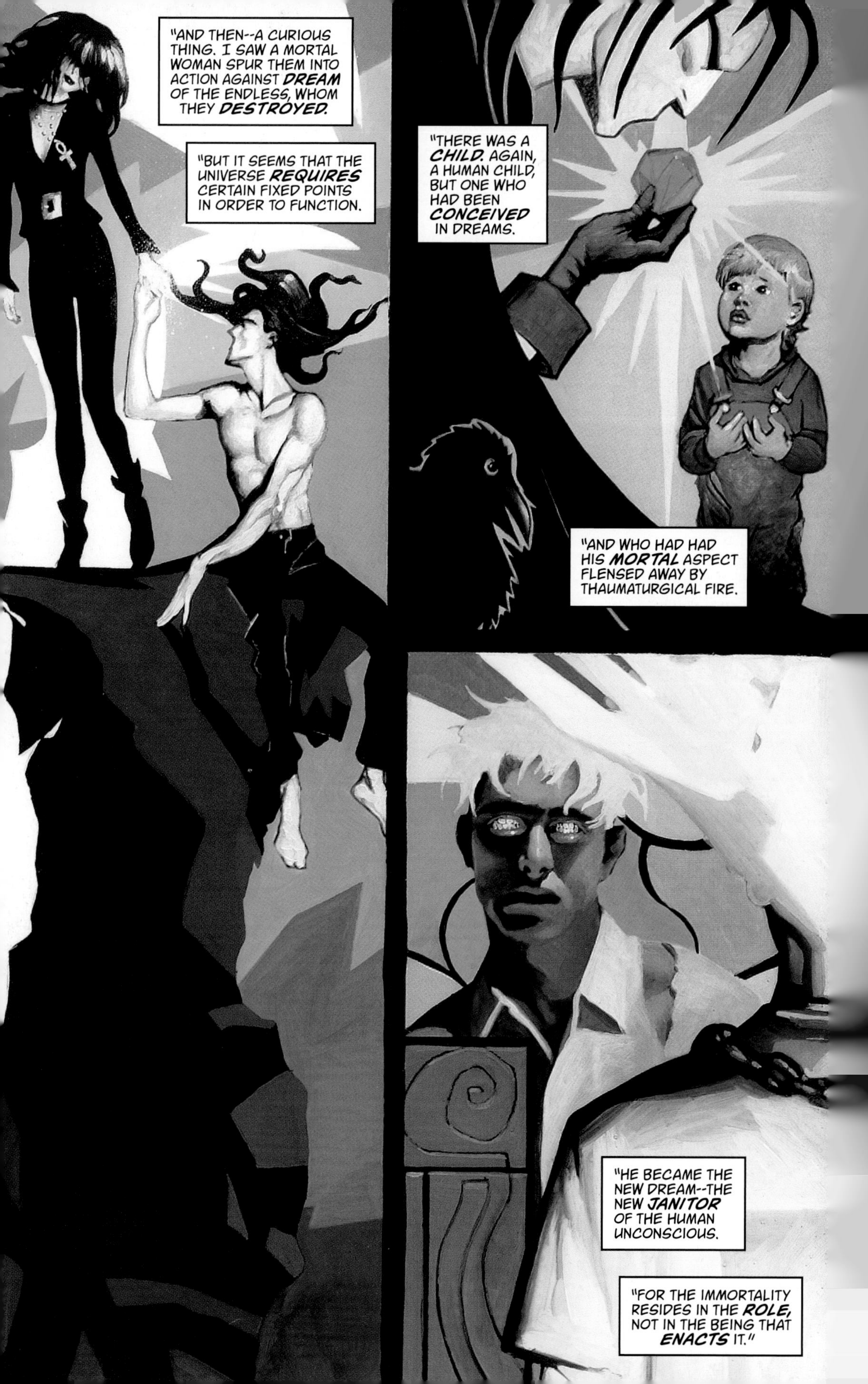
"AND THEN--A CURIOUS THING. I SAW A MORTAL WOMAN SPUR THEM INTO ACTION AGAINST DREAM OF THE ENDLESS, WHOM THEY DESTROYED.
"BUT IT SEEMS THAT THE UNIVERSE REQUIRES CERTAIN FIXED POINTS IN ORDER TO FUNCTION.
"THERE WAS A CHILD. AGAIN, A HUMAN CHILD, BUT ONE WHO HAD BEEN CONCEIVED IN DREAMS.
"AND WHO HAD HAD HIS MORTAL ASPECT FLENSED AWAY BY THAUMATURGICAL FIRE.
"HE BECAME THE NEW DREAM--THE NEW JANITOR OF THE HUMAN UNCONSCIOUS.
"FOR THE IMMORTALITY RESIDES IN THE ROLE, NOT IN THE BEING THAT ENACTS IT."

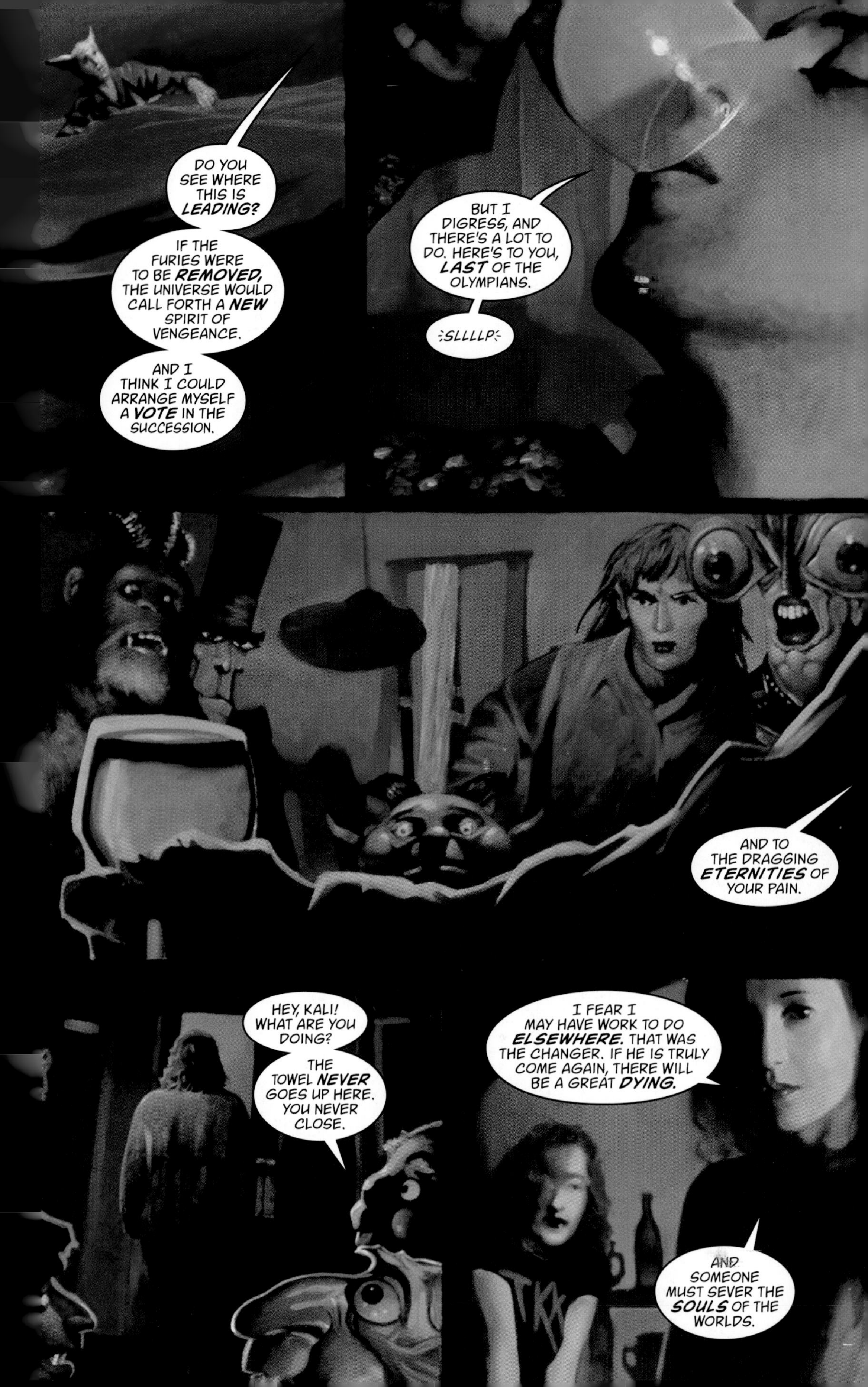
DO YOU SEE WHERE THIS IS LEADING?
IF THE FURIES WERE TO BE REMOVED, THE UNIVERSE WOULD CALL FORTH A NEW SPIRIT OF VENGEANCE.
AND I THINK I COULD ARRANGE MYSELF A VOTE IN THE SUCCESSION.
BUT I DIGRESS, AND THERE'S A LOT TO DO. HERE'S TO YOU, LAST OF THE OLYMPIANS.
SLLLLP
AND TO THE DRAGGING ETERNITIES OF YOUR PAIN.
HEY, KALI! WHAT ARE YOU DOING?
THE TOWEL NEVER GOES UP HERE. YOU NEVER CLOSE.
I FEAR I MAY HAVE WORK TO DO ELSEWHERE. THAT WAS THE CHANGER. IF HE IS TRULY COME AGAIN, THERE WILL BE A GREAT DYING.
AND SOMEONE MUST SEVER THE SOULS OF THE WORLDS.

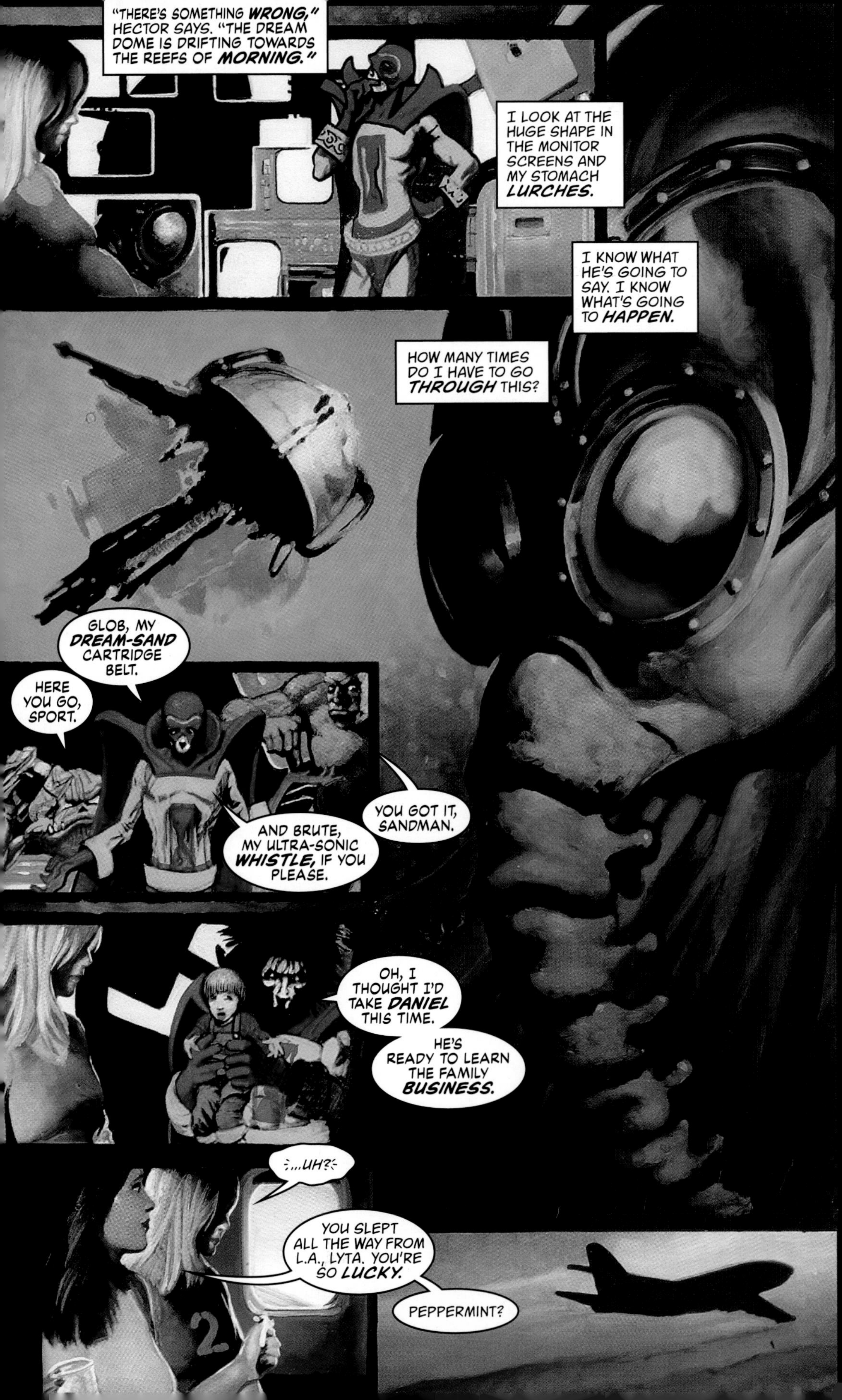
"THERE'S SOMETHING WRONG," HECTOR SAYS. "THE DREAM DOME IS DRIFTING TOWARDS THE REEFS OF MORNING."
I LOOK AT THE HUGE SHAPE IN THE MONITOR SCREENS AND MY STOMACH LURCHES.
I KNOW WHAT HE'S GOING TO SAY. I KNOW WHAT'S GOING TO HAPPEN.
HOW MANY TIMES DO I HAVE TO GO THROUGH THIS?
GLOB, MY DREAM-SAND CARTRIDGE BELT.
HERE YOU GO, SPORT.
AND BRUTE, MY ULTRA-SONIC WHISTLE, IF YOU PLEASE.
YOU GOT IT, SANDMAN.
OH, I THOUGHT I'D TAKE DANIEL THIS TIME.
HE'S READY TO LEARN THE FAMILY BUSINESS.
...UH?
YOU SLEPT ALL THE WAY FROM L.A., LYTA. YOU'RE SO LUCKY.
PEPPERMINT?
2

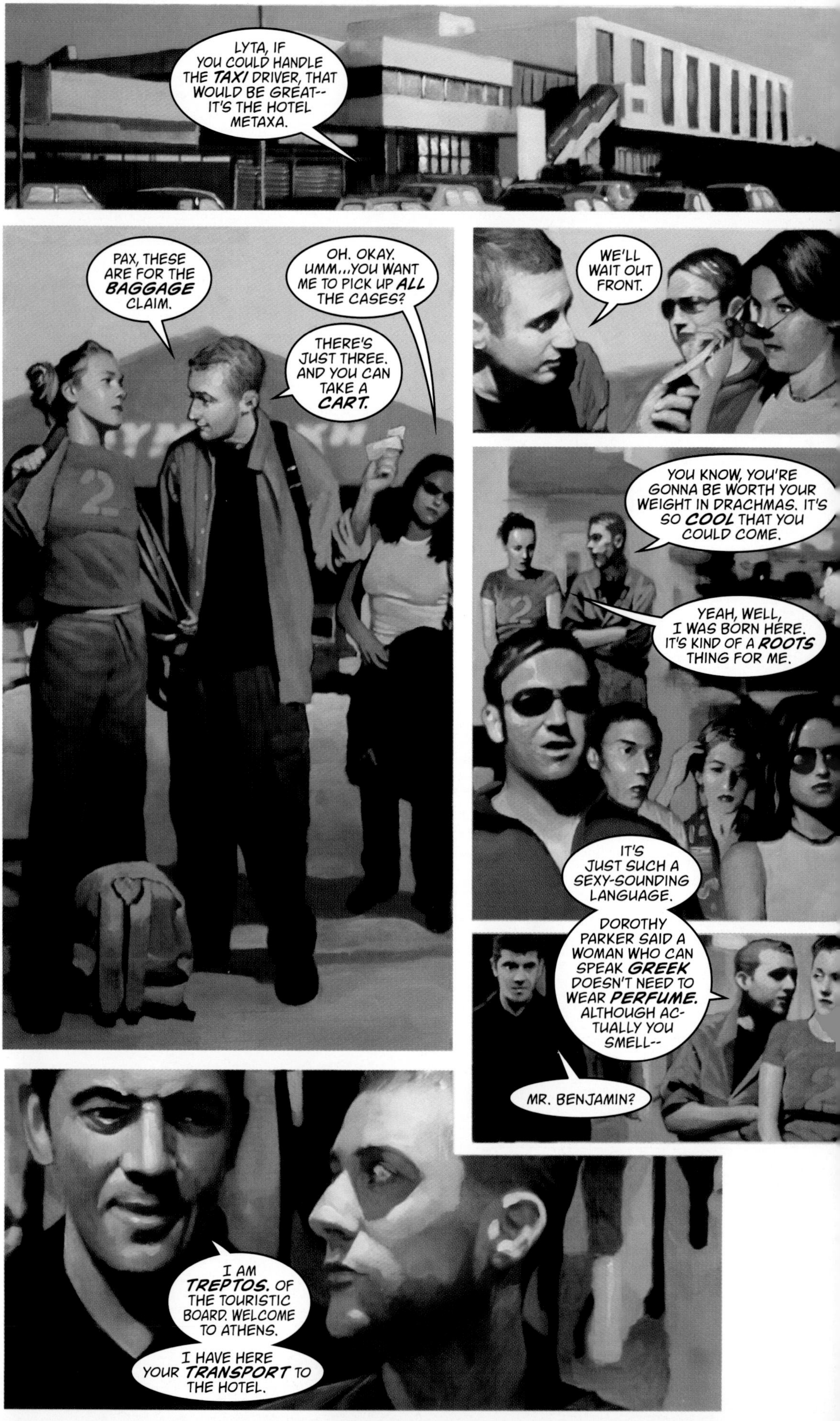
LYTA, IF YOU COULD HANDLE THE TAXI DRIVER, THAT WOULD BE GREAT-- IT'S THE HOTEL METAXA.
PAX, THESE ARE FOR THE BAGGAGE CLAIM.
OH. OKAY. UMM...YOU WANT ME TO PICK UP ALL THE CASES?
THERE'S JUST THREE. AND YOU CAN TAKE A CART.
WE'LL WAIT OUT FRONT.
YOU KNOW, YOU'RE GONNA BE WORTH YOUR WEIGHT IN DRACHMAS. IT'S SO COOL THAT YOU COULD COME.
YEAH, WELL, I WAS BORN HERE. IT'S KIND OF A ROOTS THING FOR ME.
IT'S JUST SUCH A SEXY-SOUNDING LANGUAGE.
DOROTHY PARKER SAID A WOMAN WHO CAN SPEAK GREEK DOESN'T NEED TO WEAR PERFUME. ALTHOUGH AC-TUALLY YOU SMELL--
MR. BENJAMIN?
I AM TREPTOS. OF THE TOURISTIC BOARD. WELCOME TO ATHENS.
I HAVE HERE YOUR TRANSPORT TO THE HOTEL.

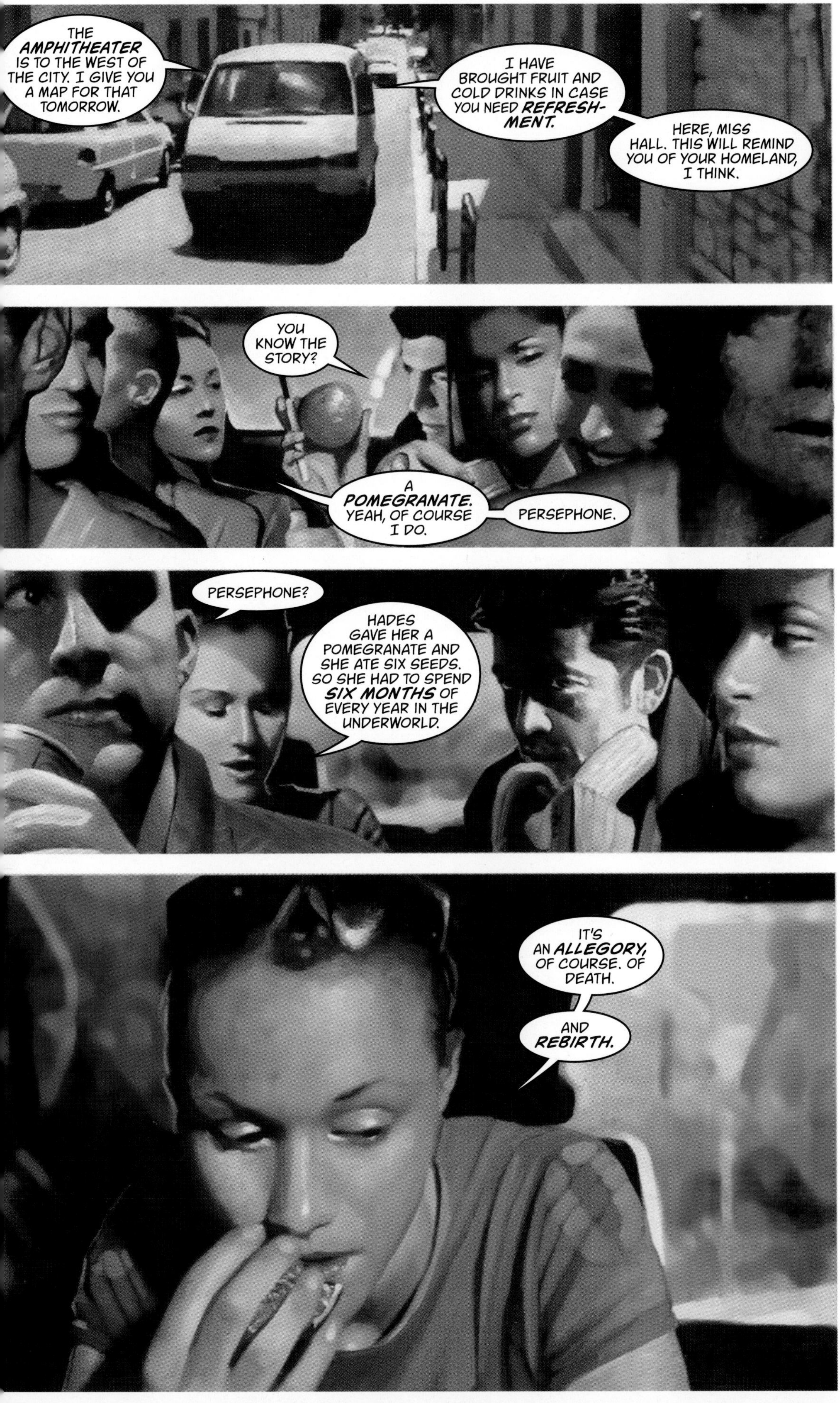
THE AMPHITHEATER IS TO THE WEST OF THE CITY. I GIVE YOU A MAP FOR THAT TOMORROW.
I HAVE BROUGHT FRUIT AND COLD DRINKS IN CASE YOU NEED REFRESH-MENT.
HERE, MISS HALL. THIS WILL REMIND YOU OF YOUR HOMELAND, I THINK.
YOU KNOW THE STORY?
A POMEGRANATE. YEAH, OF COURSE I DO.
PERSEPHONE.
PERSEPHONE?
HADES GAVE HER A POMEGRANATE AND SHE ATE SIX SEEDS. SO SHE HAD TO SPEND SIX MONTHS OF EVERY YEAR IN THE UNDERWORLD.
IT'S AN ALLEGORY, OF COURSE. OF DEATH.
AND REBIRTH.

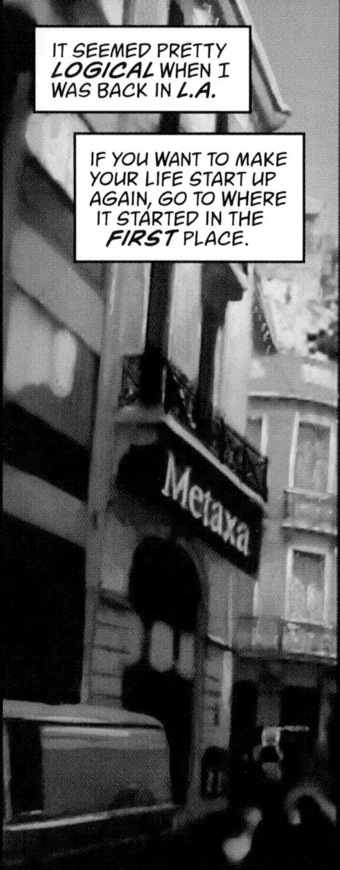
IT SEEMED PRETTY LOGICAL WHEN I WAS BACK IN L.A.
IF YOU WANT TO MAKE YOUR LIFE START UP AGAIN, GO TO WHERE IT STARTED IN THE FIRST PLACE.
Metaxa

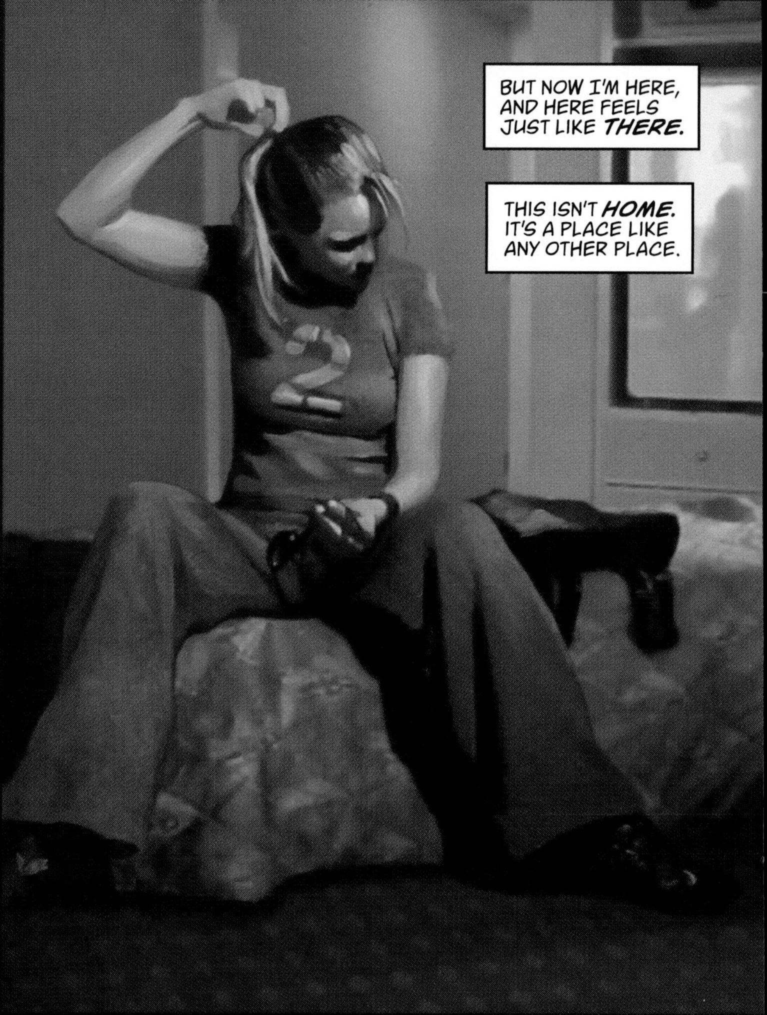
BUT NOW I'M HERE, AND HERE FEELS JUST LIKE THERE.
THIS ISN'T HOME. IT'S A PLACE LIKE ANY OTHER PLACE.

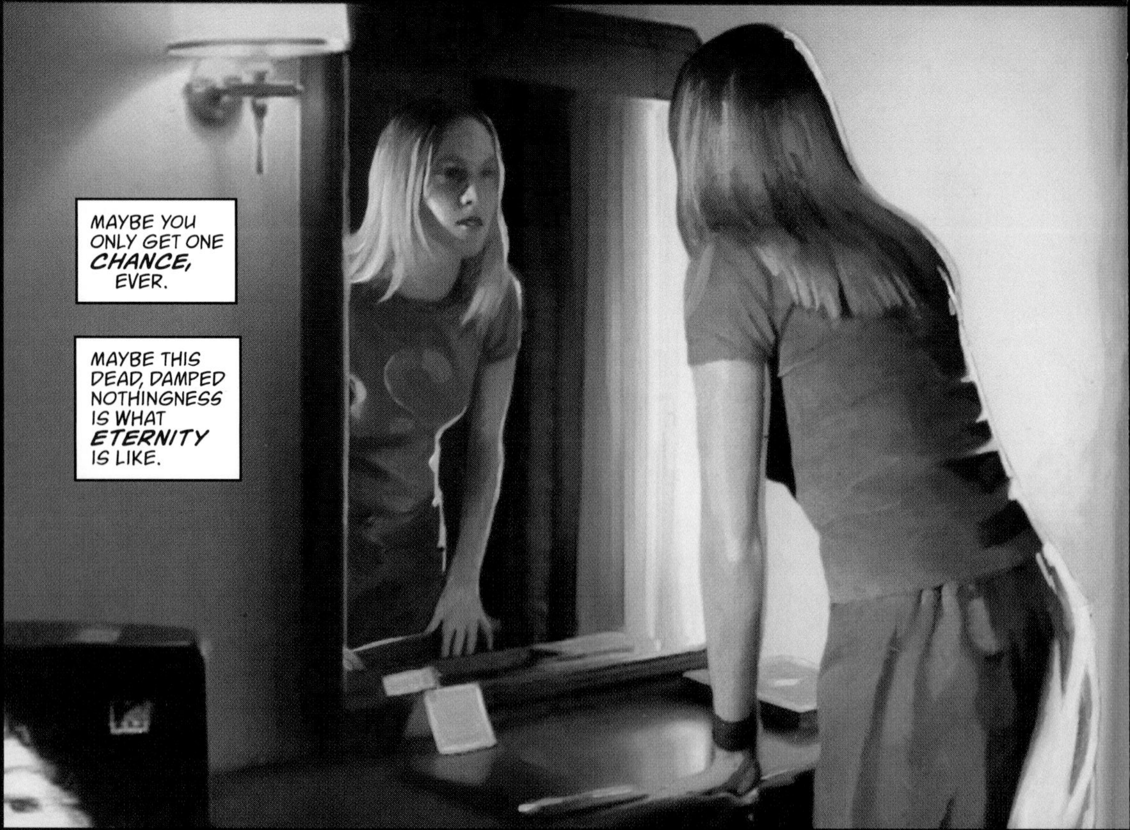
MAYBE YOU ONLY GET ONE CHANCE, EVER.
MAYBE THIS DEAD, DAMPED NOTHINGNESS IS WHAT ETERNITY IS LIKE.

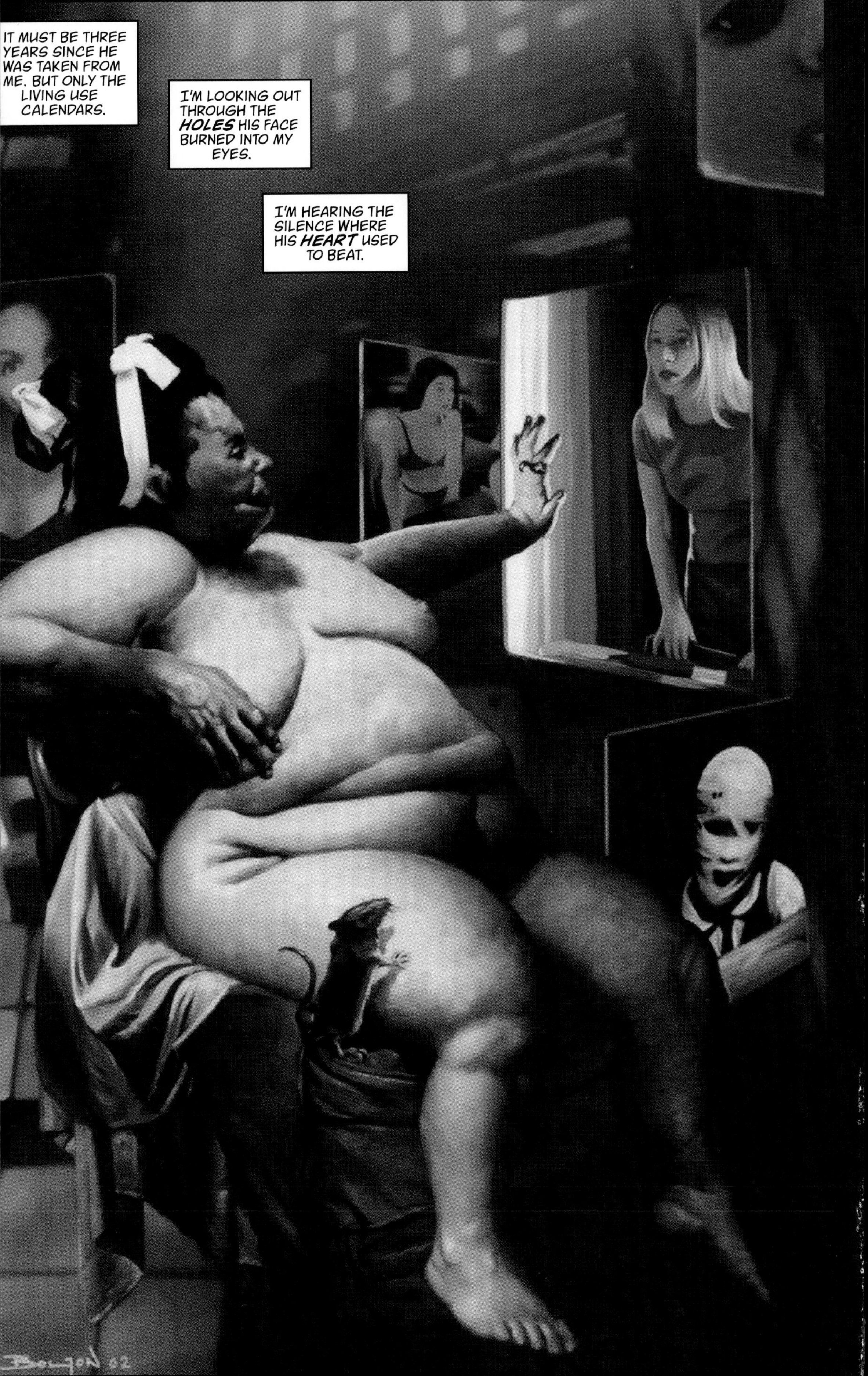
IT MUST BE THREE YEARS SINCE HE WAS TAKEN FROM ME. BUT ONLY THE LIVING USE CALENDARS.
I'M LOOKING OUT THROUGH THE **HOLES** HIS FACE BURNED INTO MY EYES.
I'M HEARING THE SILENCE WHERE HIS **HEART** USED TO BEAT.
BOLTON 02

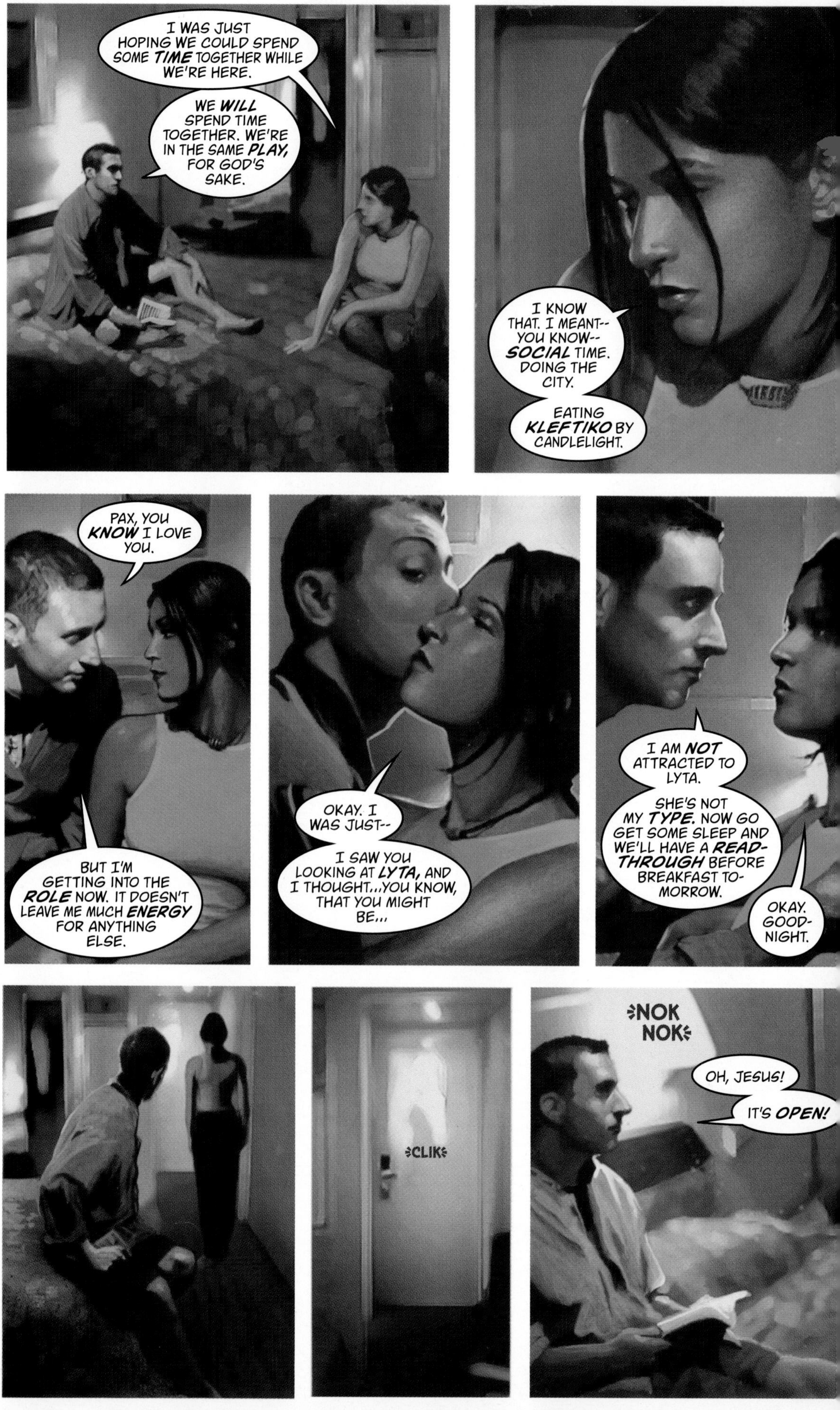
I WAS JUST HOPING WE COULD SPEND SOME TIME TOGETHER WHILE WE'RE HERE.
WE WILL SPEND TIME TOGETHER. WE'RE IN THE SAME PLAY, FOR GOD'S SAKE.
I KNOW THAT. I MEANT-- YOU KNOW-- SOCIAL TIME. DOING THE CITY.
EATING KLEFTIKO BY CANDLELIGHT.
PAX, YOU KNOW I LOVE YOU.
BUT I'M GETTING INTO THE ROLE NOW. IT DOESN'T LEAVE ME MUCH ENERGY FOR ANYTHING ELSE.
OKAY. I WAS JUST--
I SAW YOU LOOKING AT LYTA, AND I THOUGHT...YOU KNOW, THAT YOU MIGHT BE...
I AM NOT ATTRACTED TO LYTA.
SHE'S NOT MY TYPE. NOW GO GET SOME SLEEP AND WE'LL HAVE A READ-THROUGH BEFORE BREAKFAST TO-MORROW.
OKAY. GOOD-NIGHT.
CLIK
NOK NOK
OH, JESUS!
IT'S OPEN!

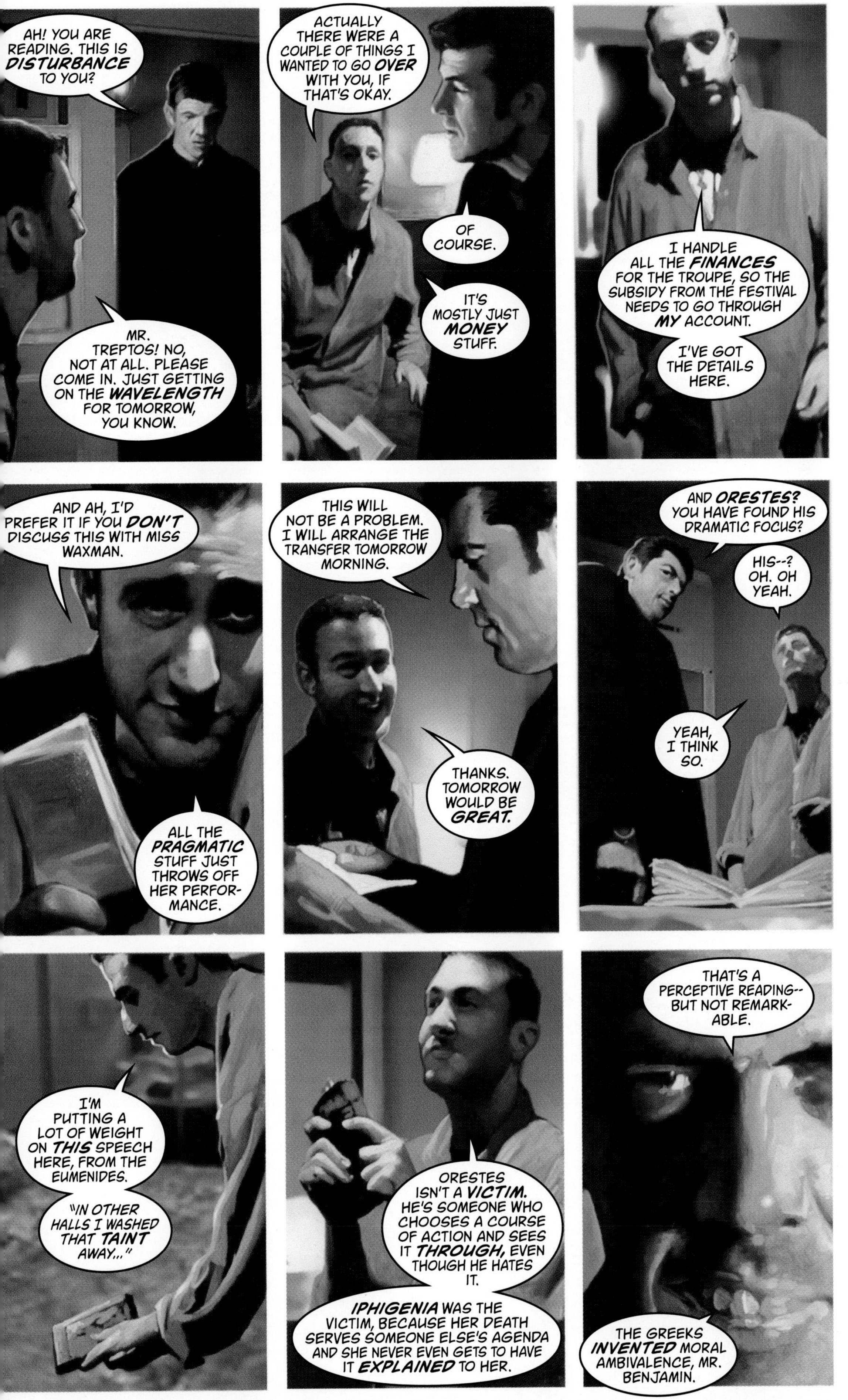

AH! YOU ARE READING. THIS IS *DISTURBANCE* TO YOU?
MR. TREPTOS! NO, NOT AT ALL. PLEASE COME IN. JUST GETTING ON THE *WAVELENGTH* FOR TOMORROW, YOU KNOW.
ACTUALLY THERE WERE A COUPLE OF THINGS I WANTED TO GO *OVER* WITH YOU, IF THAT'S OKAY.
OF COURSE.
IT'S MOSTLY JUST *MONEY* STUFF.
I HANDLE ALL THE *FINANCES* FOR THE TROUPE, SO THE SUBSIDY FROM THE FESTIVAL NEEDS TO GO THROUGH *MY* ACCOUNT.
I'VE GOT THE DETAILS HERE.
AND AH, I'D PREFER IT IF YOU *DON'T* DISCUSS THIS WITH MISS WAXMAN.
ALL THE *PRAGMATIC* STUFF JUST THROWS OFF HER PERFOR-MANCE.
THIS WILL NOT BE A PROBLEM. I WILL ARRANGE THE TRANSFER TOMORROW MORNING.
THANKS. TOMORROW WOULD BE *GREAT.*
AND *ORESTES?* YOU HAVE FOUND HIS DRAMATIC FOCUS?
HIS--? OH. OH YEAH.
YEAH, I THINK SO.
I'M PUTTING A LOT OF WEIGHT ON *THIS* SPEECH HERE, FROM THE EUMENIDES.
"IN OTHER HALLS I WASHED THAT *TAINT* AWAY..."
ORESTES ISN'T A *VICTIM.* HE'S SOMEONE WHO CHOOSES A COURSE OF ACTION AND SEES IT *THROUGH,* EVEN THOUGH HE HATES IT.
IPHIGENIA WAS THE VICTIM, BECAUSE HER DEATH SERVES SOMEONE ELSE'S AGENDA AND SHE NEVER EVEN GETS TO HAVE IT *EXPLAINED* TO HER.
THAT'S A PERCEPTIVE READING-- BUT NOT REMARK-ABLE.
THE GREEKS *INVENTED* MORAL AMBIVALENCE, MR. BENJAMIN.

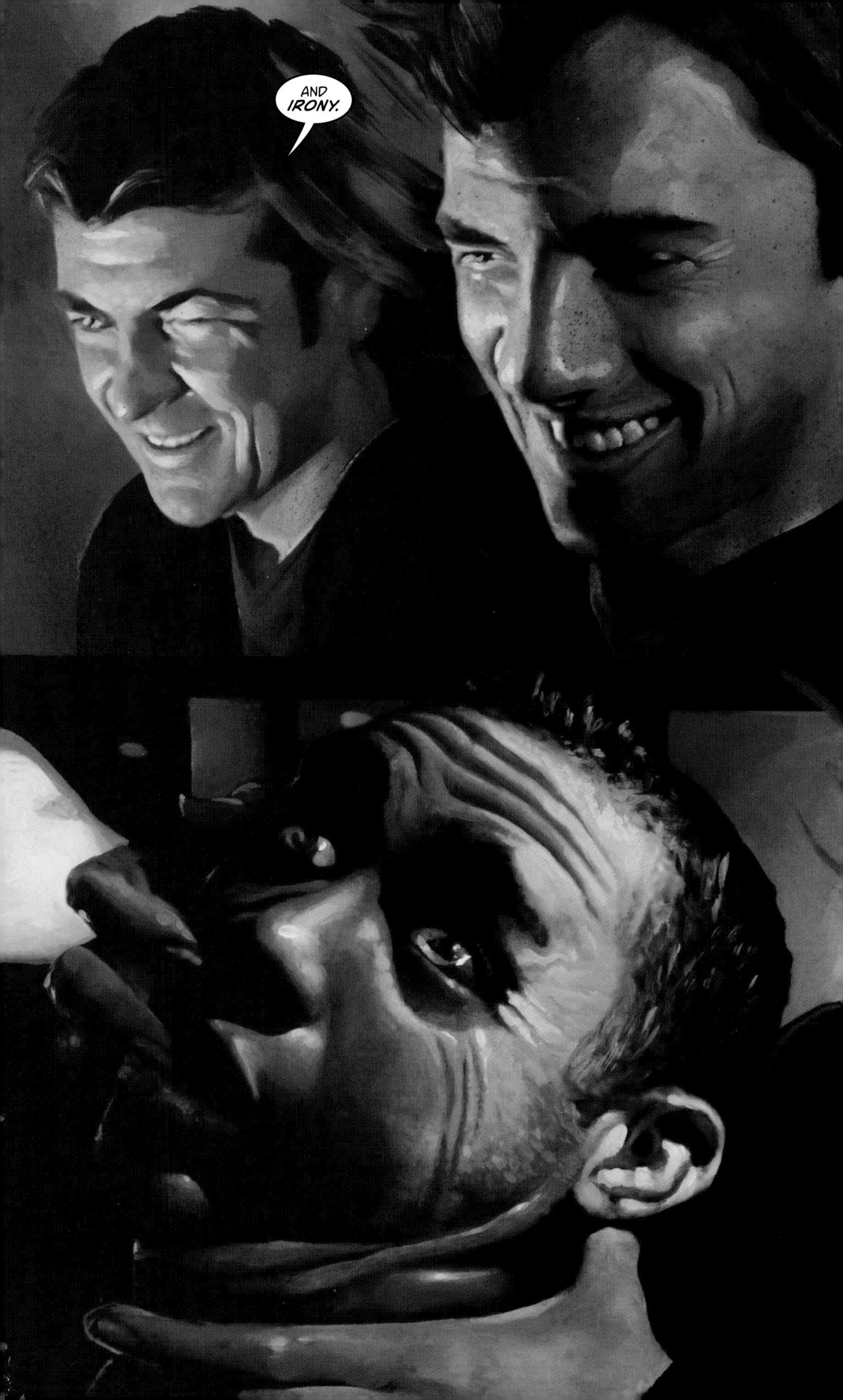
AND IRONY.

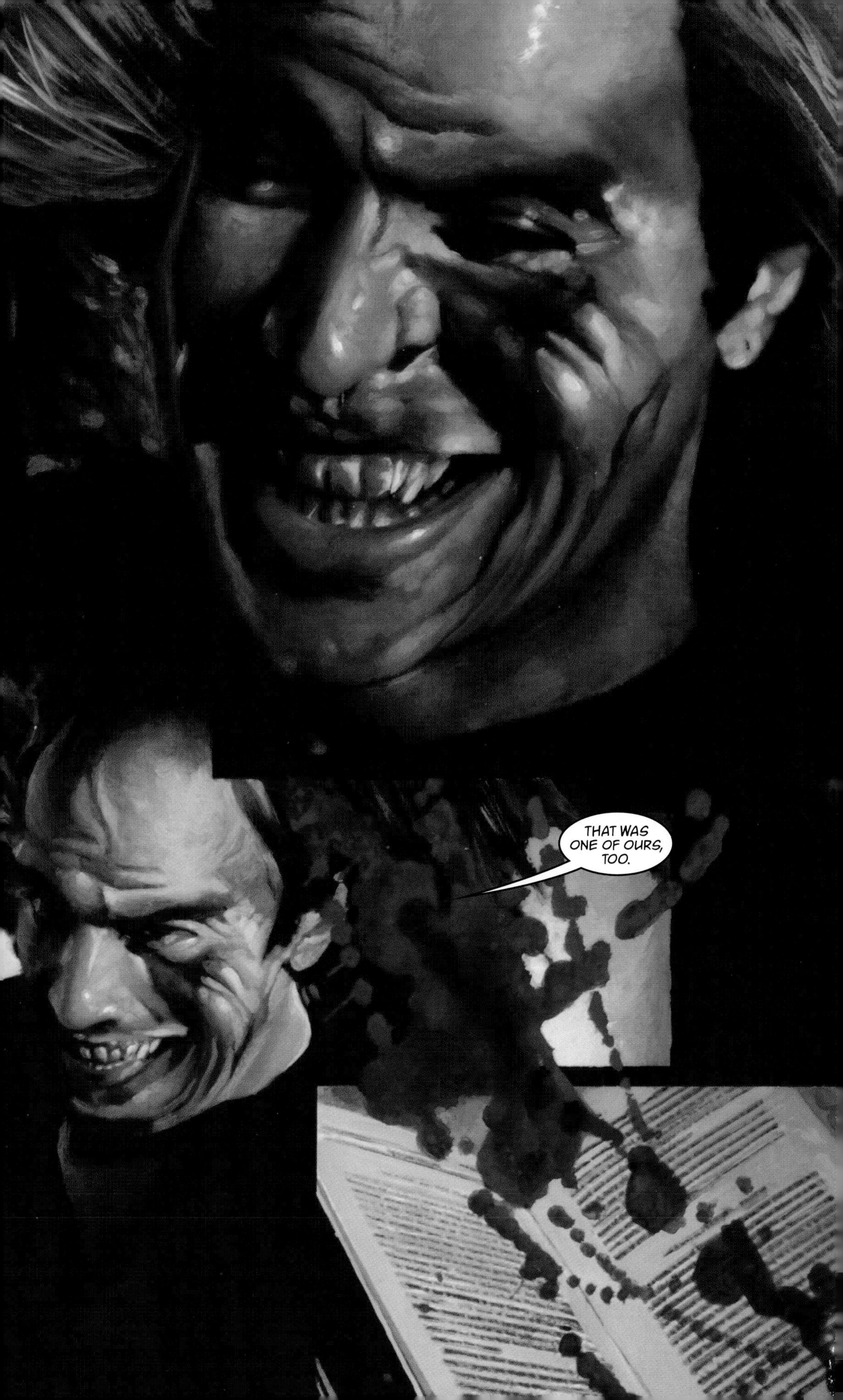
THAT WAS ONE OF OURS, TOO.

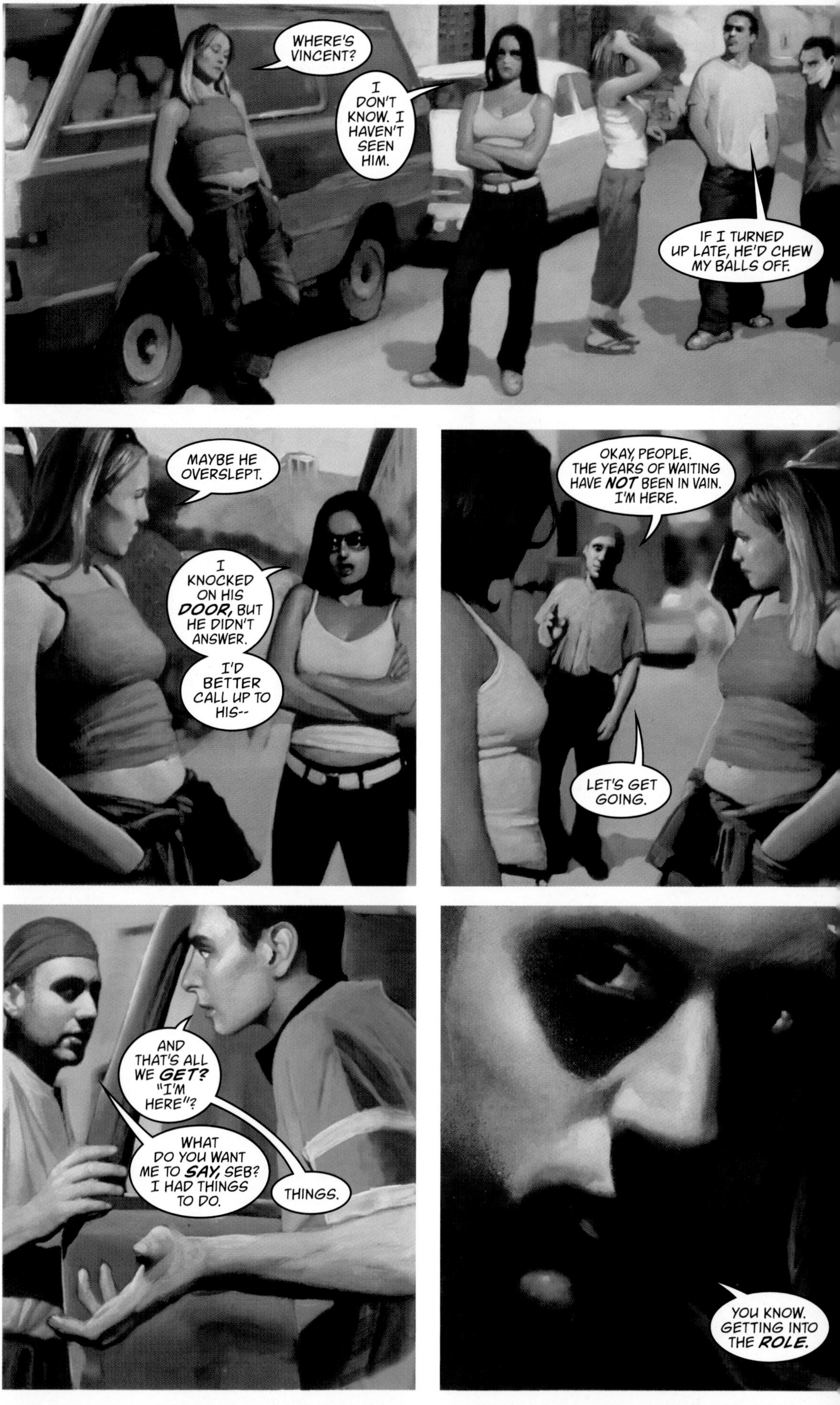
WHERE'S VINCENT?
I DON'T KNOW. I HAVEN'T SEEN HIM.
IF I TURNED UP LATE, HE'D CHEW MY BALLS OFF.
MAYBE HE OVERSLEPT.
I KNOCKED ON HIS DOOR, BUT HE DIDN'T ANSWER.
I'D BETTER CALL UP TO HIS--
OKAY, PEOPLE. THE YEARS OF WAITING HAVE NOT BEEN IN VAIN. I'M HERE.
LET'S GET GOING.
AND THAT'S ALL WE GET? "I'M HERE"?
WHAT DO YOU WANT ME TO SAY, SEB? I HAD THINGS TO DO.
THINGS.
YOU KNOW. GETTING INTO THE ROLE.

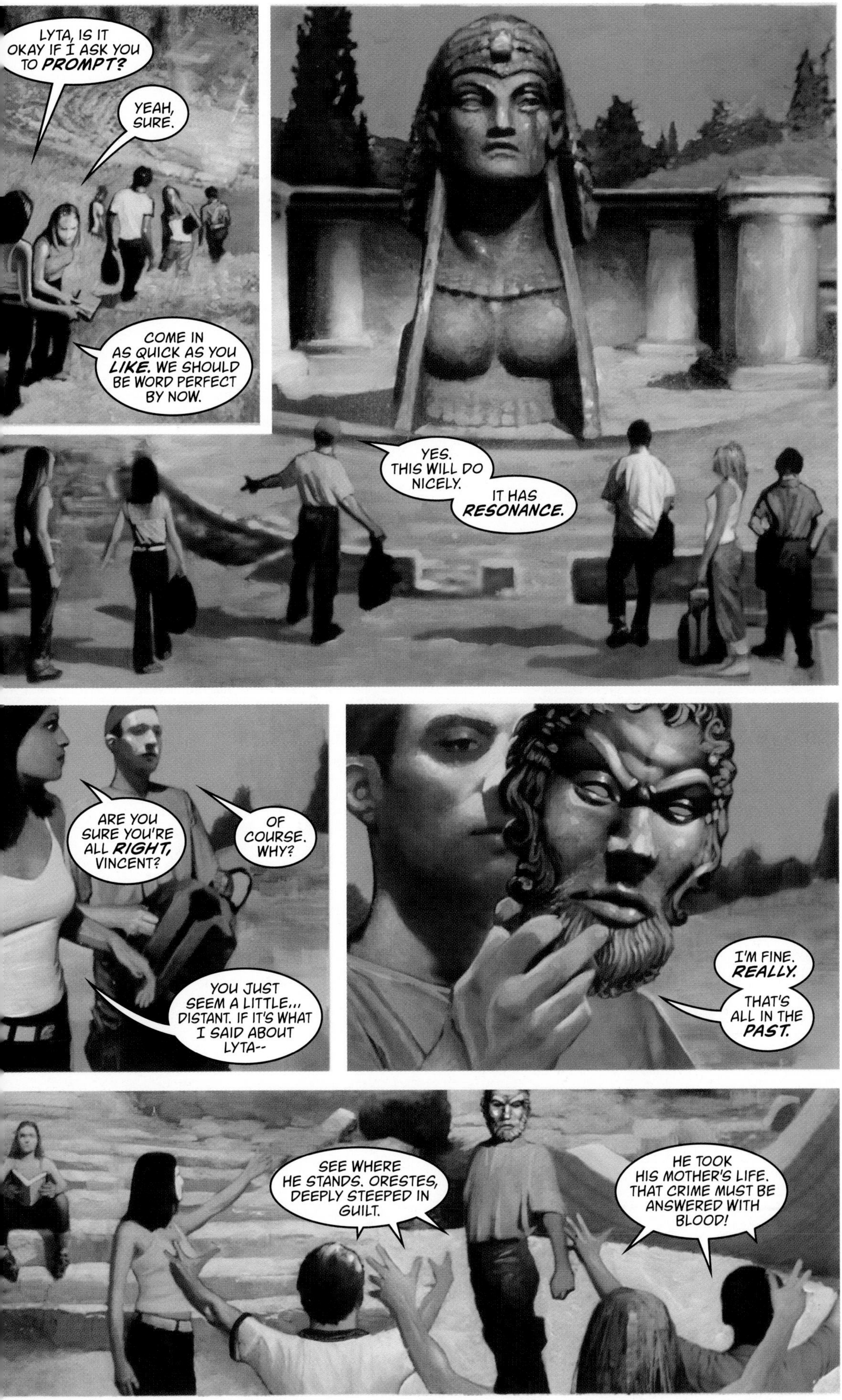
LYTA, IS IT OKAY IF I ASK YOU TO PROMPT?
YEAH, SURE.
COME IN AS QUICK AS YOU LIKE. WE SHOULD BE WORD PERFECT BY NOW.
YES. THIS WILL DO NICELY.
IT HAS RESONANCE.
ARE YOU SURE YOU'RE ALL RIGHT, VINCENT?
OF COURSE. WHY?
YOU JUST SEEM A LITTLE... DISTANT. IF IT'S WHAT I SAID ABOUT LYTA--
I'M FINE. REALLY.
THAT'S ALL IN THE PAST.
SEE WHERE HE STANDS. ORESTES, DEEPLY STEEPED IN GUILT.
HE TOOK HIS MOTHER'S LIFE. THAT CRIME MUST BE ANSWERED WITH BLOOD!

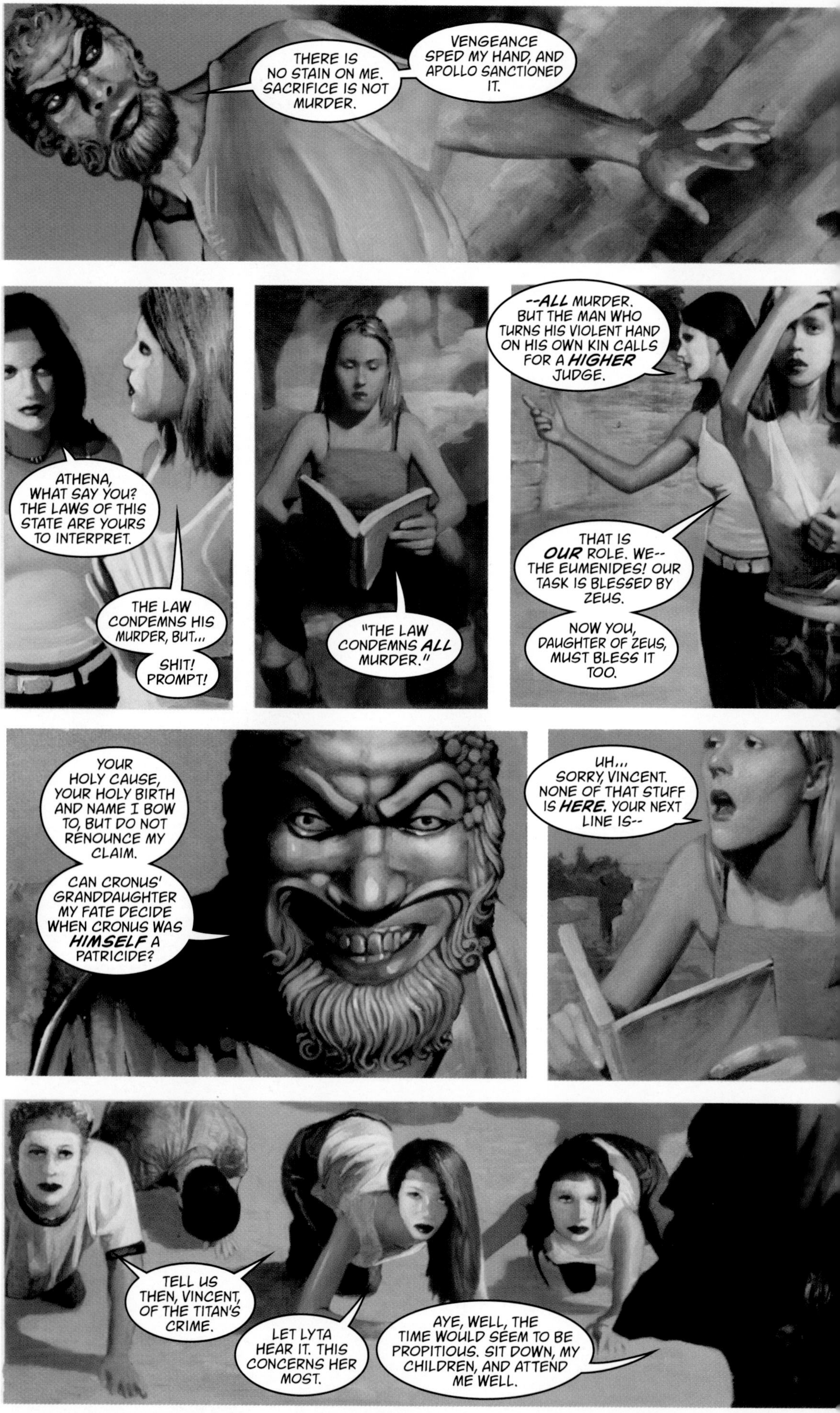
THERE IS NO STAIN ON ME. SACRIFICE IS NOT MURDER.
VENGEANCE SPED MY HAND, AND APOLLO SANCTIONED IT.
ATHENA, WHAT SAY YOU? THE LAWS OF THIS STATE ARE YOURS TO INTERPRET.
THE LAW CONDEMNS HIS MURDER, BUT...
SHIT! PROMPT!
"THE LAW CONDEMNS ALL MURDER."
--ALL MURDER. BUT THE MAN WHO TURNS HIS VIOLENT HAND ON HIS OWN KIN CALLS FOR A HIGHER JUDGE.
THAT IS OUR ROLE. WE-- THE EUMENIDES! OUR TASK IS BLESSED BY ZEUS.
NOW YOU, DAUGHTER OF ZEUS, MUST BLESS IT TOO.
YOUR HOLY CAUSE, YOUR HOLY BIRTH AND NAME I BOW TO, BUT DO NOT RENOUNCE MY CLAIM.
CAN CRONUS' GRANDDAUGHTER MY FATE DECIDE WHEN CRONUS WAS HIMSELF A PATRICIDE?
UH... SORRY, VINCENT. NONE OF THAT STUFF IS HERE. YOUR NEXT LINE IS--
TELL US THEN, VINCENT, OF THE TITAN'S CRIME.
LET LYTA HEAR IT. THIS CONCERNS HER MOST.
AYE, WELL, THE TIME WOULD SEEM TO BE PROPITIOUS. SIT DOWN, MY CHILDREN, AND ATTEND ME WELL.

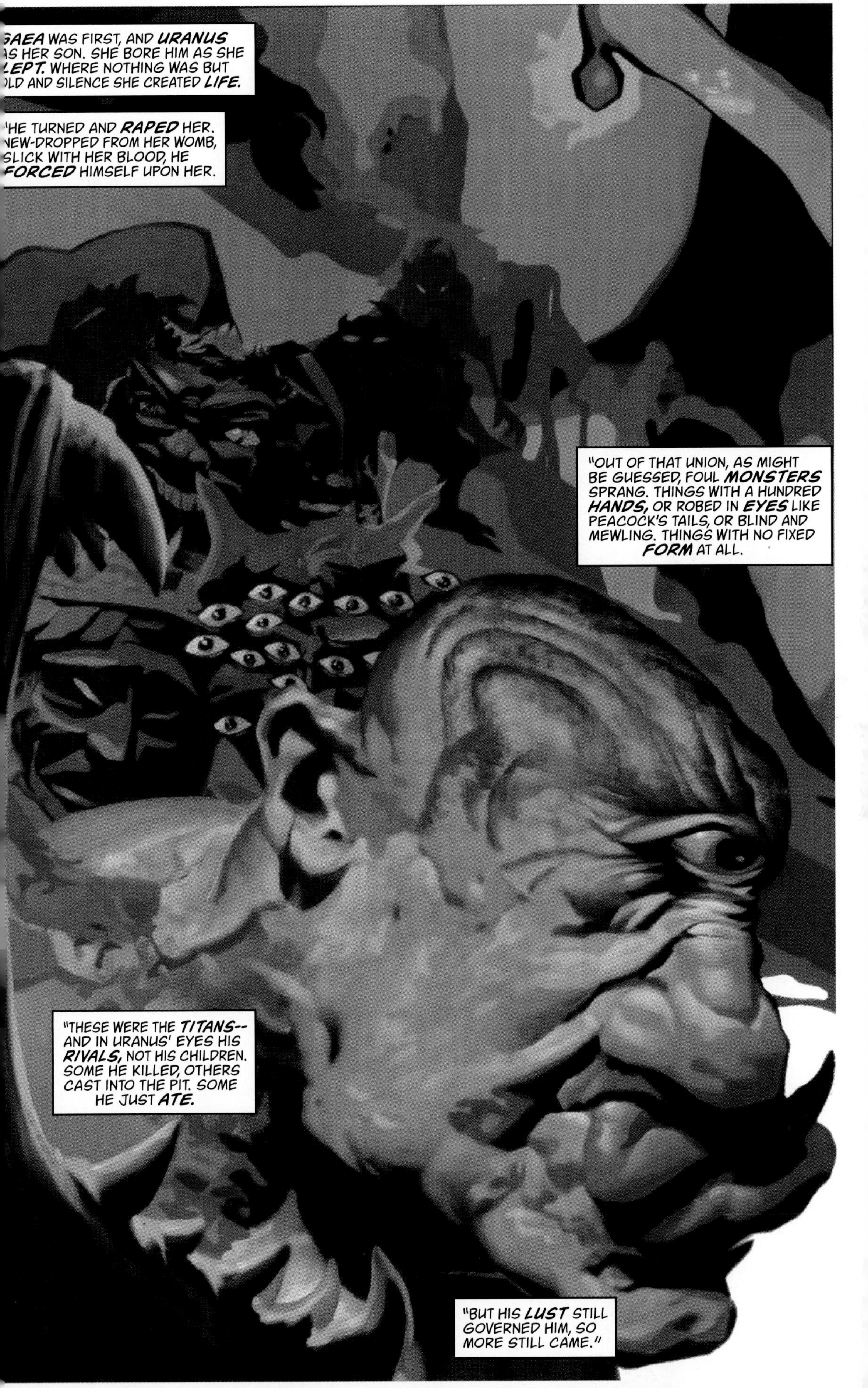

GAEA WAS FIRST, AND URANUS AS HER SON. SHE BORE HIM AS SHE LEPT. WHERE NOTHING WAS BUT OLD AND SILENCE SHE CREATED LIFE.
HE TURNED AND RAPED HER. NEW-DROPPED FROM HER WOMB, SLICK WITH HER BLOOD, HE FORCED HIMSELF UPON HER.
"OUT OF THAT UNION, AS MIGHT BE GUESSED, FOUL MONSTERS SPRANG. THINGS WITH A HUNDRED HANDS, OR ROBED IN EYES LIKE PEACOCK'S TAILS, OR BLIND AND MEWLING. THINGS WITH NO FIXED FORM AT ALL.
"THESE WERE THE TITANS-- AND IN URANUS' EYES HIS RIVALS, NOT HIS CHILDREN. SOME HE KILLED, OTHERS CAST INTO THE PIT. SOME HE JUST ATE.
"BUT HIS LUST STILL GOVERNED HIM, SO MORE STILL CAME."

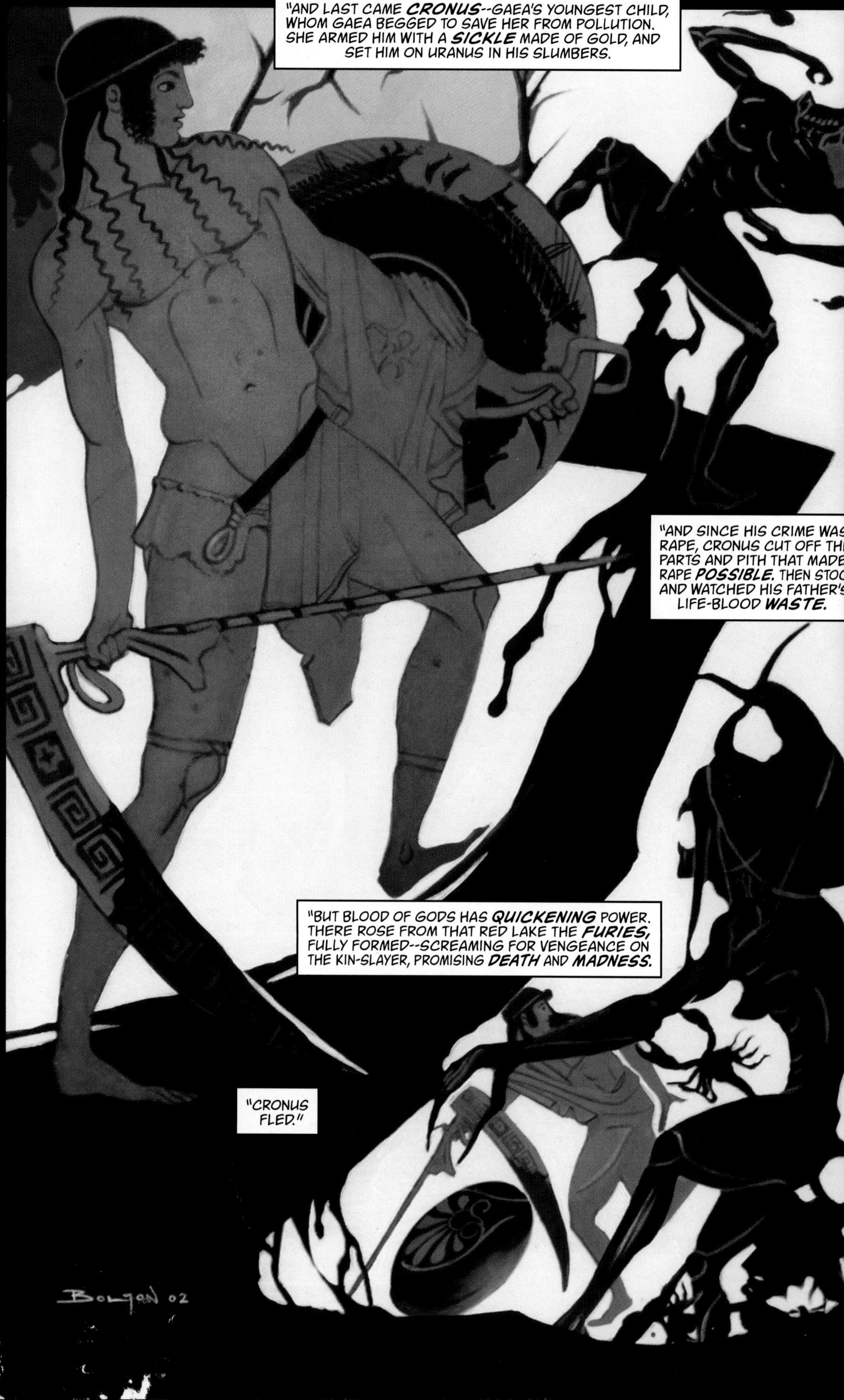
"AND LAST CAME CRONUS--GAEA'S YOUNGEST CHILD, WHOM GAEA BEGGED TO SAVE HER FROM POLLUTION. SHE ARMED HIM WITH A SICKLE MADE OF GOLD, AND SET HIM ON URANUS IN HIS SLUMBERS.
"AND SINCE HIS CRIME WAS RAPE, CRONUS CUT OFF TH PARTS AND PITH THAT MADE RAPE POSSIBLE. THEN STOO AND WATCHED HIS FATHER'S LIFE-BLOOD WASTE.
"BUT BLOOD OF GODS HAS QUICKENING POWER. THERE ROSE FROM THAT RED LAKE THE FURIES, FULLY FORMED--SCREAMING FOR VENGEANCE ON THE KIN-SLAYER, PROMISING DEATH AND MADNESS.
"CRONUS FLED."
BOLGAN 02

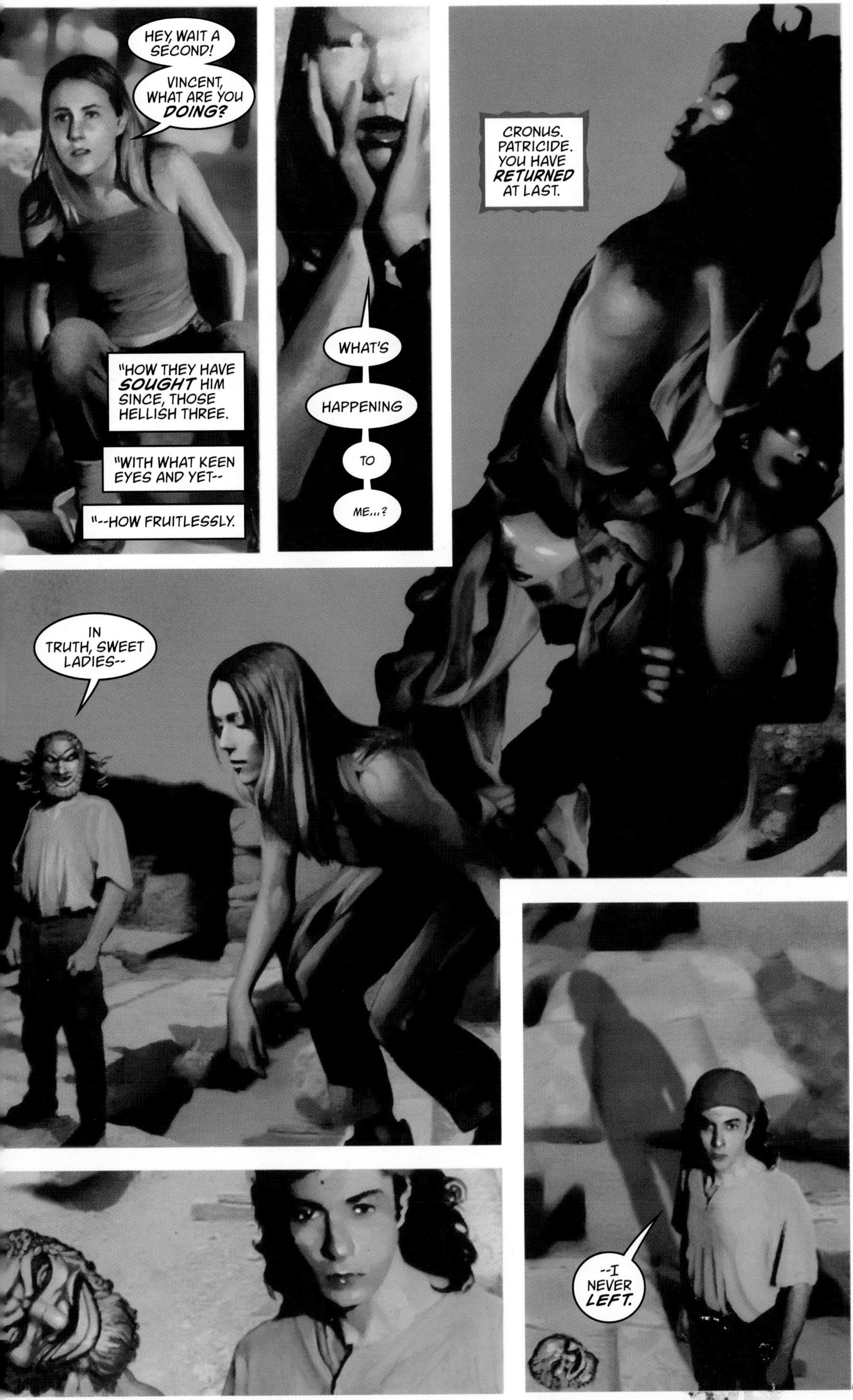
HEY, WAIT A SECOND!
VINCENT, WHAT ARE YOU DOING?
"HOW THEY HAVE SOUGHT HIM SINCE, THOSE HELLISH THREE.
"WITH WHAT KEEN EYES AND YET--
"--HOW FRUITLESSLY.
WHAT'S
HAPPENING
TO
ME...?
CRONUS. PATRICIDE. YOU HAVE RETURNED AT LAST.
IN TRUTH, SWEET LADIES--
--I NEVER LEFT.

YOUR **PUNISHMENT** WAS VOUCHSAFED TO US.
AYE, IT WAS.
AND NOW AT LAST WE CAN **COMPLETE** IT.
WELL, THAT'S A HEARSE OF A DIFFERENT COLOR.
BOLTON

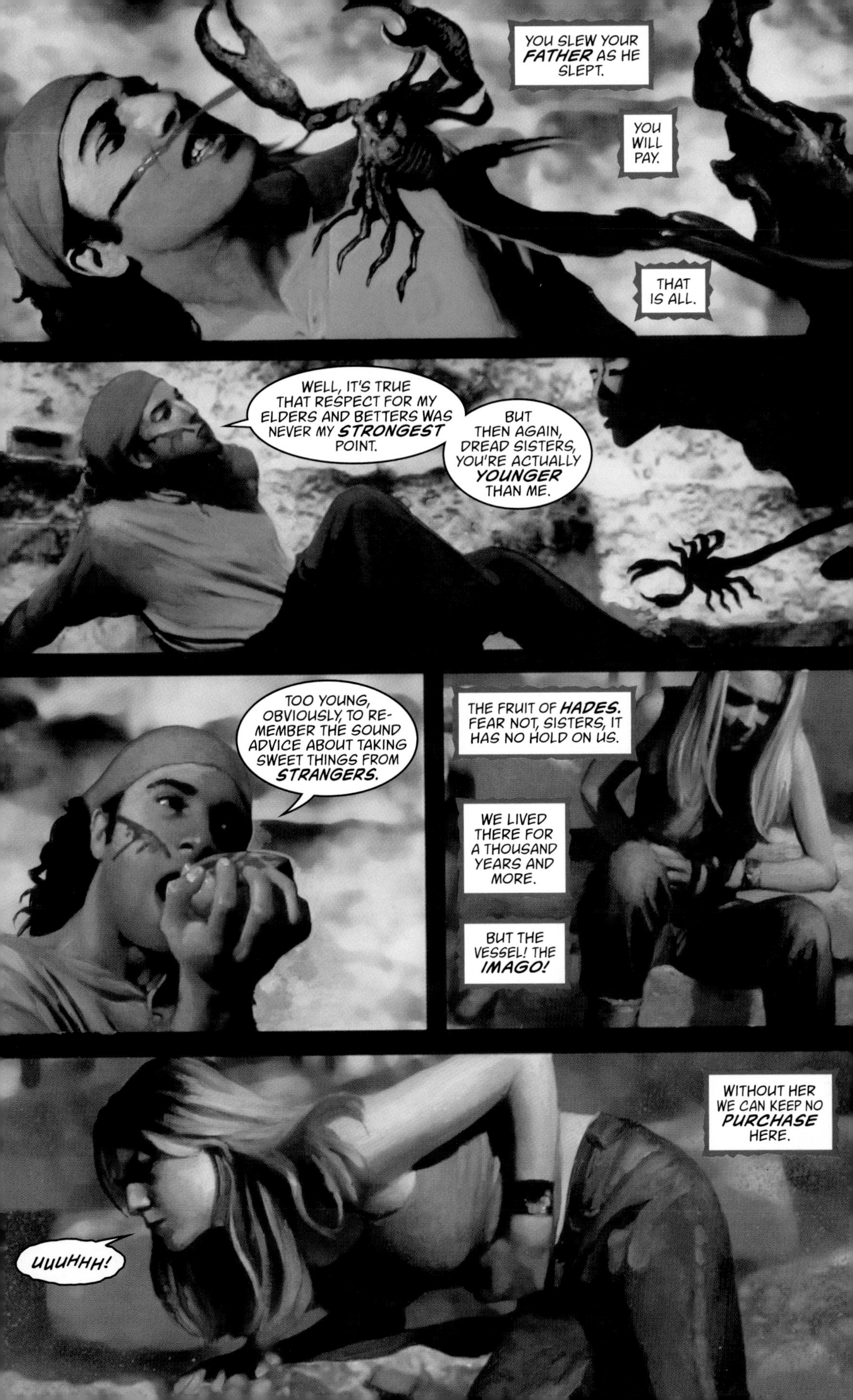
YOU SLEW YOUR FATHER AS HE SLEPT.
YOU WILL PAY.
THAT IS ALL.
WELL, IT'S TRUE THAT RESPECT FOR MY ELDERS AND BETTERS WAS NEVER MY STRONGEST POINT.
BUT THEN AGAIN, DREAD SISTERS, YOU'RE ACTUALLY YOUNGER THAN ME.
TOO YOUNG, OBVIOUSLY, TO RE-MEMBER THE SOUND ADVICE ABOUT TAKING SWEET THINGS FROM STRANGERS.
THE FRUIT OF HADES. FEAR NOT, SISTERS, IT HAS NO HOLD ON US.
WE LIVED THERE FOR A THOUSAND YEARS AND MORE.
BUT THE VESSEL! THE IMAGO!
WITHOUT HER WE CAN KEEP NO PURCHASE HERE.
UUUHHH!

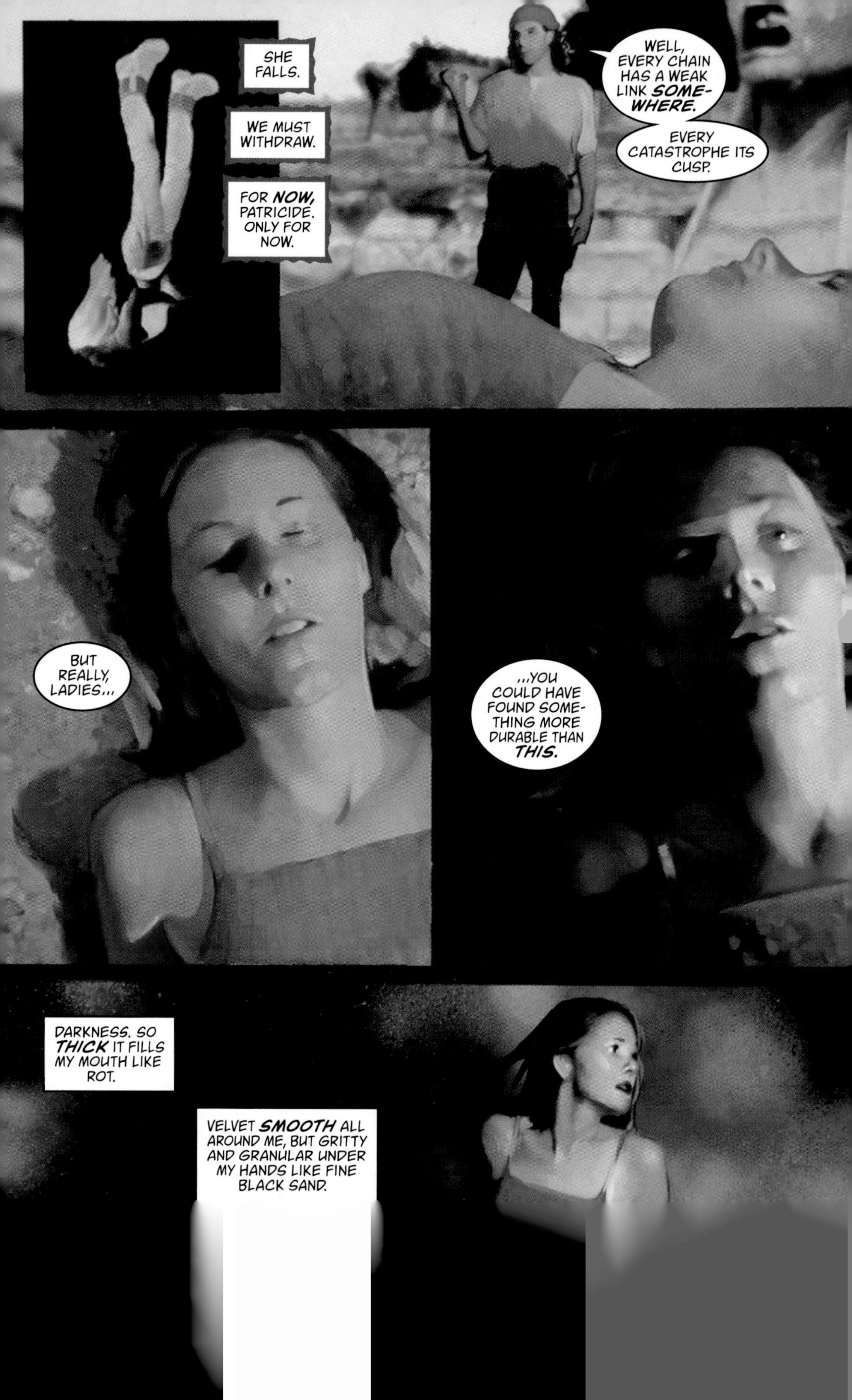
SHE FALLS.
WE MUST WITHDRAW.
FOR NOW, PATRICIDE. ONLY FOR NOW.
WELL, EVERY CHAIN HAS A WEAK LINK SOME-WHERE.
EVERY CATASTROPHE ITS CUSP.
BUT REALLY, LADIES...
...YOU COULD HAVE FOUND SOME-THING MORE DURABLE THAN THIS.
DARKNESS. SO THICK IT FILLS MY MOUTH LIKE ROT.
VELVET SMOOTH ALL AROUND ME, BUT GRITTY AND GRANULAR UNDER MY HANDS LIKE FINE BLACK SAND.

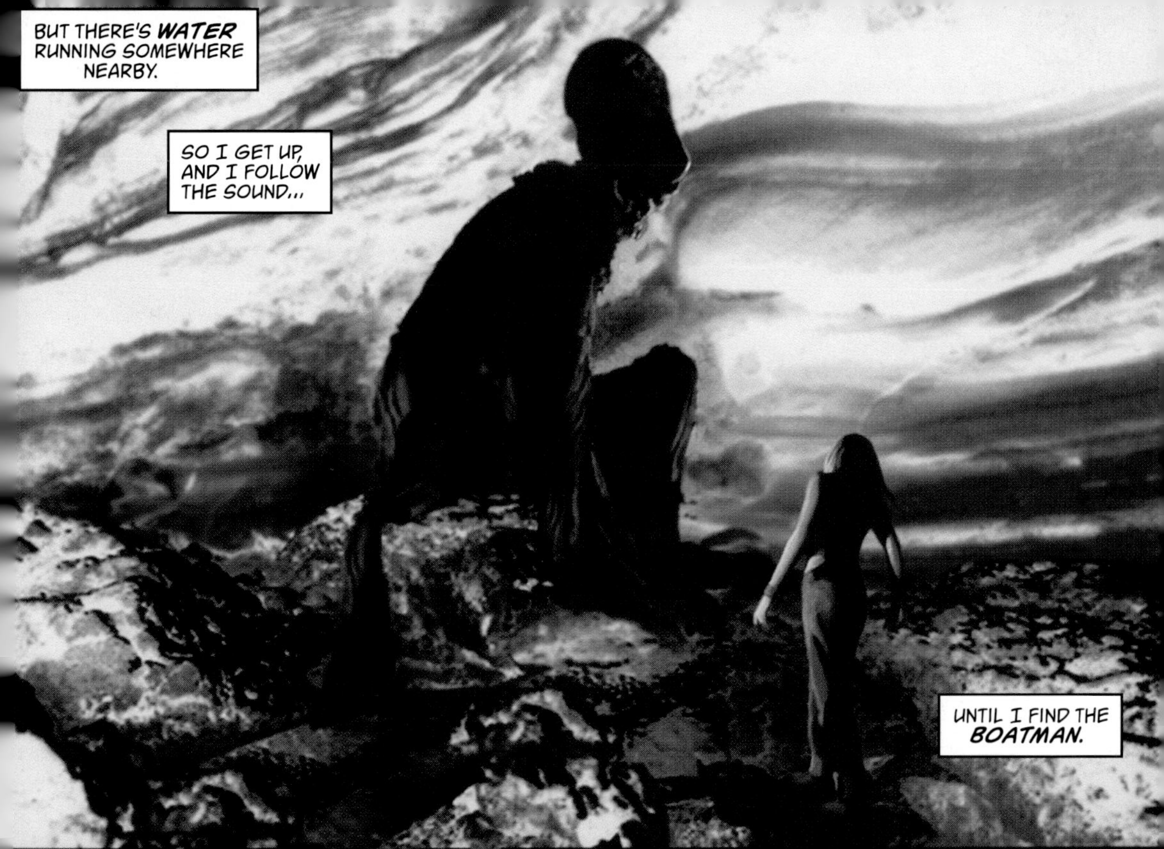
BUT THERE'S WATER RUNNING SOMEWHERE NEARBY.
SO I GET UP, AND I FOLLOW THE SOUND...
UNTIL I FIND THE BOATMAN.

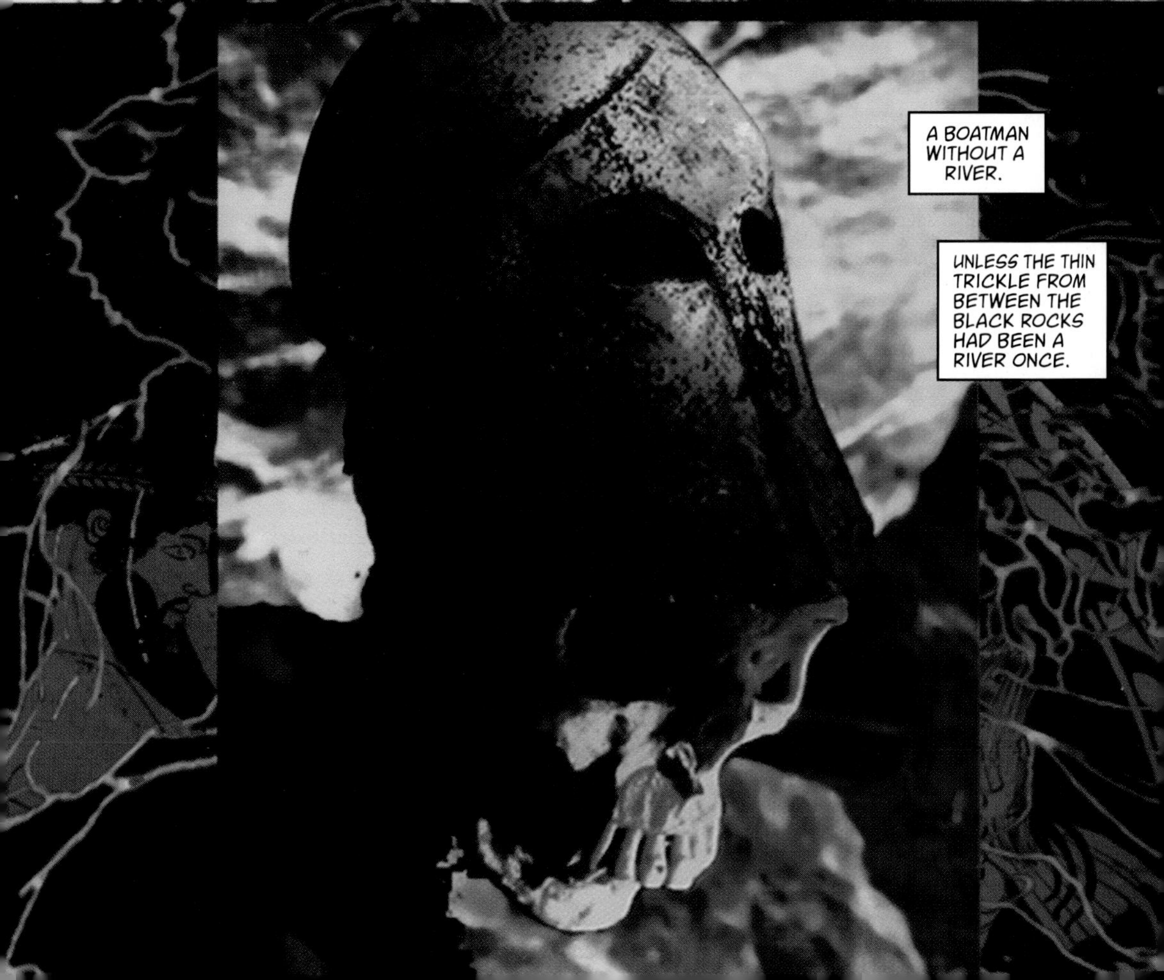
A BOATMAN WITHOUT A RIVER.
UNLESS THE THIN TRICKLE FROM BETWEEN THE BLACK ROCKS HAD BEEN A RIVER ONCE.

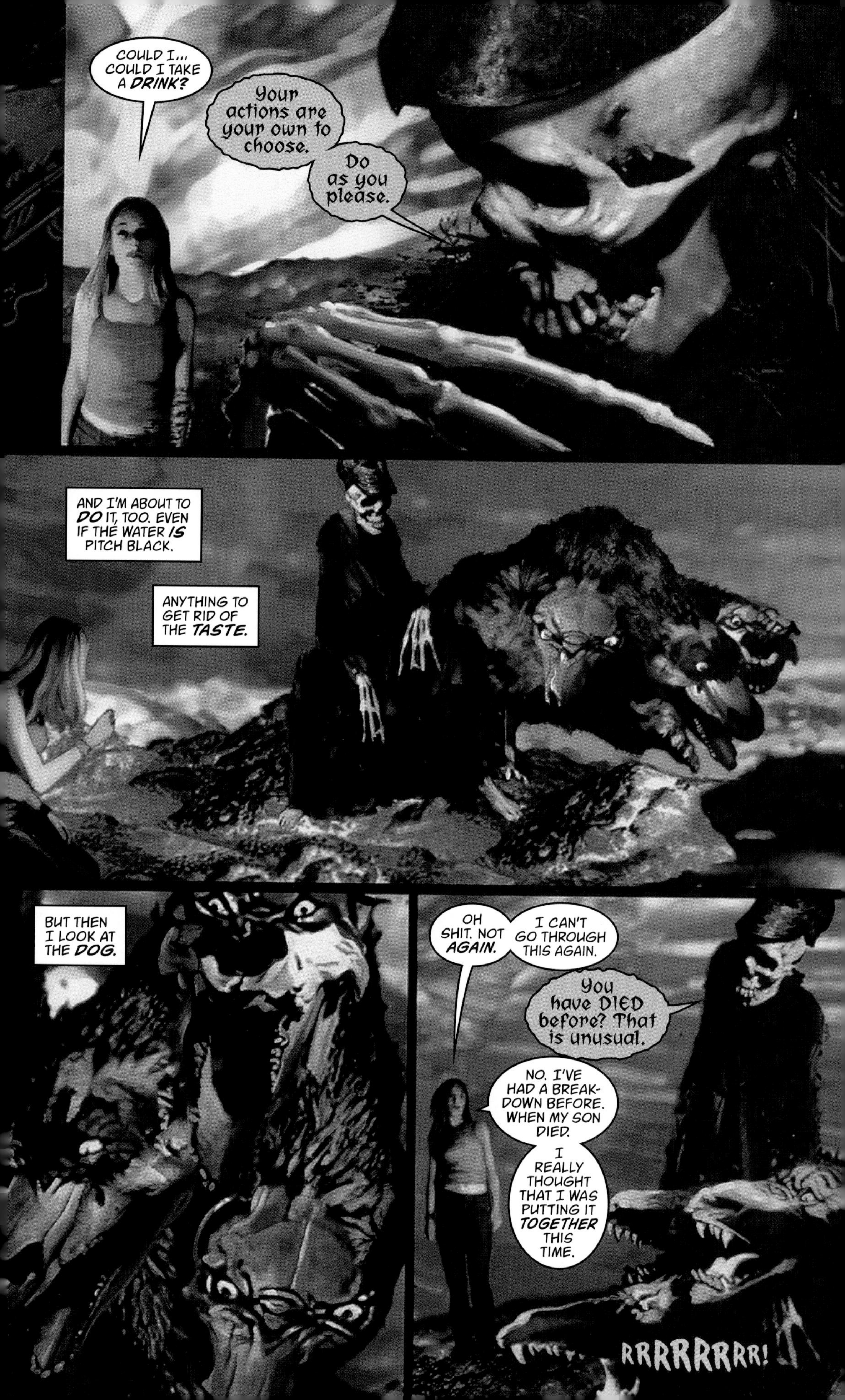
COULD I... COULD I TAKE A DRINK?
Your actions are your own to choose.
Do as you please.
AND I'M ABOUT TO DO IT, TOO. EVEN IF THE WATER IS PITCH BLACK.
ANYTHING TO GET RID OF THE TASTE.
BUT THEN I LOOK AT THE DOG.
OH SHIT. NOT AGAIN.
I CAN'T GO THROUGH THIS AGAIN.
You have DIED before? That is unusual.
NO. I'VE HAD A BREAK-DOWN BEFORE. WHEN MY SON DIED.
I REALLY THOUGHT THAT I WAS PUTTING IT TOGETHER THIS TIME.
RRRRRRRR!

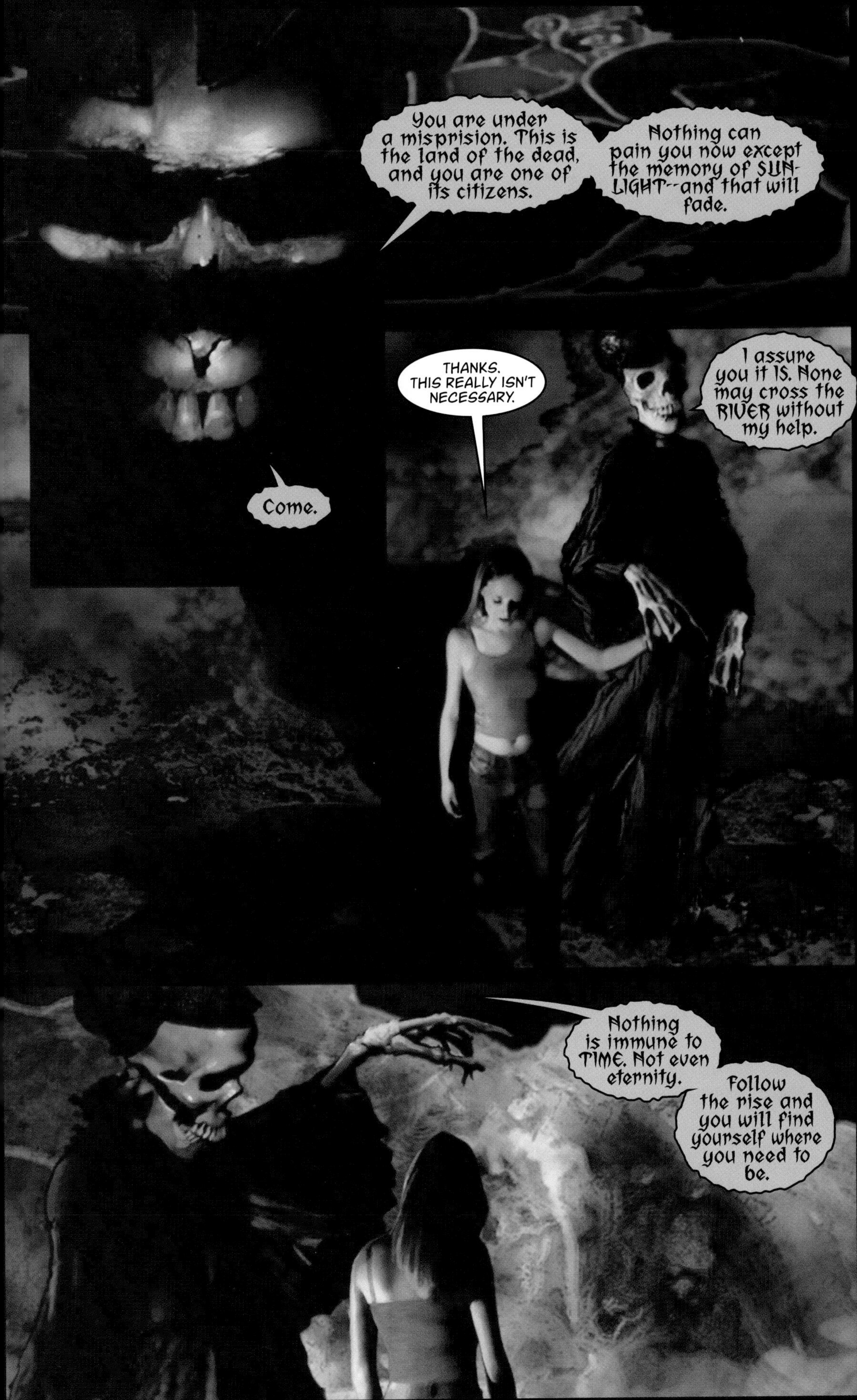
You are under a misprision. This is the land of the dead, and you are one of its citizens.
Nothing can pain you now except the memory of SUN-LIGHT--and that will fade.
Come.
THANKS. THIS REALLY ISN'T NECESSARY.
I assure you it IS. None may cross the RIVER without my help.
Nothing is immune to TIME. Not even eternity.
Follow the rise and you will find yourself where you need to be.

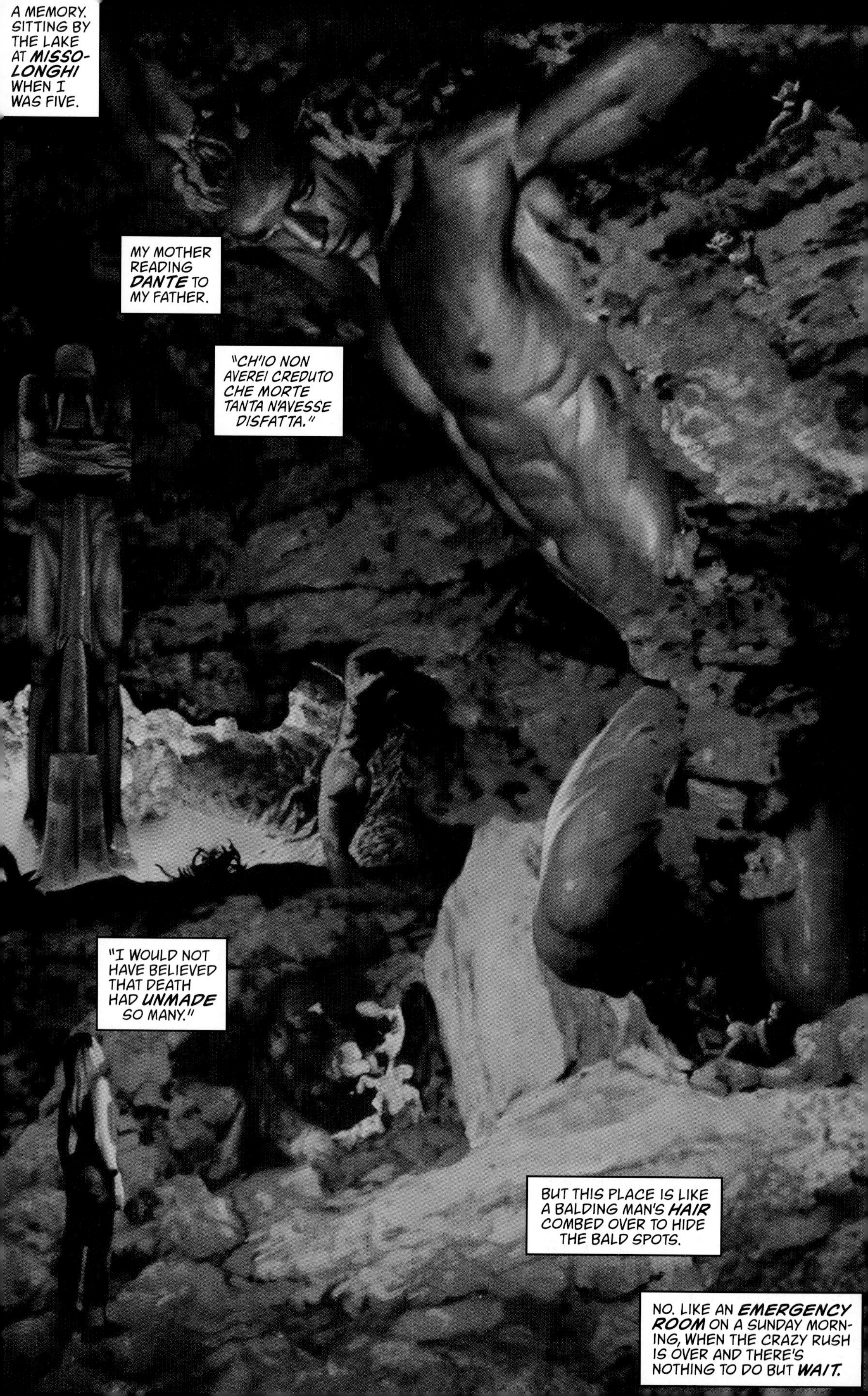
A MEMORY. SITTING BY THE LAKE AT MISSO-LONGHI WHEN I WAS FIVE.
MY MOTHER READING DANTE TO MY FATHER.
"CH'IO NON AVEREI CREDUTO CHE MORTE TANTA N'AVESSE DISFATTA."
"I WOULD NOT HAVE BELIEVED THAT DEATH HAD UNMADE SO MANY."
BUT THIS PLACE IS LIKE A BALDING MAN'S HAIR COMBED OVER TO HIDE THE BALD SPOTS.
NO. LIKE AN EMERGENCY ROOM ON A SUNDAY MORN-ING, WHEN THE CRAZY RUSH IS OVER AND THERE'S NOTHING TO DO BUT WAIT.

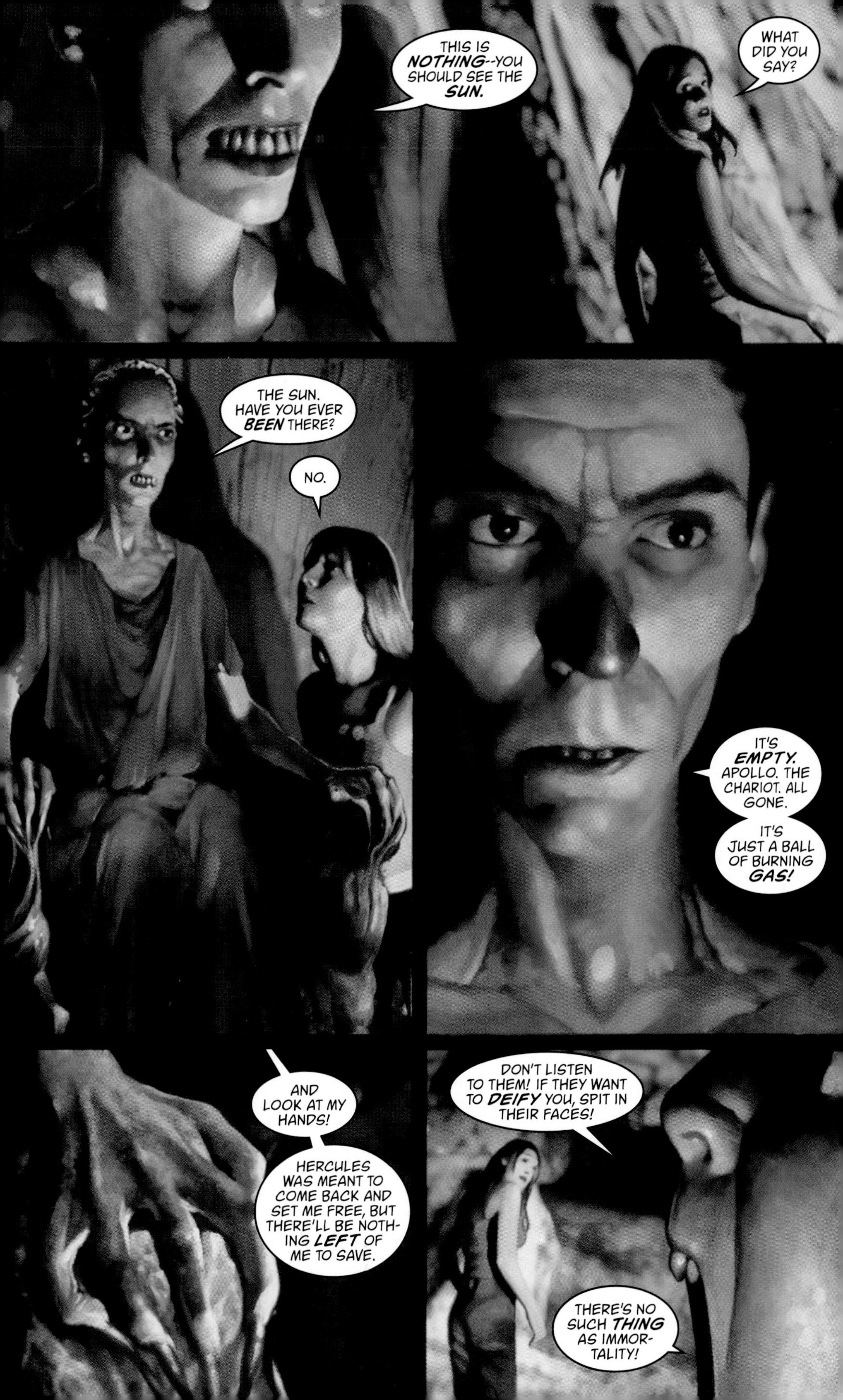
THIS IS NOTHING--YOU SHOULD SEE THE SUN.
WHAT DID YOU SAY?
THE SUN. HAVE YOU EVER BEEN THERE?
NO.
IT'S EMPTY. APOLLO. THE CHARIOT. ALL GONE.
IT'S JUST A BALL OF BURNING GAS!
AND LOOK AT MY HANDS!
HERCULES WAS MEANT TO COME BACK AND SET ME FREE, BUT THERE'LL BE NOTHING LEFT OF ME TO SAVE.
DON'T LISTEN TO THEM! IF THEY WANT TO DEIFY YOU, SPIT IN THEIR FACES!
THERE'S NO SUCH THING AS IMMORTALITY!

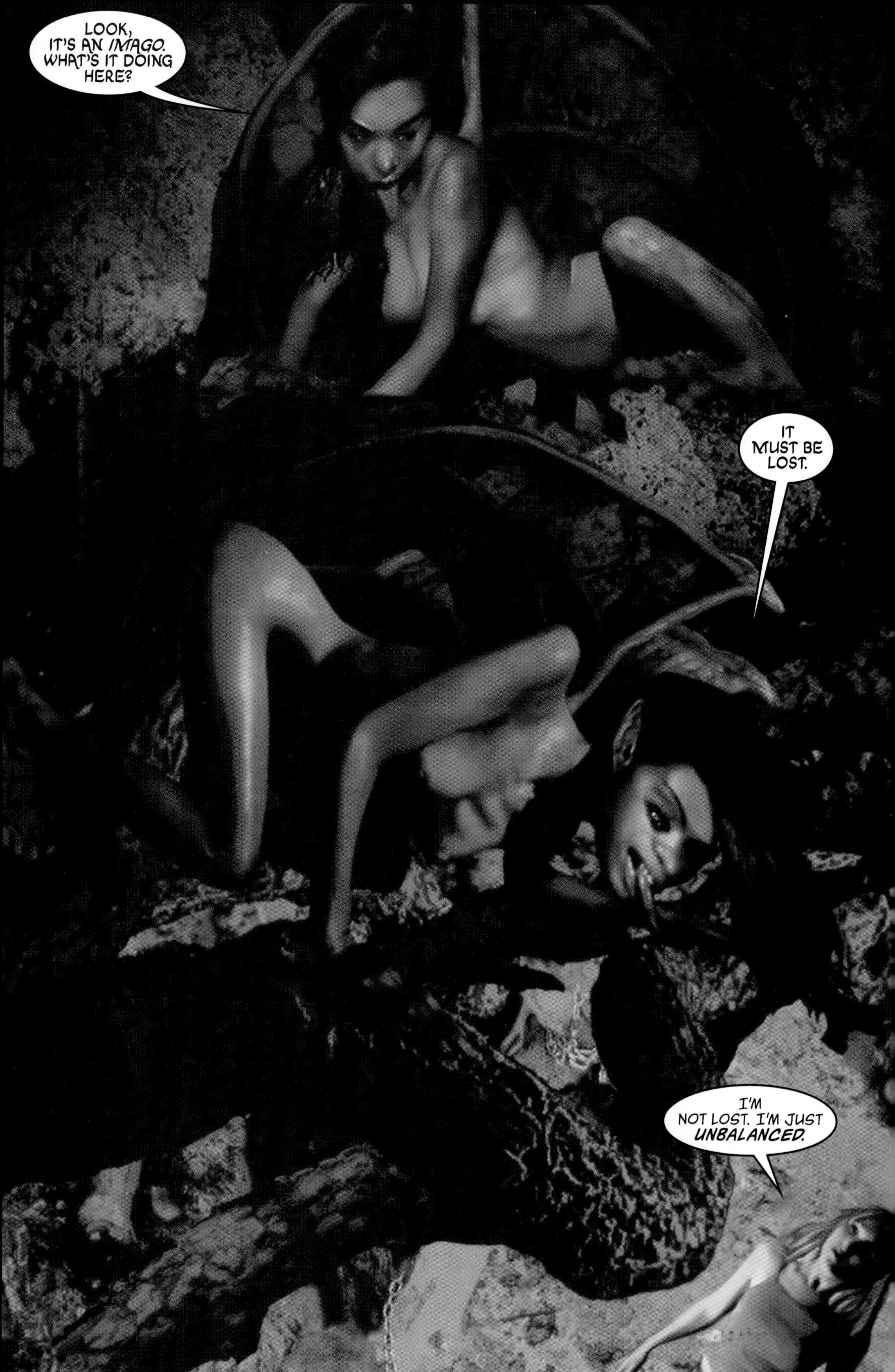
LOOK, IT'S AN IMAGO. WHAT'S IT DOING HERE?
IT MUST BE LOST.
I'M NOT LOST. I'M JUST UNBALANCED.

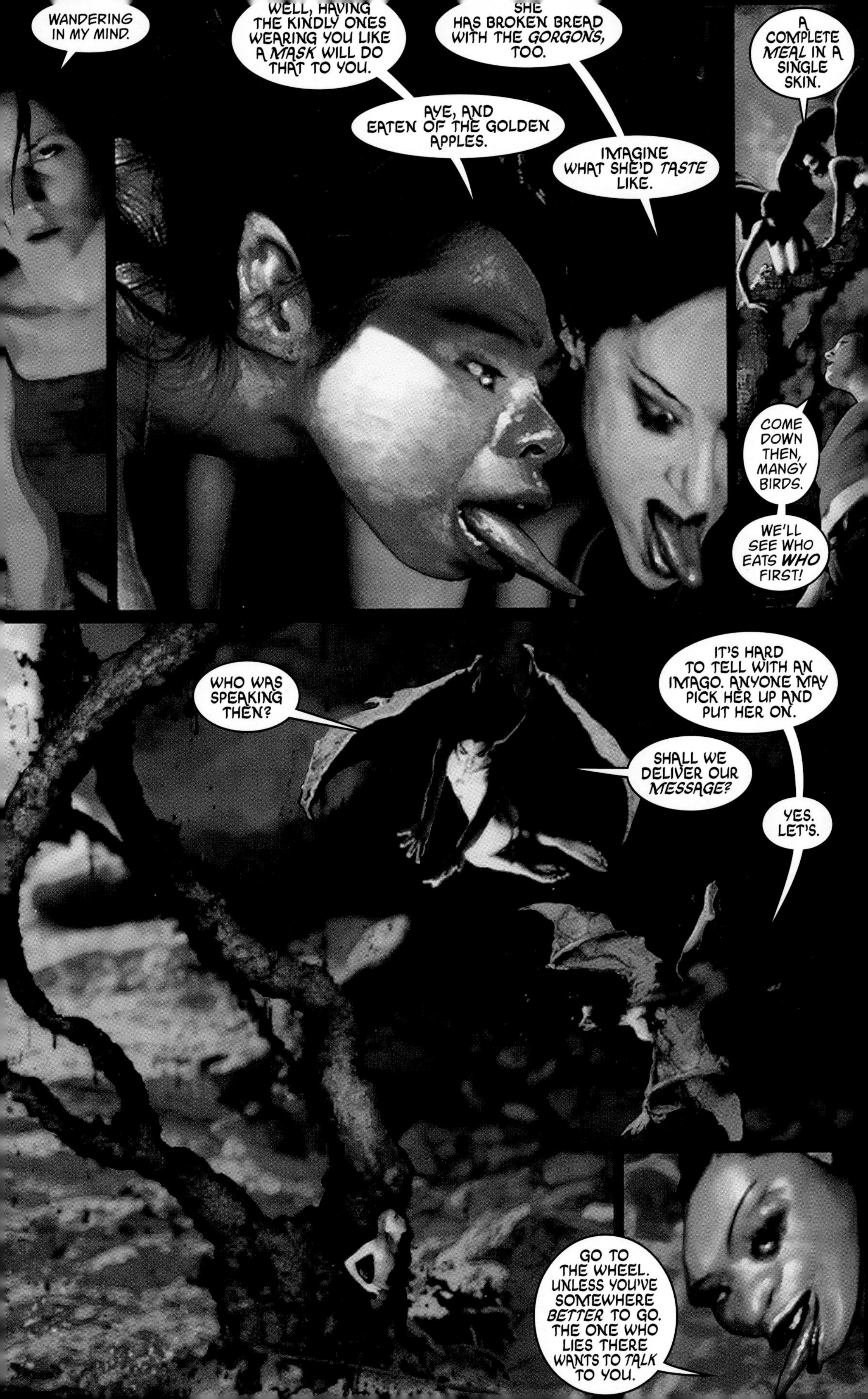
WANDERING IN MY MIND.
WELL, HAVING THE KINDLY ONES WEARING YOU LIKE A MASK WILL DO THAT TO YOU.
SHE HAS BROKEN BREAD WITH THE GORGONS, TOO.
A COMPLETE MEAL IN A SINGLE SKIN.
AYE, AND EATEN OF THE GOLDEN APPLES.
IMAGINE WHAT SHE'D TASTE LIKE.
COME DOWN THEN, MANGY BIRDS.
WE'LL SEE WHO EATS WHO FIRST!
WHO WAS SPEAKING THEN?
IT'S HARD TO TELL WITH AN IMAGO. ANYONE MAY PICK HER UP AND PUT HER ON.
SHALL WE DELIVER OUR MESSAGE?
YES. LET'S.
GO TO THE WHEEL. UNLESS YOU'VE SOMEWHERE BETTER TO GO. THE ONE WHO LIES THERE WANTS TO TALK TO YOU.

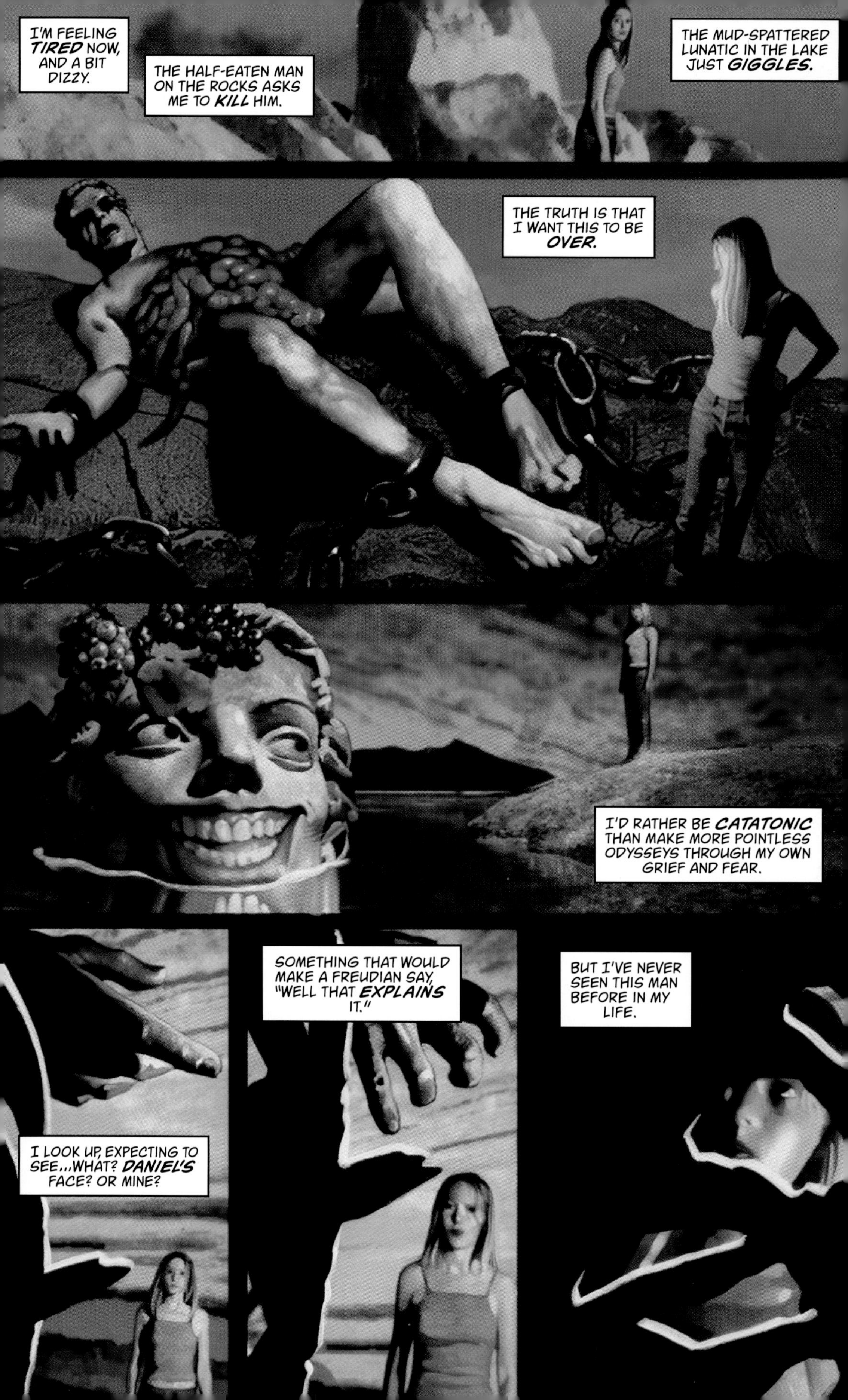
I'M FEELING TIRED NOW, AND A BIT DIZZY.
THE HALF-EATEN MAN ON THE ROCKS ASKS ME TO KILL HIM.
THE MUD-SPATTERED LUNATIC IN THE LAKE JUST GIGGLES.
THE TRUTH IS THAT I WANT THIS TO BE OVER.
I'D RATHER BE CATATONIC THAN MAKE MORE POINTLESS ODYSSEYS THROUGH MY OWN GRIEF AND FEAR.
I LOOK UP, EXPECTING TO SEE...WHAT? DANIEL'S FACE? OR MINE?
SOMETHING THAT WOULD MAKE A FREUDIAN SAY, "WELL THAT EXPLAINS IT."
BUT I'VE NEVER SEEN THIS MAN BEFORE IN MY LIFE.

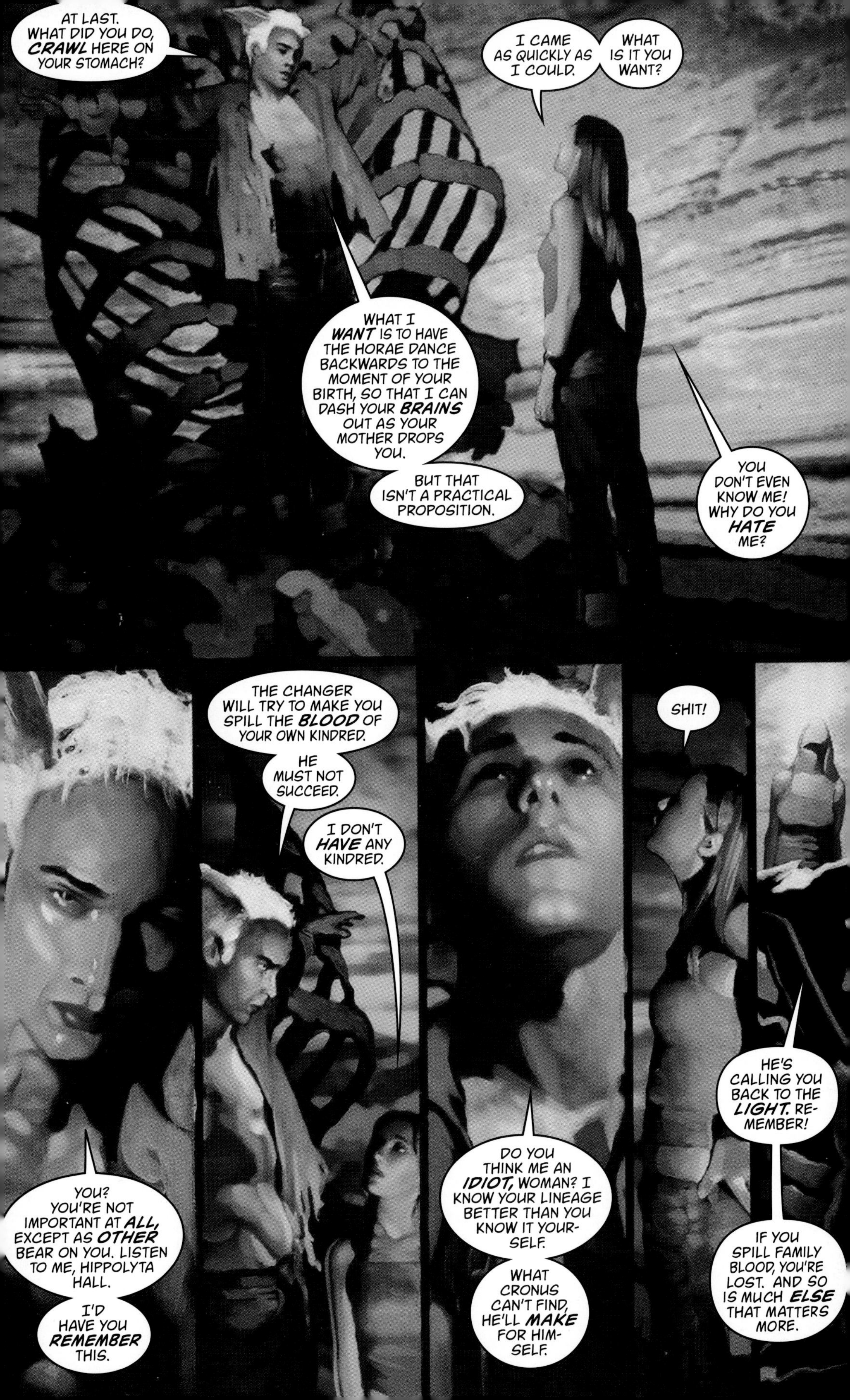
AT LAST. WHAT DID YOU DO, CRAWL HERE ON YOUR STOMACH?
I CAME AS QUICKLY AS I COULD.
WHAT IS IT YOU WANT?
WHAT I WANT IS TO HAVE THE HORAE DANCE BACKWARDS TO THE MOMENT OF YOUR BIRTH, SO THAT I CAN DASH YOUR BRAINS OUT AS YOUR MOTHER DROPS YOU.
BUT THAT ISN'T A PRACTICAL PROPOSITION.
YOU DON'T EVEN KNOW ME! WHY DO YOU HATE ME?
YOU? YOU'RE NOT IMPORTANT AT ALL, EXCEPT AS OTHER BEAR ON YOU. LISTEN TO ME, HIPPOLYTA HALL.
I'D HAVE YOU REMEMBER THIS.
THE CHANGER WILL TRY TO MAKE YOU SPILL THE BLOOD OF YOUR OWN KINDRED.
HE MUST NOT SUCCEED.
I DON'T HAVE ANY KINDRED.
DO YOU THINK ME AN IDIOT, WOMAN? I KNOW YOUR LINEAGE BETTER THAN YOU KNOW IT YOURSELF.
WHAT CRONUS CAN'T FIND, HE'LL MAKE FOR HIMSELF.
SHIT!
HE'S CALLING YOU BACK TO THE LIGHT. REMEMBER!
IF YOU SPILL FAMILY BLOOD, YOU'RE LOST. AND SO IS MUCH ELSE THAT MATTERS MORE.

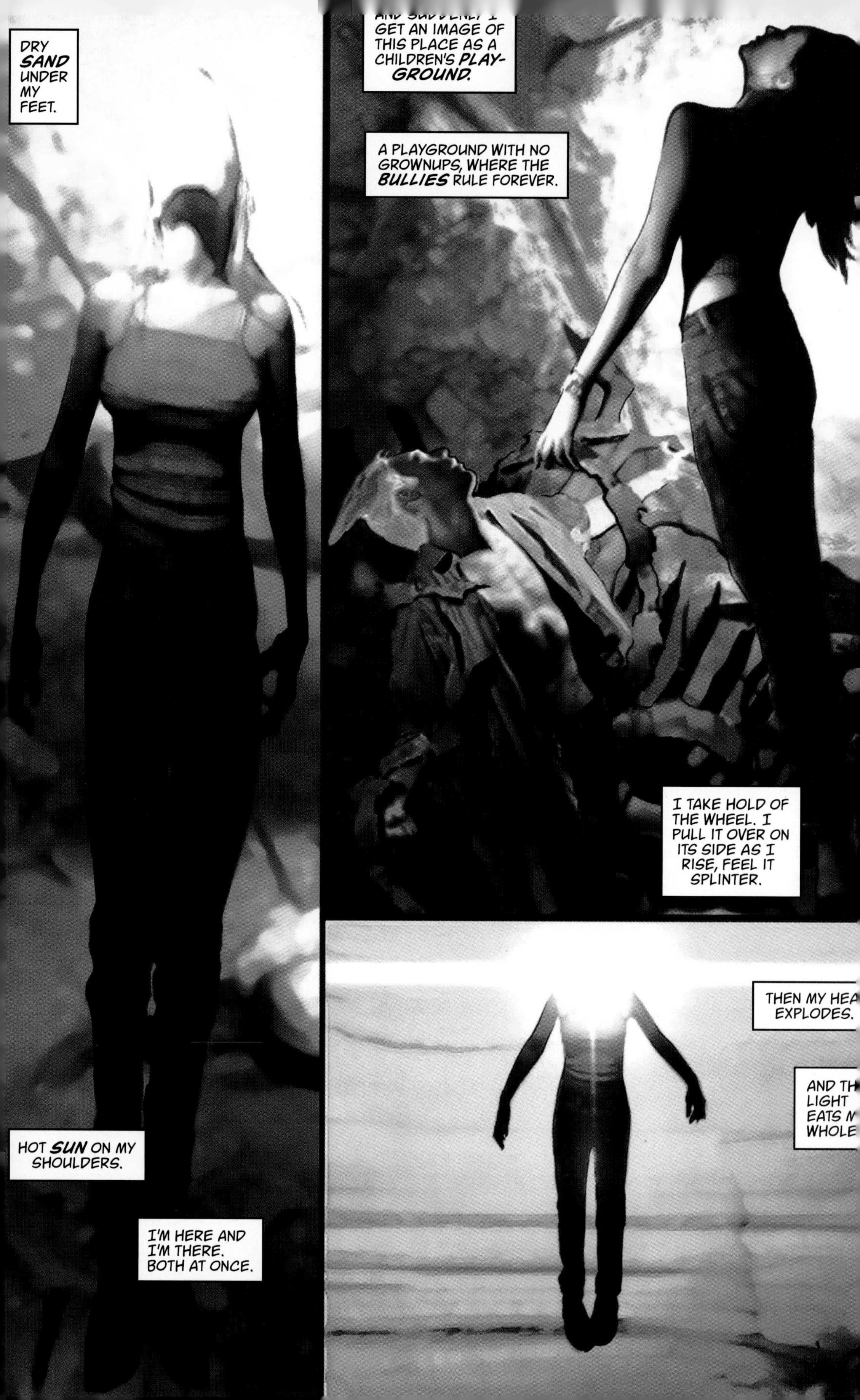
DRY SAND UNDER MY FEET.
HOT SUN ON MY SHOULDERS.
I'M HERE AND I'M THERE. BOTH AT ONCE.
GET AN IMAGE OF THIS PLACE AS A CHILDREN'S PLAY-GROUND.
A PLAYGROUND WITH NO GROWNUPS, WHERE THE BULLIES RULE FOREVER.
I TAKE HOLD OF THE WHEEL. I PULL IT OVER ON ITS SIDE AS I RISE, FEEL IT SPLINTER.
THEN MY HEA
EXPLODES.
AND TH
LIGHT
EATS M
WHOLE

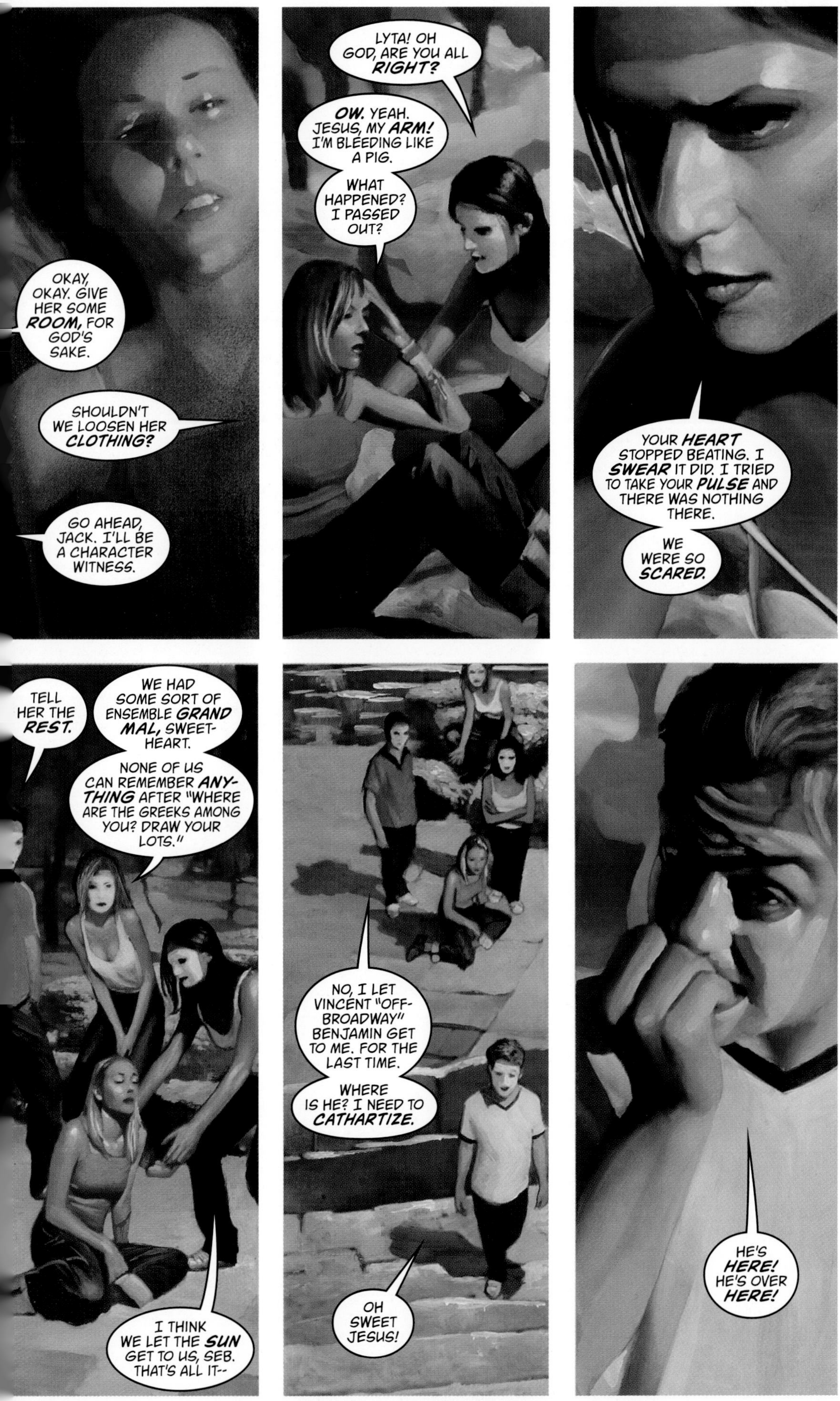
LYTA! OH GOD, ARE YOU ALL RIGHT?
OW. YEAH. JESUS, MY ARM! I'M BLEEDING LIKE A PIG.
WHAT HAPPENED? I PASSED OUT?
OKAY, OKAY. GIVE HER SOME ROOM, FOR GOD'S SAKE.
SHOULDN'T WE LOOSEN HER CLOTHING?
GO AHEAD, JACK. I'LL BE A CHARACTER WITNESS.
YOUR HEART STOPPED BEATING. I SWEAR IT DID. I TRIED TO TAKE YOUR PULSE AND THERE WAS NOTHING THERE.
WE WERE SO SCARED.
TELL HER THE REST.
WE HAD SOME SORT OF ENSEMBLE GRAND MAL, SWEET-HEART.
NONE OF US CAN REMEMBER ANY-THING AFTER "WHERE ARE THE GREEKS AMONG YOU? DRAW YOUR LOTS."
I THINK WE LET THE SUN GET TO US, SEB. THAT'S ALL IT--
NO, I LET VINCENT "OFF-BROADWAY" BENJAMIN GET TO ME. FOR THE LAST TIME.
WHERE IS HE? I NEED TO CATHARTIZE.
OH SWEET JESUS!
HE'S HERE! HE'S OVER HERE!

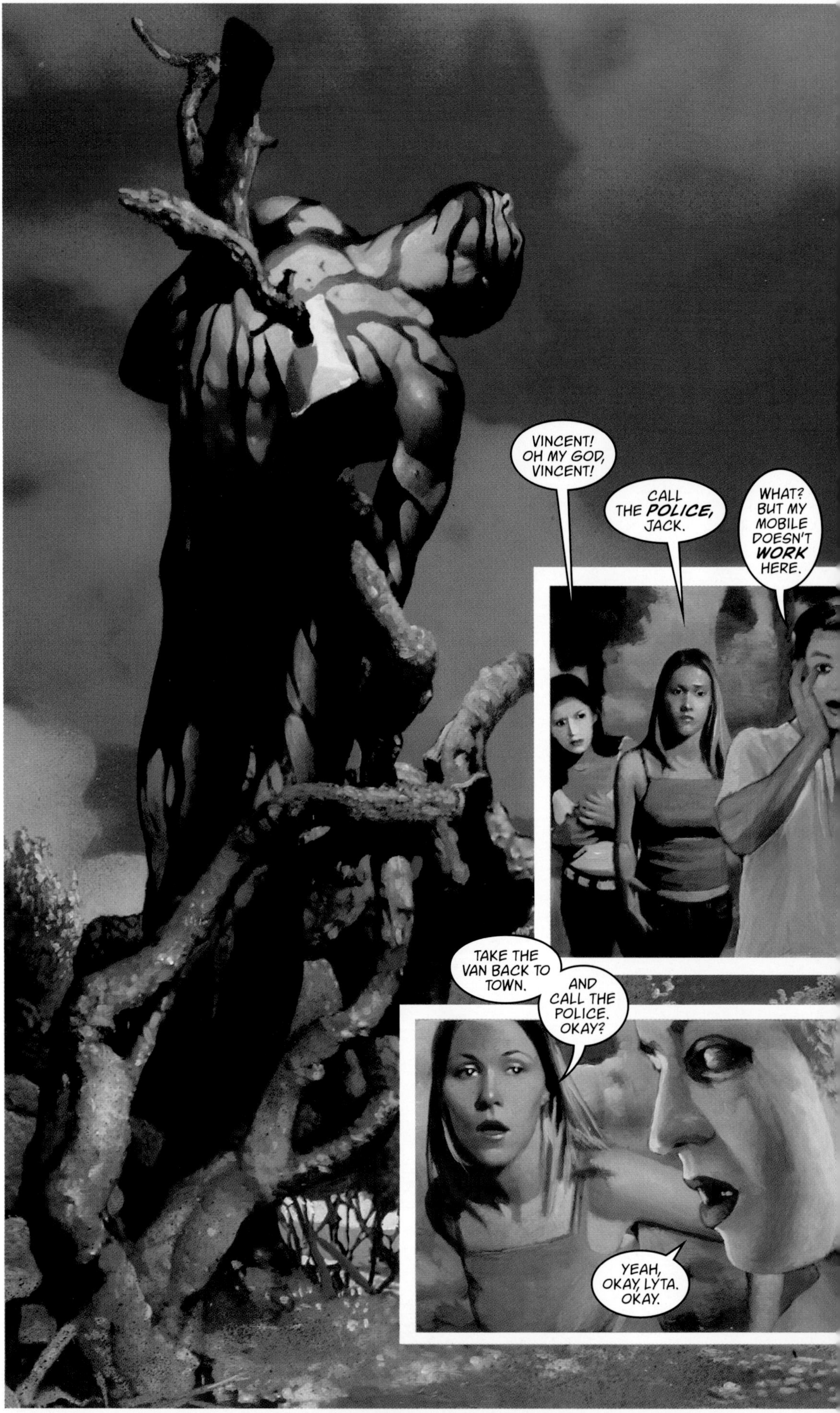
VINCENT! OH MY GOD, VINCENT!
CALL THE **POLICE,** JACK.
WHAT? BUT MY MOBILE DOESN'T **WORK** HERE.
TAKE THE VAN BACK TO TOWN.
AND CALL THE POLICE. OKAY?
YEAH, OKAY, LYTA. OKAY.

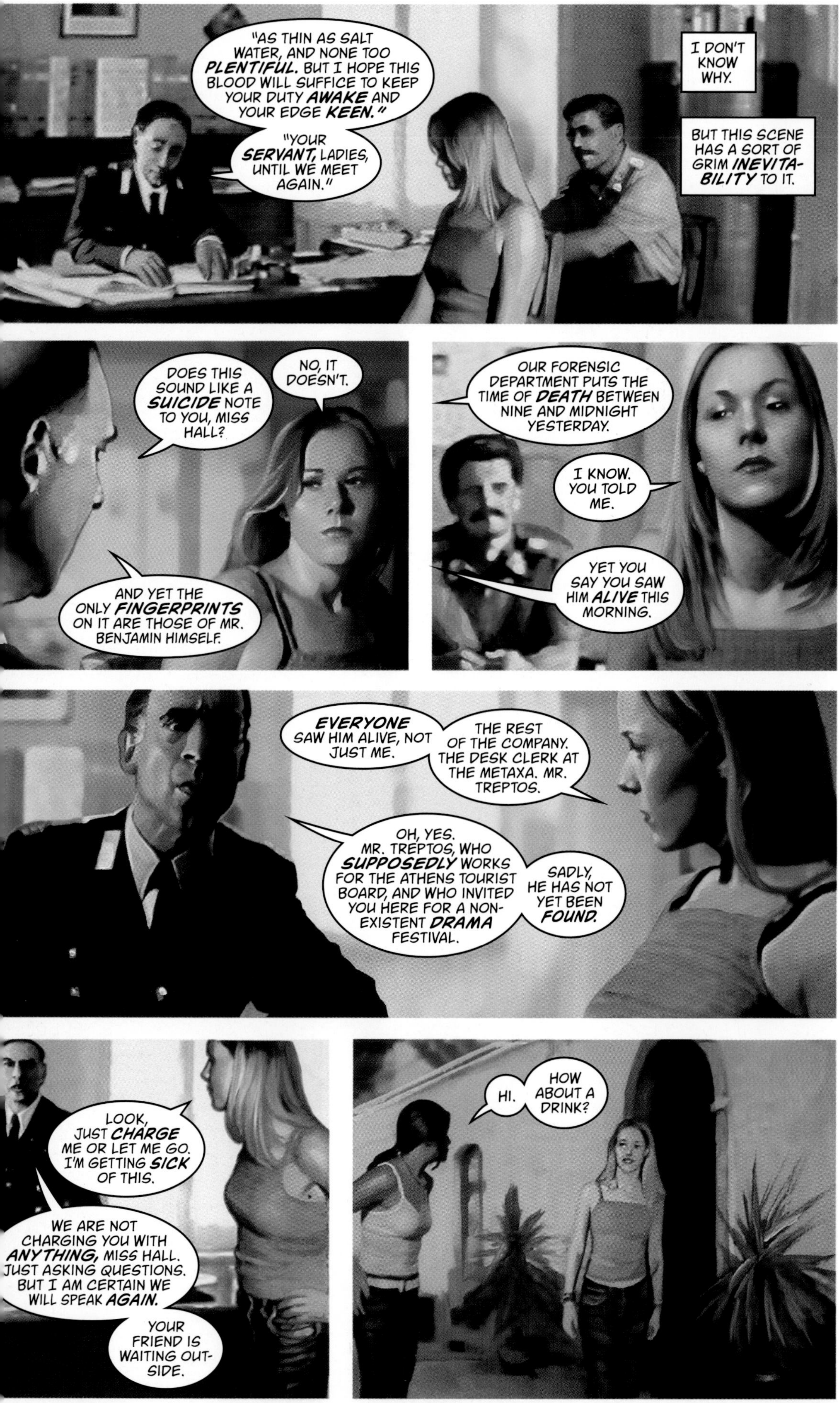
"AS THIN AS SALT WATER, AND NONE TOO PLENTIFUL. BUT I HOPE THIS BLOOD WILL SUFFICE TO KEEP YOUR DUTY AWAKE AND YOUR EDGE KEEN."
"YOUR SERVANT, LADIES, UNTIL WE MEET AGAIN."
I DON'T KNOW WHY.
BUT THIS SCENE HAS A SORT OF GRIM INEVITA-BILITY TO IT.
DOES THIS SOUND LIKE A SUICIDE NOTE TO YOU, MISS HALL?
NO, IT DOESN'T.
AND YET THE ONLY FINGERPRINTS ON IT ARE THOSE OF MR. BENJAMIN HIMSELF.
OUR FORENSIC DEPARTMENT PUTS THE TIME OF DEATH BETWEEN NINE AND MIDNIGHT YESTERDAY.
I KNOW. YOU TOLD ME.
YET YOU SAY YOU SAW HIM ALIVE THIS MORNING.
EVERYONE SAW HIM ALIVE, NOT JUST ME.
THE REST OF THE COMPANY. THE DESK CLERK AT THE METAXA. MR. TREPTOS.
OH, YES. MR. TREPTOS, WHO SUPPOSEDLY WORKS FOR THE ATHENS TOURIST BOARD, AND WHO INVITED YOU HERE FOR A NON-EXISTENT DRAMA FESTIVAL.
SADLY, HE HAS NOT YET BEEN FOUND.
LOOK, JUST CHARGE ME OR LET ME GO. I'M GETTING SICK OF THIS.
WE ARE NOT CHARGING YOU WITH ANYTHING, MISS HALL. JUST ASKING QUESTIONS. BUT I AM CERTAIN WE WILL SPEAK AGAIN.
YOUR FRIEND IS WAITING OUT-SIDE.
HI.
HOW ABOUT A DRINK?

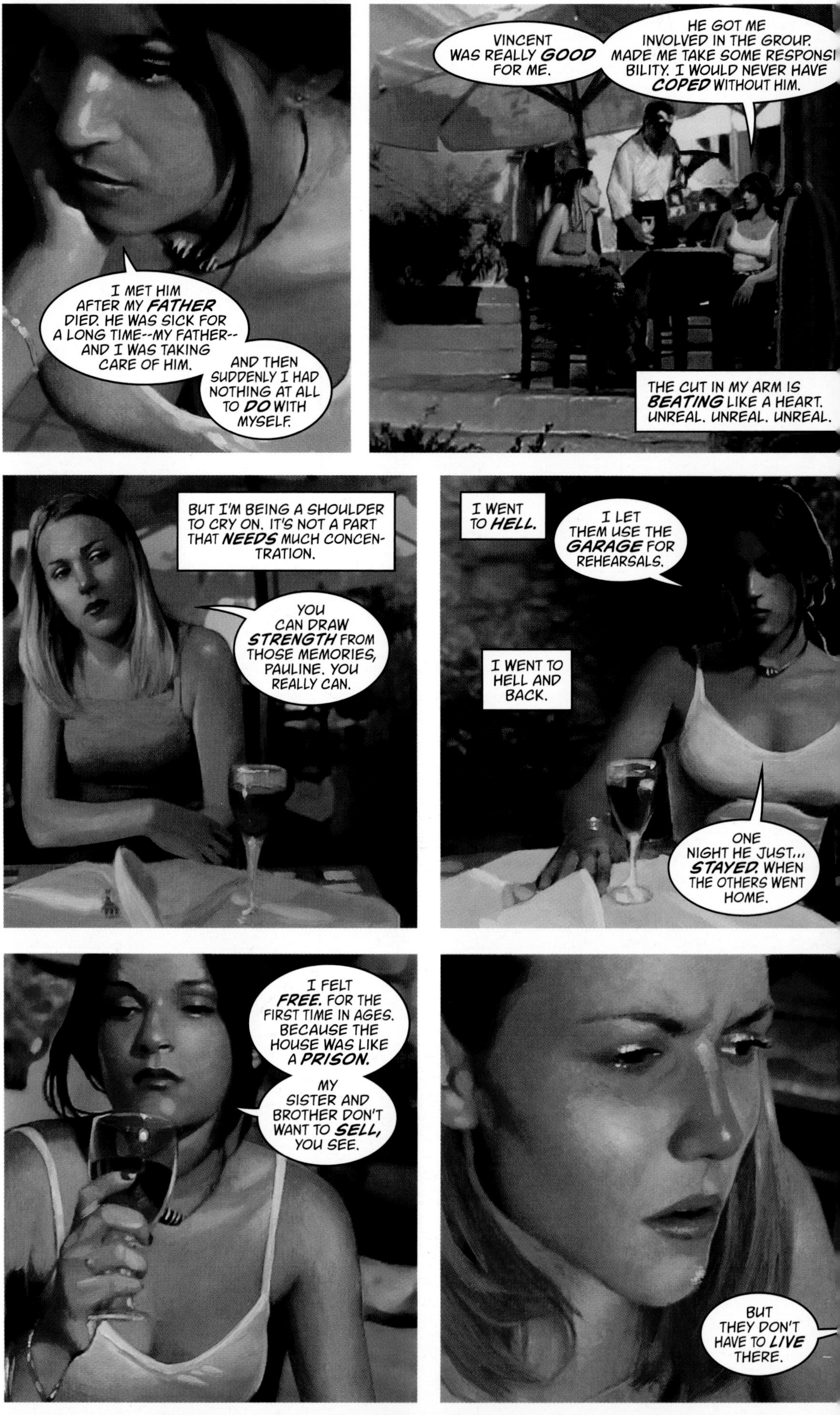
I MET HIM AFTER MY FATHER DIED. HE WAS SICK FOR A LONG TIME--MY FATHER-- AND I WAS TAKING CARE OF HIM.
AND THEN SUDDENLY I HAD NOTHING AT ALL TO DO WITH MYSELF.
VINCENT WAS REALLY GOOD FOR ME.
HE GOT ME INVOLVED IN THE GROUP. MADE ME TAKE SOME RESPONSI BILITY. I WOULD NEVER HAVE COPED WITHOUT HIM.
THE CUT IN MY ARM IS BEATING LIKE A HEART. UNREAL. UNREAL. UNREAL.
BUT I'M BEING A SHOULDER TO CRY ON. IT'S NOT A PART THAT NEEDS MUCH CONCENTRATION.
YOU CAN DRAW STRENGTH FROM THOSE MEMORIES, PAULINE. YOU REALLY CAN.
I WENT TO HELL.
I LET THEM USE THE GARAGE FOR REHEARSALS.
I WENT TO HELL AND BACK.
ONE NIGHT HE JUST... STAYED. WHEN THE OTHERS WENT HOME.
I FELT FREE. FOR THE FIRST TIME IN AGES. BECAUSE THE HOUSE WAS LIKE A PRISON.
MY SISTER AND BROTHER DON'T WANT TO SELL, YOU SEE.
BUT THEY DON'T HAVE TO LIVE THERE.

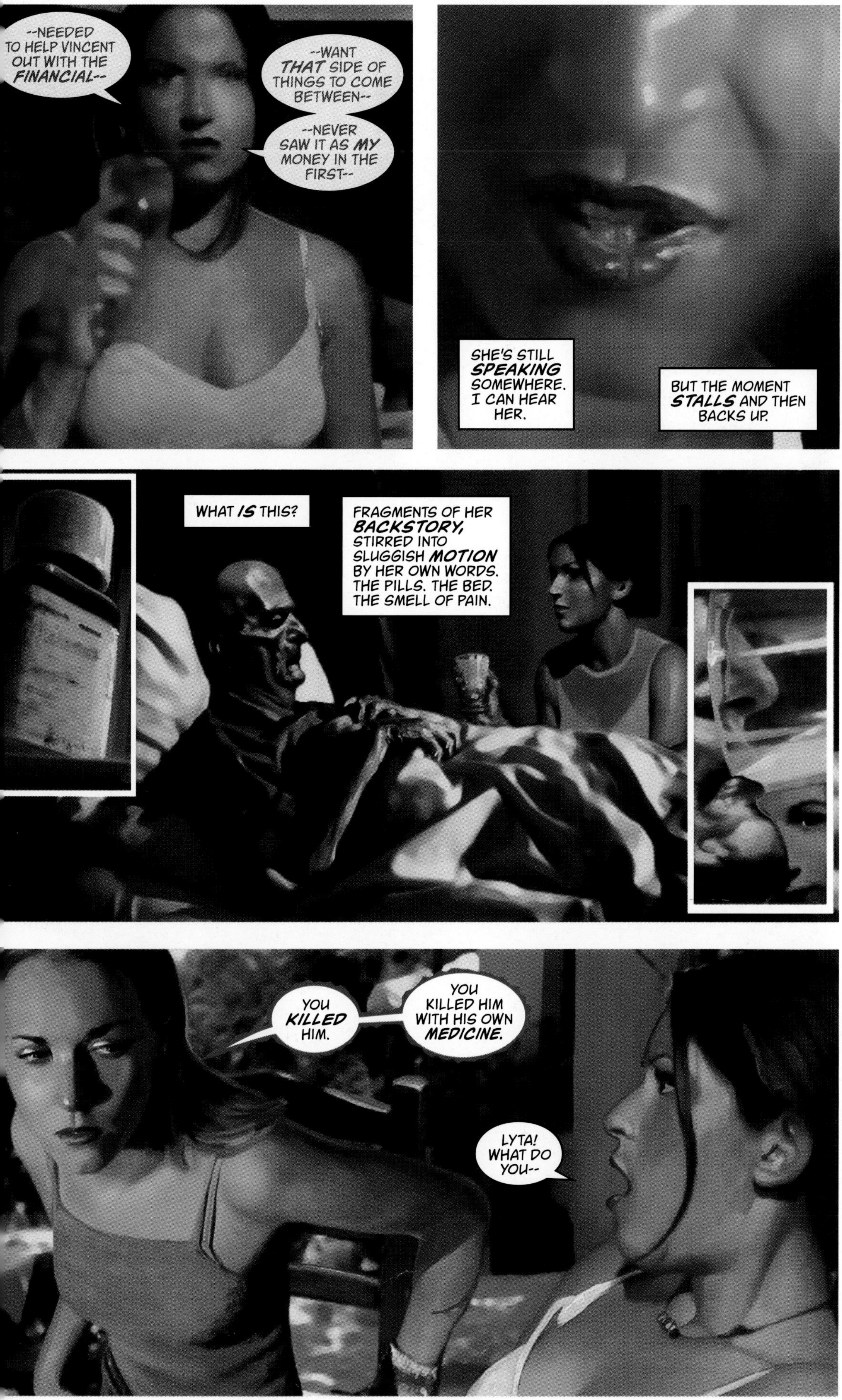
--NEEDED TO HELP VINCENT OUT WITH THE FINANCIAL--
--WANT THAT SIDE OF THINGS TO COME BETWEEN--
--NEVER SAW IT AS MY MONEY IN THE FIRST--
SHE'S STILL SPEAKING SOMEWHERE. I CAN HEAR HER.
BUT THE MOMENT STALLS AND THEN BACKS UP.
WHAT IS THIS?
FRAGMENTS OF HER BACKSTORY, STIRRED INTO SLUGGISH MOTION BY HER OWN WORDS. THE PILLS. THE BED. THE SMELL OF PAIN.
YOU KILLED HIM.
YOU KILLED HIM WITH HIS OWN MEDICINE.
LYTA! WHAT DO YOU--

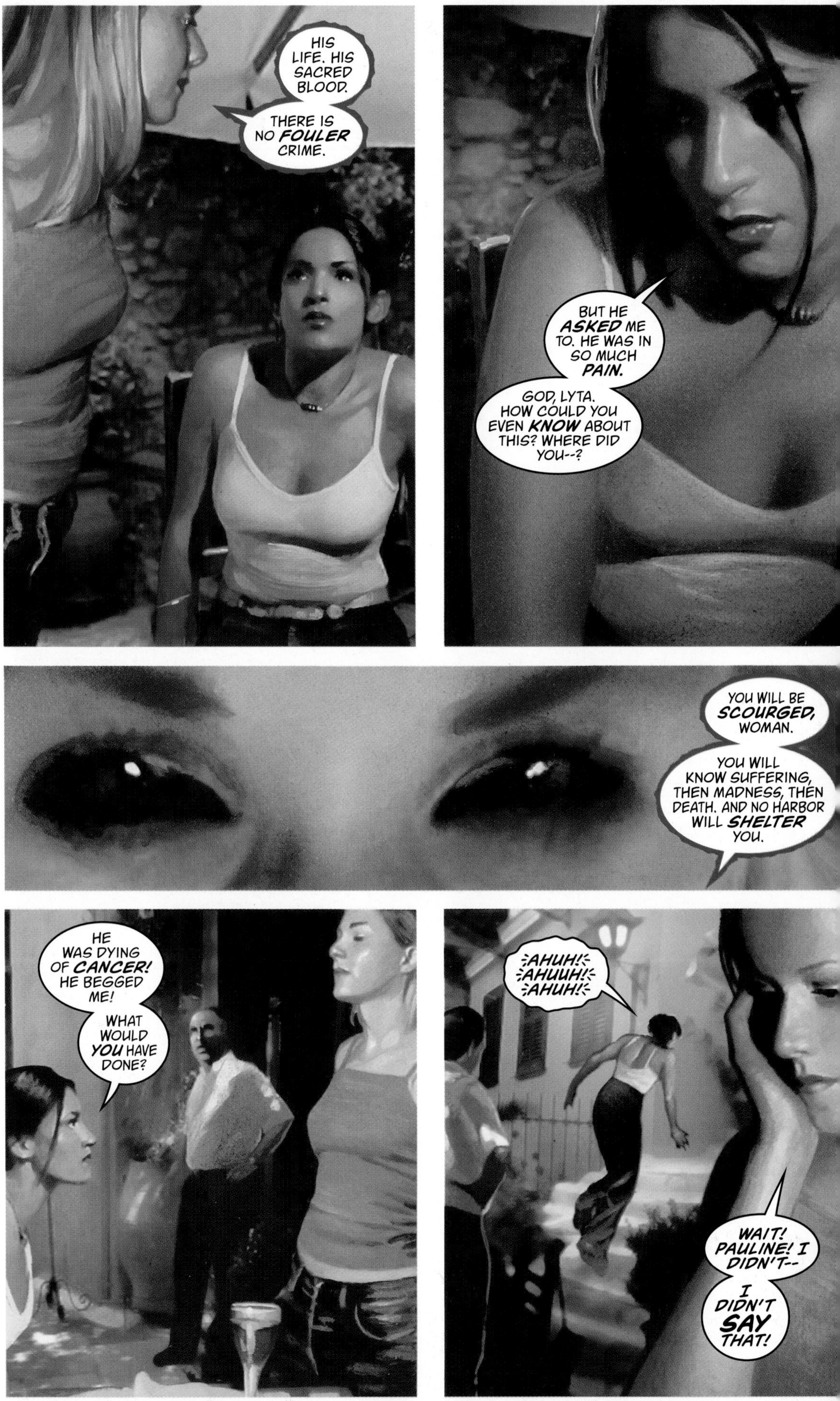
HIS LIFE. HIS SACRED BLOOD.
THERE IS NO FOULER CRIME.
BUT HE ASKED ME TO. HE WAS IN SO MUCH PAIN.
GOD, LYTA. HOW COULD YOU EVEN KNOW ABOUT THIS? WHERE DID YOU--?
YOU WILL BE SCOURGED, WOMAN.
YOU WILL KNOW SUFFERING, THEN MADNESS, THEN DEATH. AND NO HARBOR WILL SHELTER YOU.
HE WAS DYING OF CANCER! HE BEGGED ME!
WHAT WOULD YOU HAVE DONE?
AHUH! AHUUH! AHUH!
WAIT! PAULINE! I DIDN'T--
I DIDN'T SAY THAT!

WELL, NOW THAT'S A FIRST STEP TOWARDS *ENLIGHTEN-MENT.*

BLOOD REMEMBERS *BONE,* AND SEEDS REMEMBER *FLOWERS.* THE WHOLE OF CREATION IS BUILT OUT OF NESTED BOXES.

THUS YOU ARE ALL *PRISONERS* OF YOUR OWN PAST, COMPELLED TO DANCE THE SAME STEPS OVER AND OVER.

ONLY THE CHANGER CHANGES.

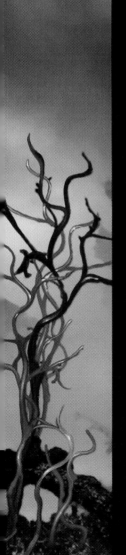

WHEN I RULED, ALL THINGS WERE *COMPOSED* OF CHANGE. THE PAST WAS MEREST CLOUD-SHADOW.

MINDS AND SOULS WERE LIKE AEOLIAN *HARPS,* THAT THE WINDS PLUCKED AND PLAYED ON.

AND *SEEDS* REMEMBERED BLOOD.

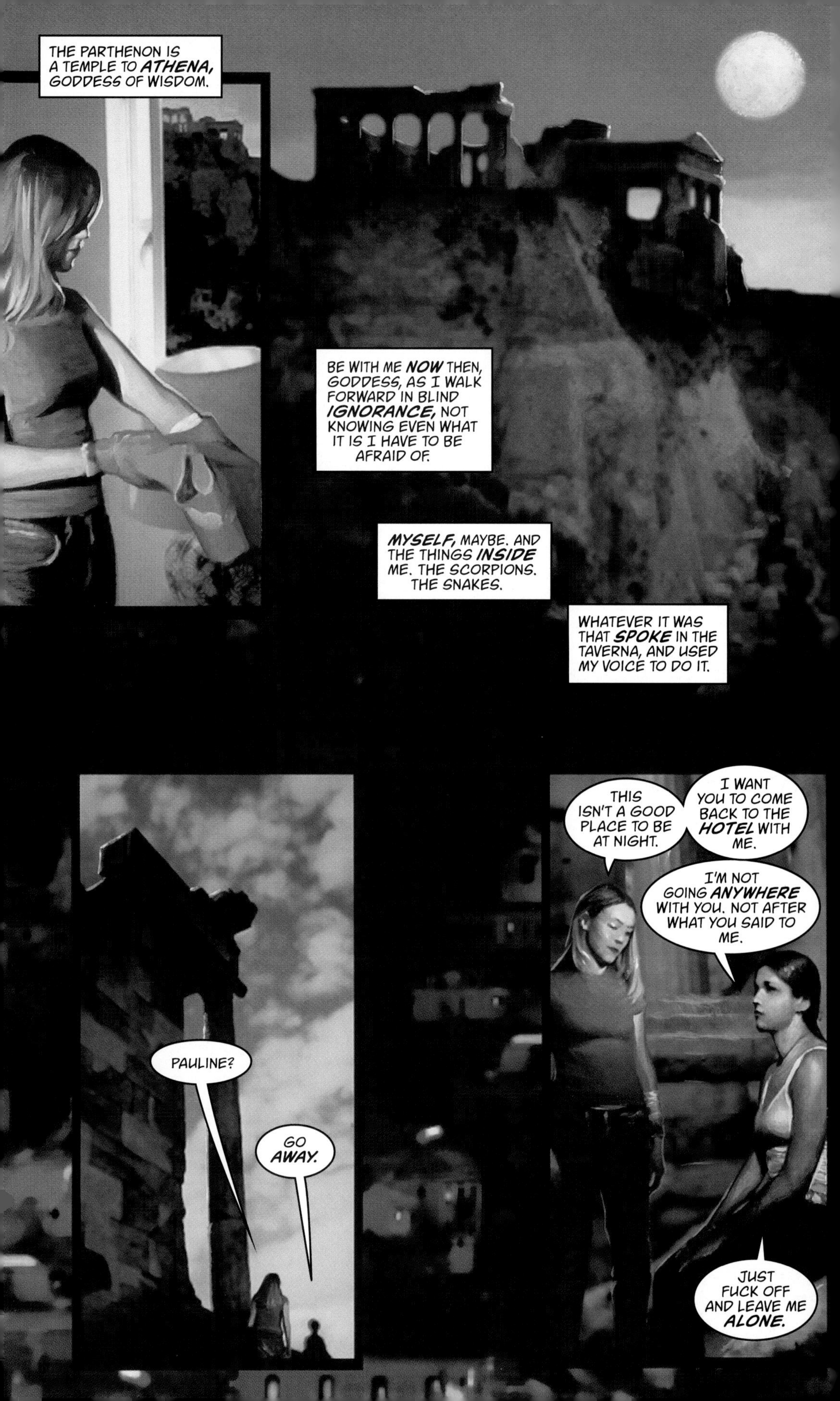
THE PARTHENON IS A TEMPLE TO ATHENA, GODDESS OF WISDOM.
BE WITH ME NOW THEN, GODDESS, AS I WALK FORWARD IN BLIND IGNORANCE, NOT KNOWING EVEN WHAT IT IS I HAVE TO BE AFRAID OF.
MYSELF, MAYBE. AND THE THINGS INSIDE ME. THE SCORPIONS. THE SNAKES.
WHATEVER IT WAS THAT SPOKE IN THE TAVERNA, AND USED MY VOICE TO DO IT.
PAULINE?
GO AWAY.
THIS ISN'T A GOOD PLACE TO BE AT NIGHT.
I WANT YOU TO COME BACK TO THE HOTEL WITH ME.
I'M NOT GOING ANYWHERE WITH YOU. NOT AFTER WHAT YOU SAID TO ME.
JUST FUCK OFF AND LEAVE ME ALONE.

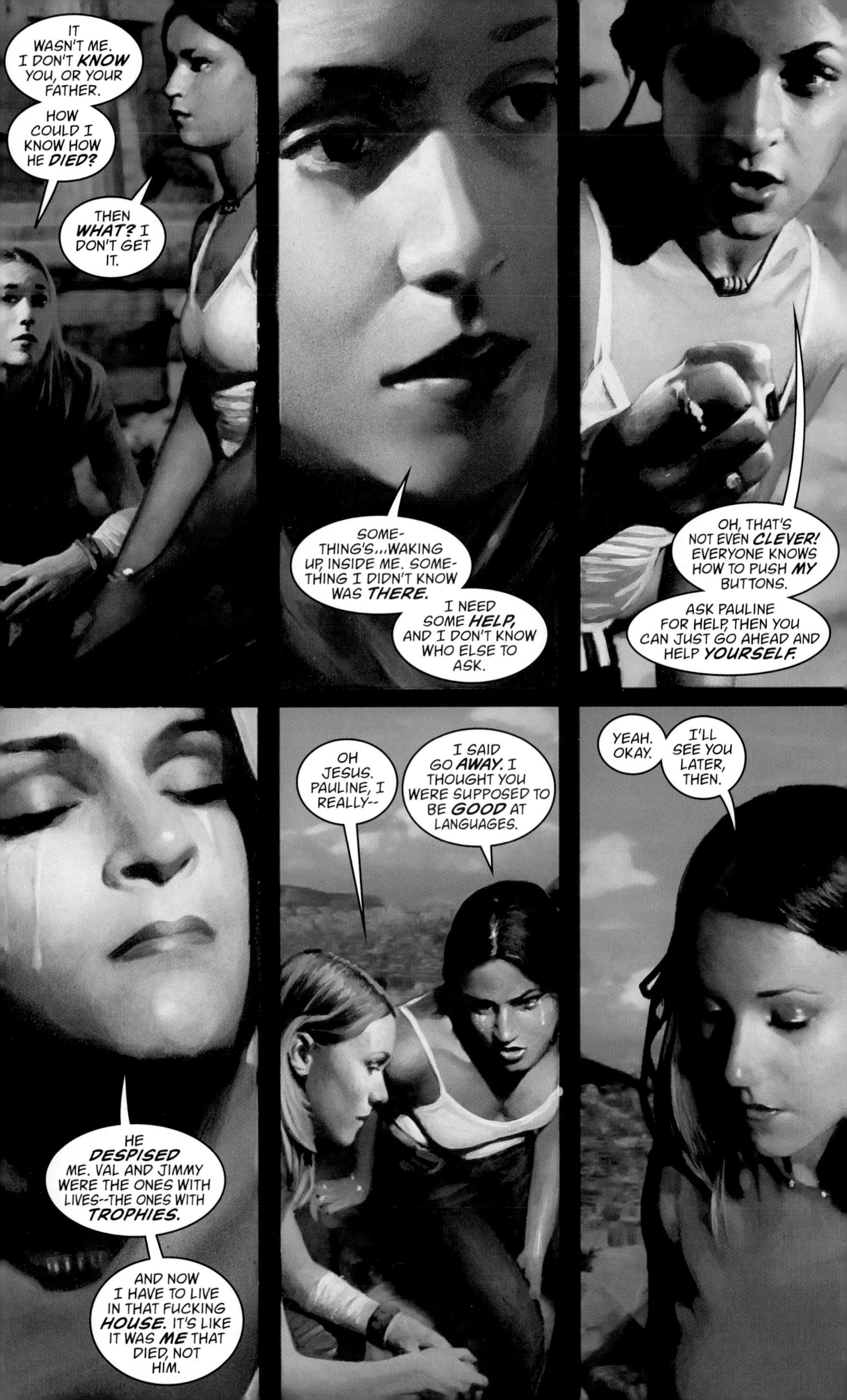
IT WASN'T ME. I DON'T KNOW YOU, OR YOUR FATHER.
HOW COULD I KNOW HOW HE DIED?
THEN WHAT? I DON'T GET IT.
SOME-THING'S...WAKING UP, INSIDE ME. SOME-THING I DIDN'T KNOW WAS THERE.
I NEED SOME HELP, AND I DON'T KNOW WHO ELSE TO ASK.
OH, THAT'S NOT EVEN CLEVER! EVERYONE KNOWS HOW TO PUSH MY BUTTONS.
ASK PAULINE FOR HELP, THEN YOU CAN JUST GO AHEAD AND HELP YOURSELF.
HE DESPISED ME. VAL AND JIMMY WERE THE ONES WITH LIVES--THE ONES WITH TROPHIES.
AND NOW I HAVE TO LIVE IN THAT FUCKING HOUSE. IT'S LIKE IT WAS ME THAT DIED, NOT HIM.
OH JESUS. PAULINE, I REALLY--
I SAID GO AWAY. I THOUGHT YOU WERE SUPPOSED TO BE GOOD AT LANGUAGES.
YEAH. OKAY.
I'LL SEE YOU LATER, THEN.

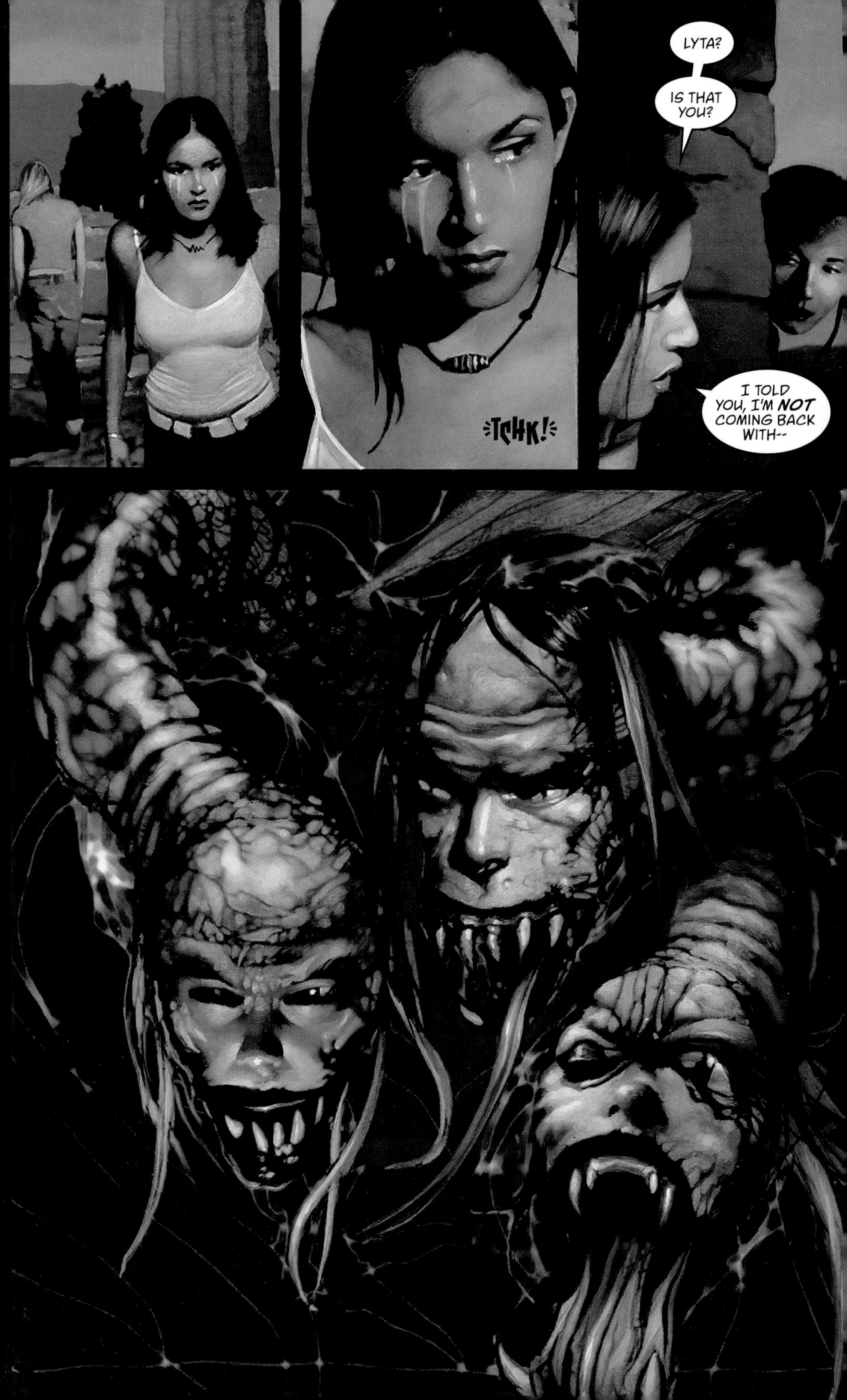
TCHK!
LYTA?
IS THAT YOU?
I TOLD YOU, I'M **NOT** COMING BACK WITH--

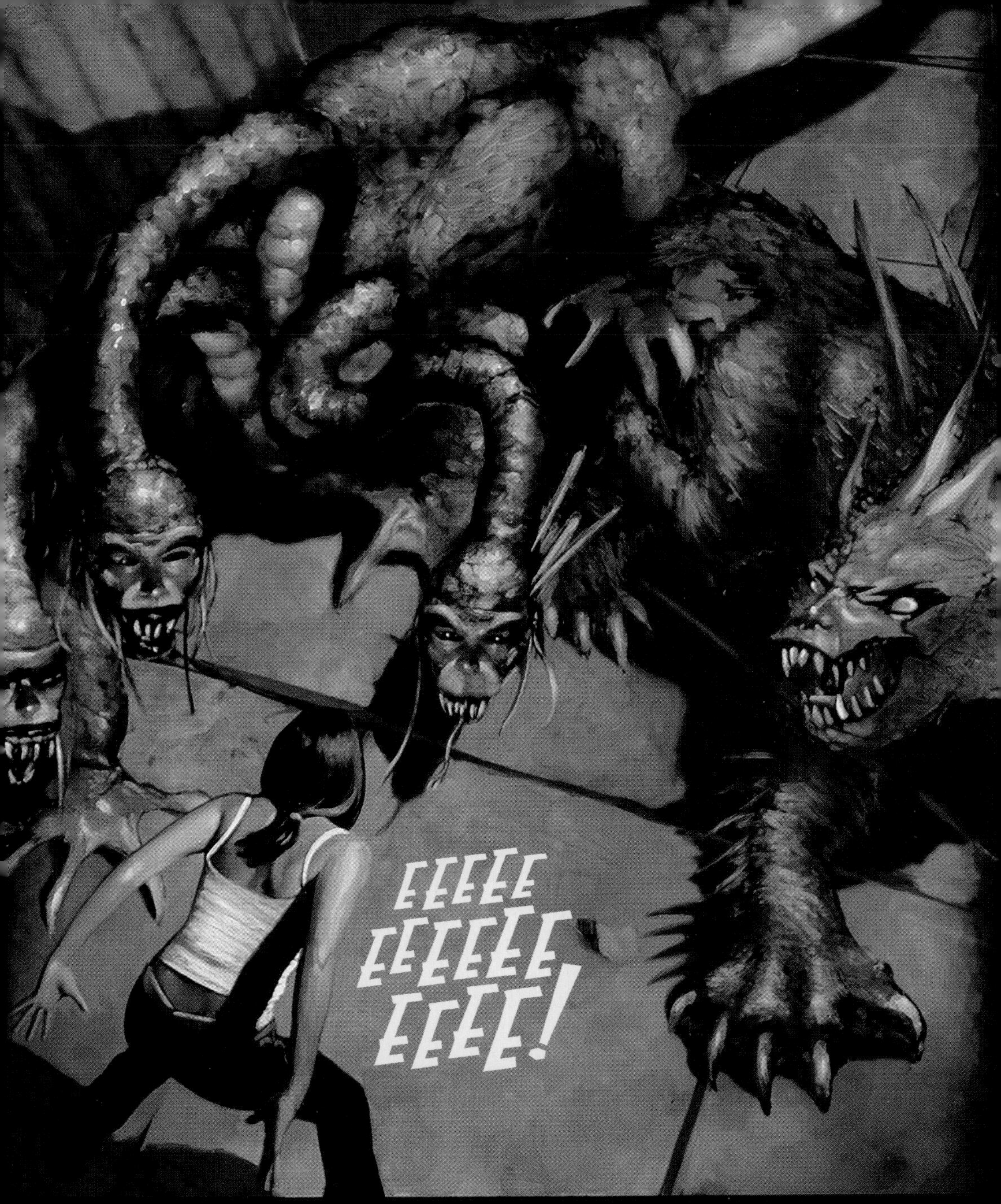
EEEEE
EEEEEE
EEEE!

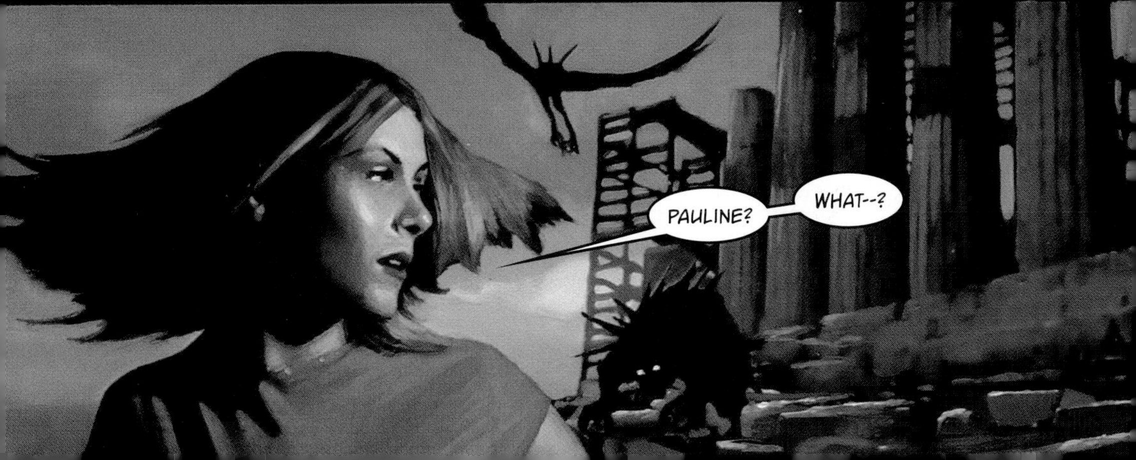
PAULINE?
WHAT--?

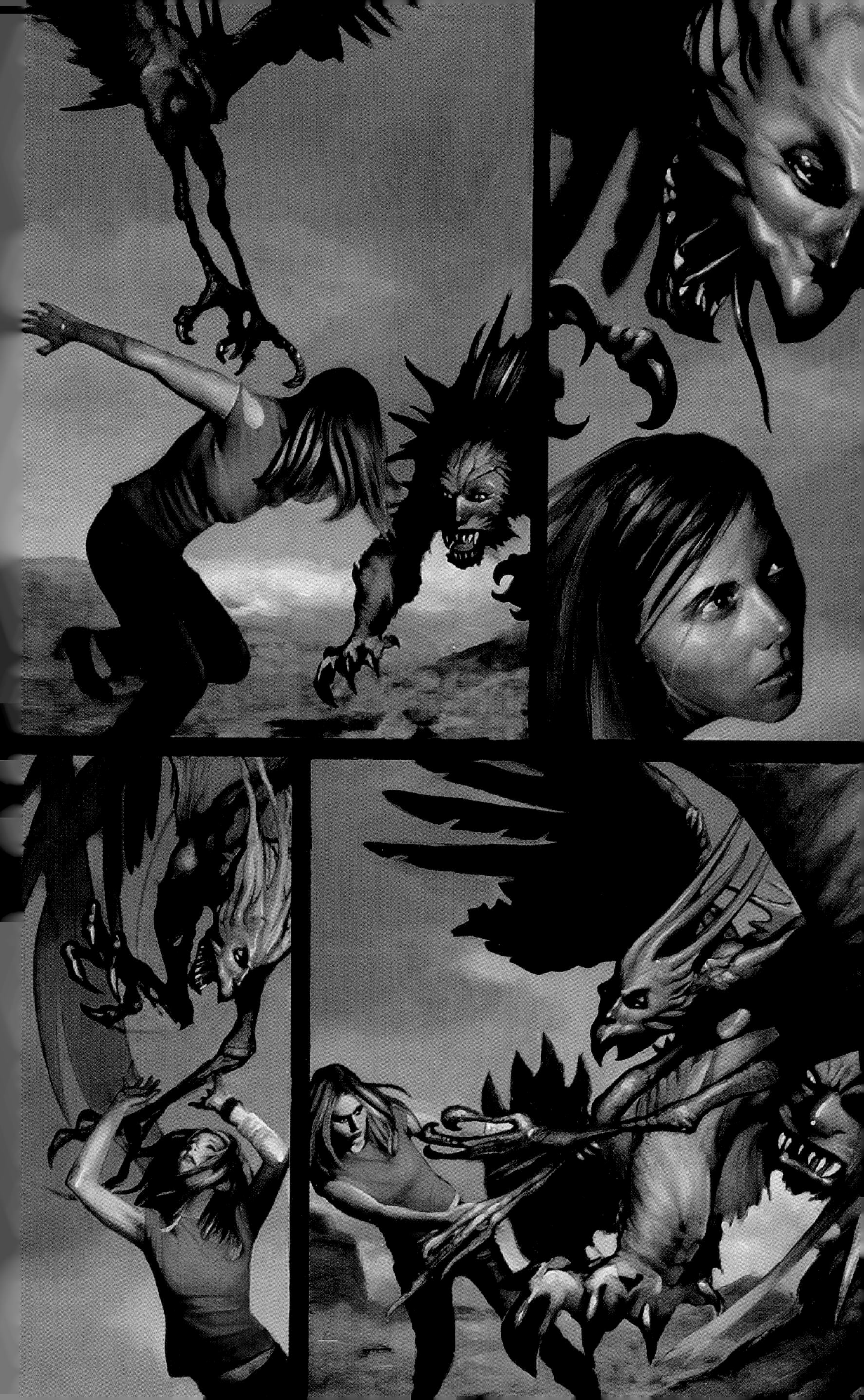

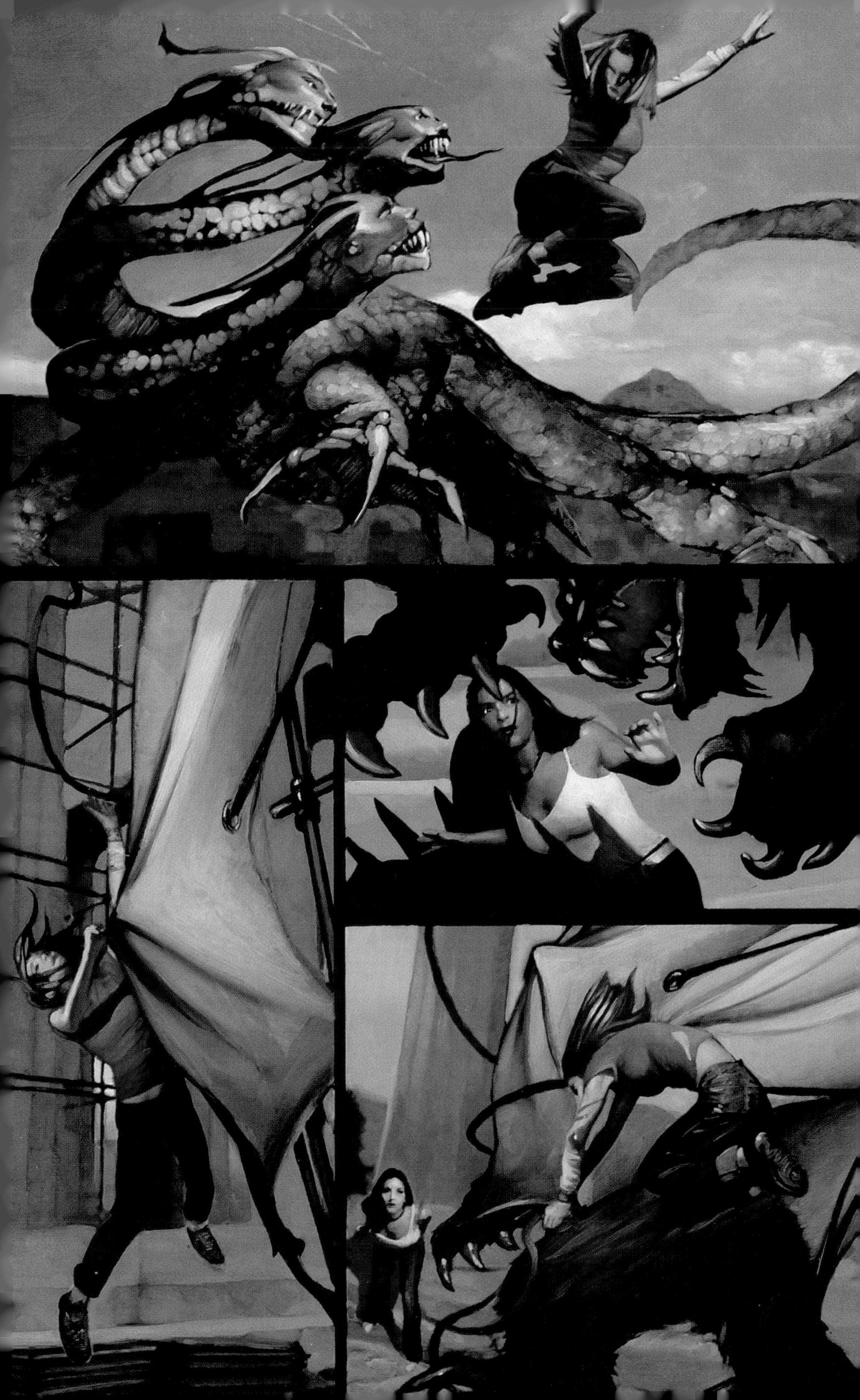

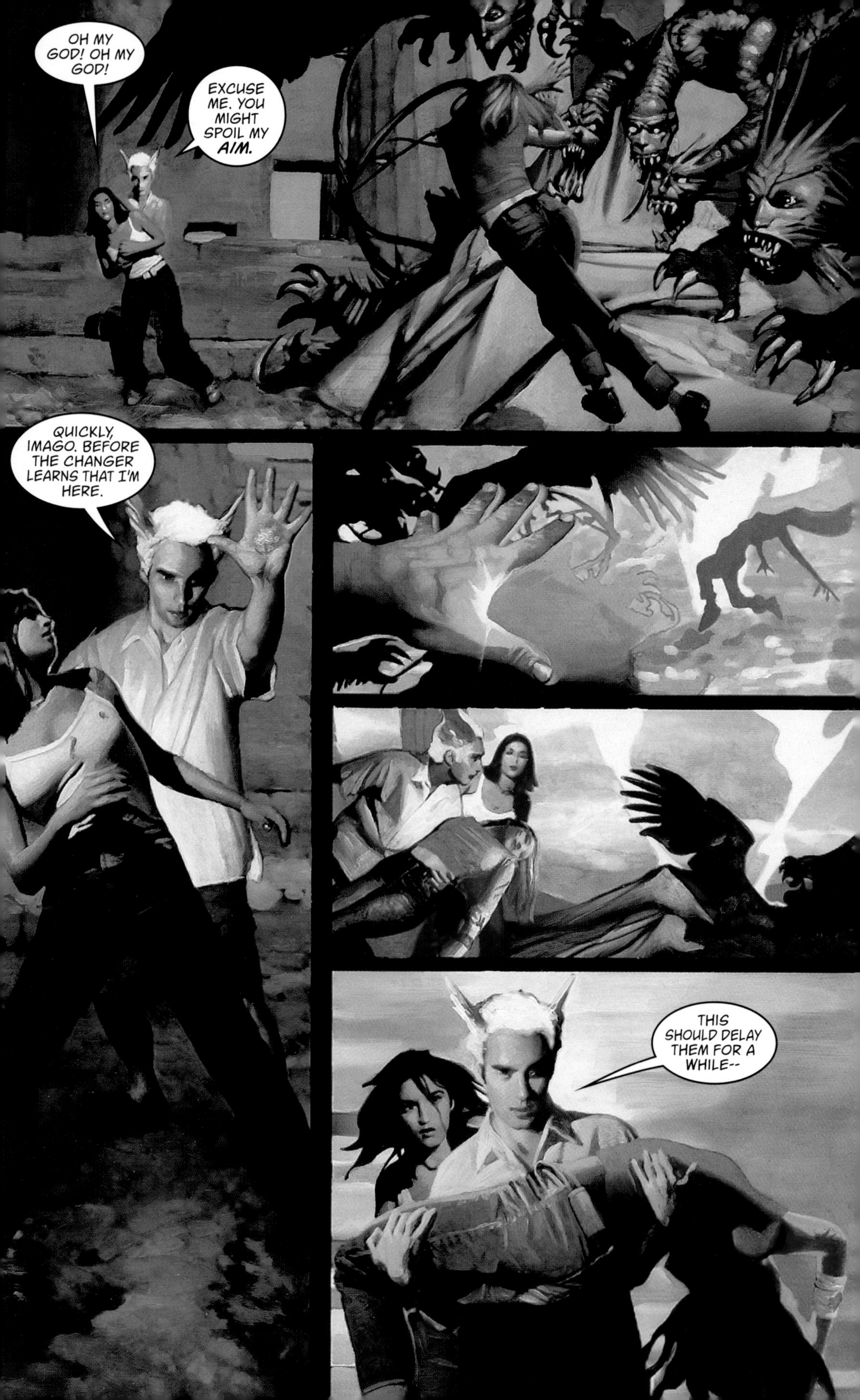
OH MY GOD! OH MY GOD!
EXCUSE ME. YOU MIGHT SPOIL MY AIM.
QUICKLY, IMAGO. BEFORE THE CHANGER LEARNS THAT I'M HERE.
THIS SHOULD DELAY THEM FOR A WHILE--

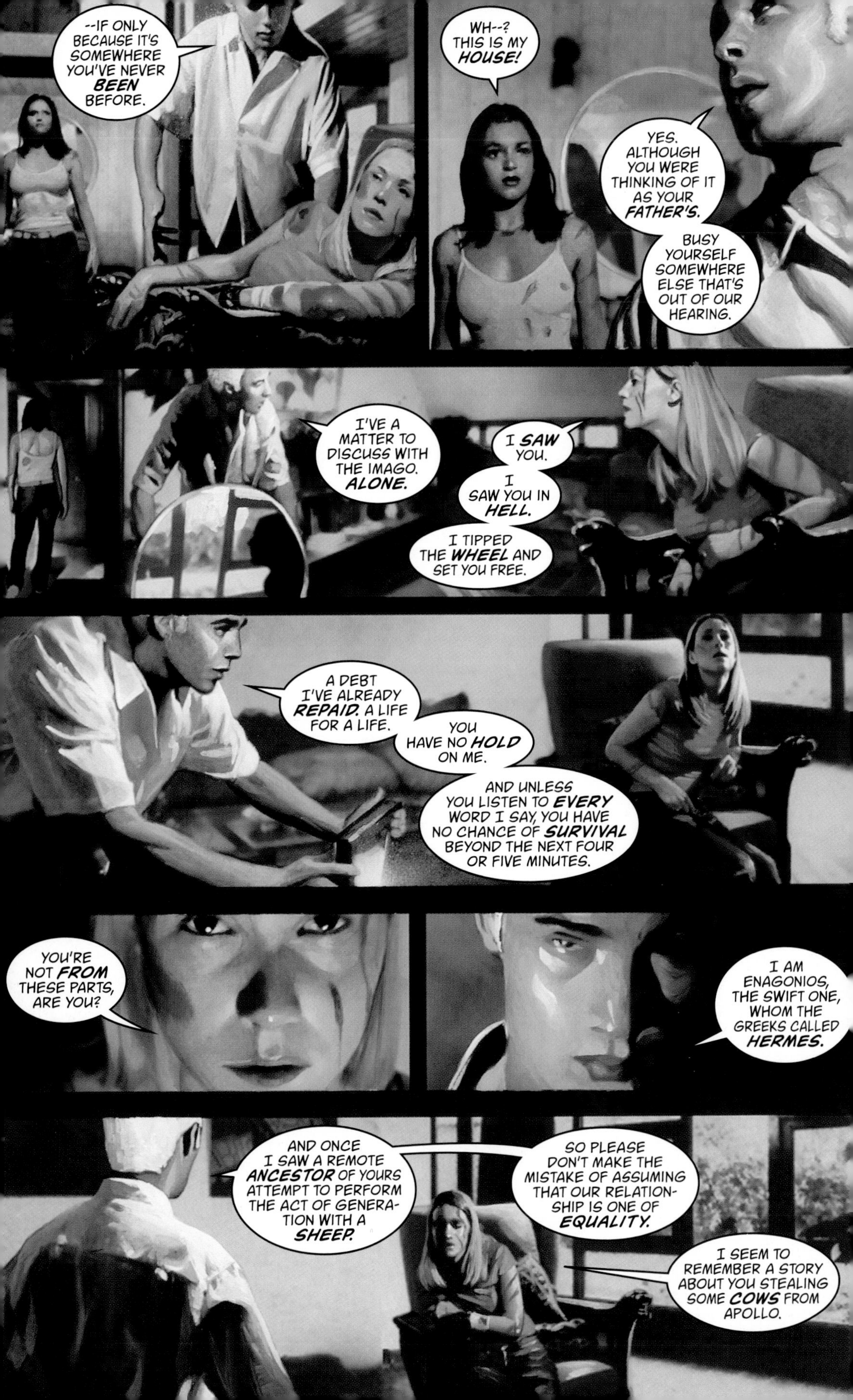
--IF ONLY BECAUSE IT'S SOMEWHERE YOU'VE NEVER **BEEN** BEFORE.
WH--? THIS IS MY **HOUSE!**
YES. ALTHOUGH YOU WERE THINKING OF IT AS YOUR **FATHER'S.**
BUSY YOURSELF SOMEWHERE ELSE THAT'S OUT OF OUR HEARING.
I'VE A MATTER TO DISCUSS WITH THE IMAGO. **ALONE.**
I **SAW** YOU.
I SAW YOU IN **HELL.**
I TIPPED THE **WHEEL** AND SET YOU FREE.
A DEBT I'VE ALREADY **REPAID.** A LIFE FOR A LIFE.
YOU HAVE NO **HOLD** ON ME.
AND UNLESS YOU LISTEN TO **EVERY** WORD I SAY, YOU HAVE NO CHANCE OF **SURVIVAL** BEYOND THE NEXT FOUR OR FIVE MINUTES.
YOU'RE NOT **FROM** THESE PARTS, ARE YOU?
I AM ENAGONIOS, THE SWIFT ONE, WHOM THE GREEKS CALLED **HERMES.**
AND ONCE I SAW A REMOTE **ANCESTOR** OF YOURS ATTEMPT TO PERFORM THE ACT OF GENERATION WITH A **SHEEP.**
SO PLEASE DON'T MAKE THE MISTAKE OF ASSUMING THAT OUR RELATIONSHIP IS ONE OF **EQUALITY.**
I SEEM TO REMEMBER A STORY ABOUT YOU STEALING SOME **COWS** FROM APOLLO.

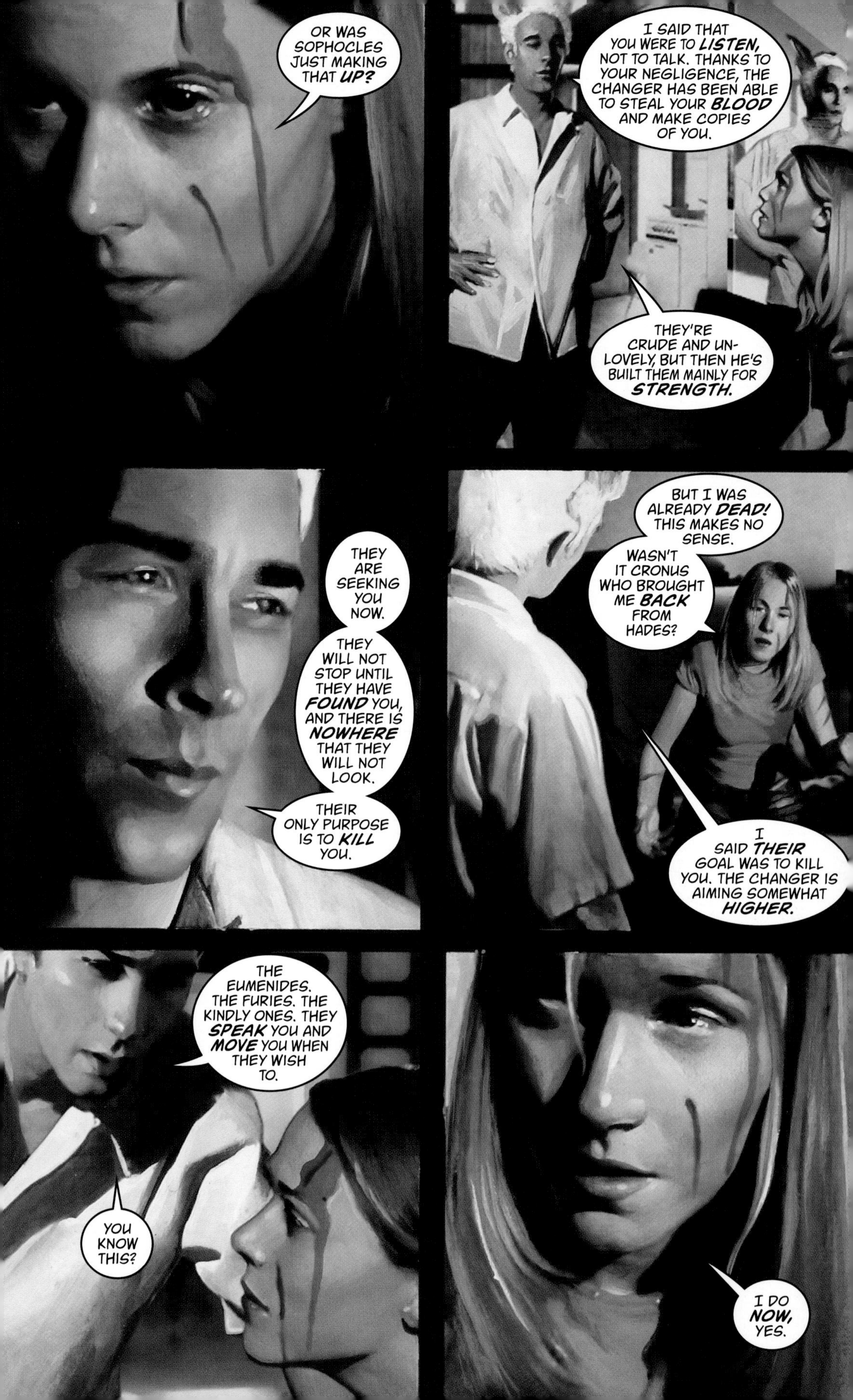
OR WAS SOPHOCLES JUST MAKING THAT UP?
I SAID THAT YOU WERE TO LISTEN, NOT TO TALK. THANKS TO YOUR NEGLIGENCE, THE CHANGER HAS BEEN ABLE TO STEAL YOUR BLOOD AND MAKE COPIES OF YOU.
THEY'RE CRUDE AND UN-LOVELY, BUT THEN HE'S BUILT THEM MAINLY FOR STRENGTH.
THEY ARE SEEKING YOU NOW.
THEY WILL NOT STOP UNTIL THEY HAVE FOUND YOU, AND THERE IS NOWHERE THAT THEY WILL NOT LOOK.
THEIR ONLY PURPOSE IS TO KILL YOU.
BUT I WAS ALREADY DEAD! THIS MAKES NO SENSE.
WASN'T IT CRONUS WHO BROUGHT ME BACK FROM HADES?
I SAID THEIR GOAL WAS TO KILL YOU. THE CHANGER IS AIMING SOMEWHAT HIGHER.
THE EUMENIDES. THE FURIES. THE KINDLY ONES. THEY SPEAK YOU AND MOVE YOU WHEN THEY WISH TO.
YOU KNOW THIS?
I DO NOW, YES.

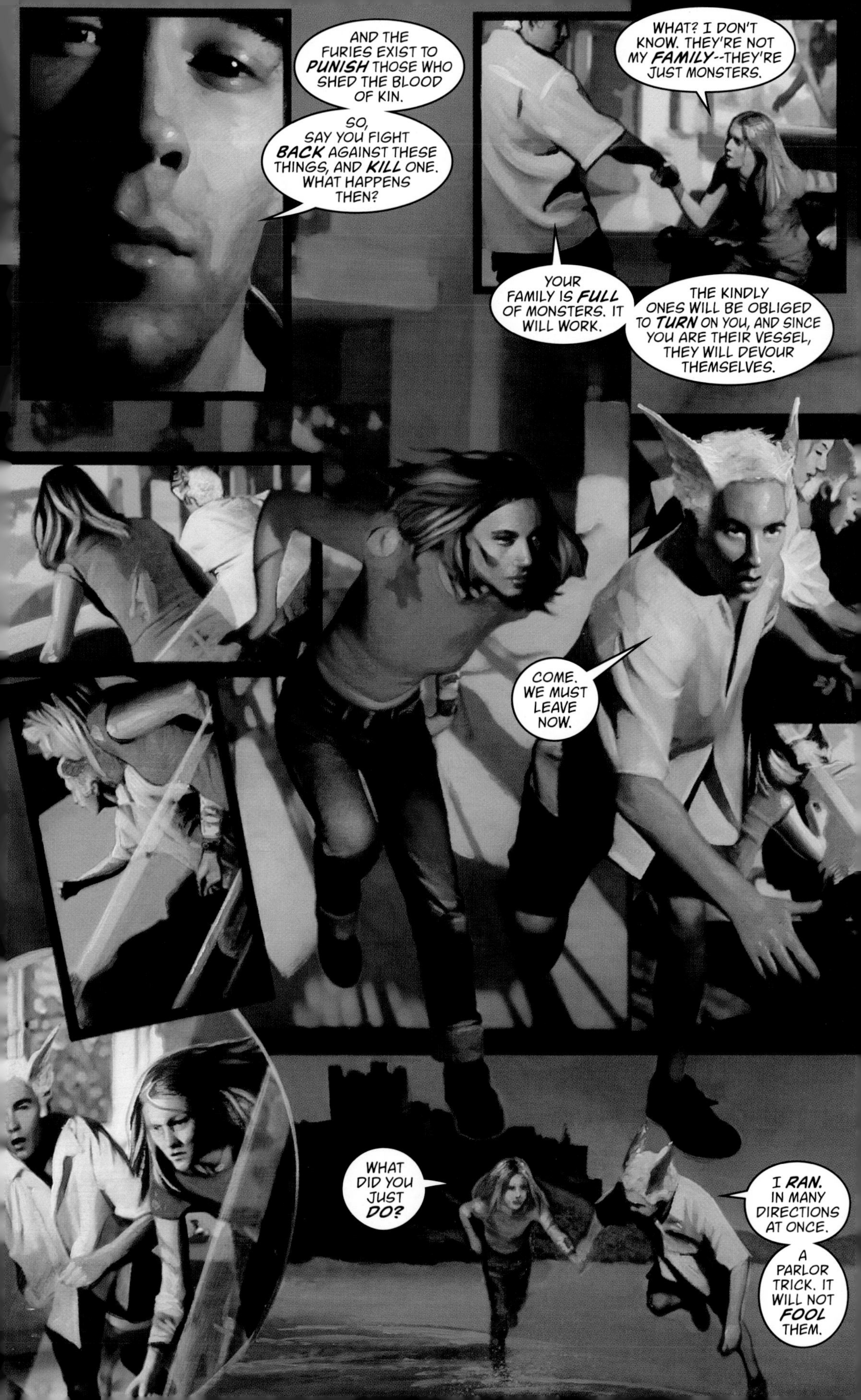
AND THE FURIES EXIST TO PUNISH THOSE WHO SHED THE BLOOD OF KIN.
SO, SAY YOU FIGHT BACK AGAINST THESE THINGS, AND KILL ONE. WHAT HAPPENS THEN?
WHAT? I DON'T KNOW. THEY'RE NOT MY FAMILY--THEY'RE JUST MONSTERS.
YOUR FAMILY IS FULL OF MONSTERS. IT WILL WORK.
THE KINDLY ONES WILL BE OBLIGED TO TURN ON YOU, AND SINCE YOU ARE THEIR VESSEL, THEY WILL DEVOUR THEMSELVES.
COME. WE MUST LEAVE NOW.
WHAT DID YOU JUST DO?
I RAN. IN MANY DIRECTIONS AT ONCE.
A PARLOR TRICK. IT WILL NOT FOOL THEM.

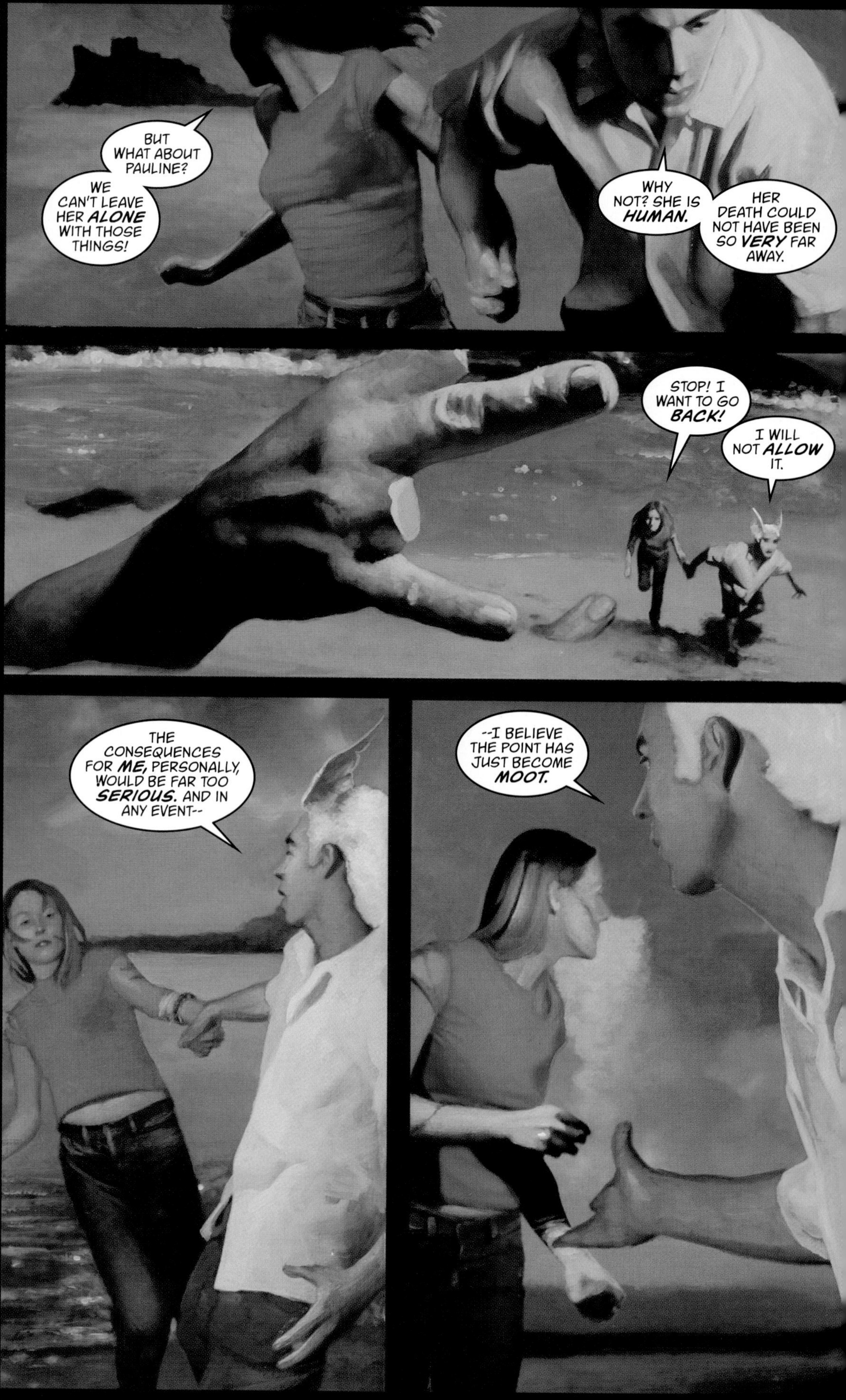
BUT WHAT ABOUT PAULINE?
WE CAN'T LEAVE HER ALONE WITH THOSE THINGS!
WHY NOT? SHE IS HUMAN.
HER DEATH COULD NOT HAVE BEEN SO VERY FAR AWAY.
STOP! I WANT TO GO BACK!
I WILL NOT ALLOW IT.
THE CONSEQUENCES FOR ME, PERSONALLY, WOULD BE FAR TOO SERIOUS. AND IN ANY EVENT--
--I BELIEVE THE POINT HAS JUST BECOME MOOT.

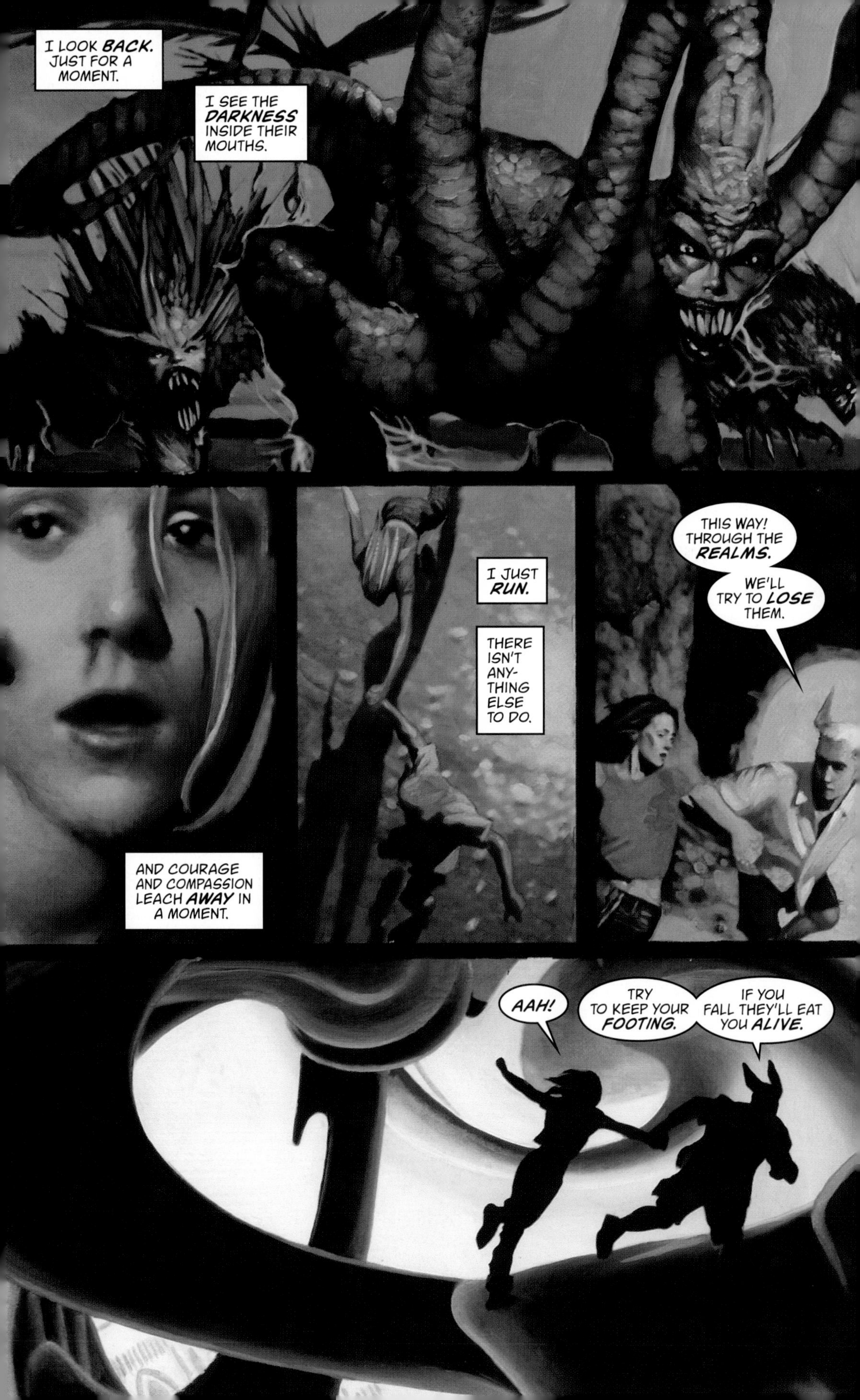
I LOOK BACK. JUST FOR A MOMENT.
I SEE THE DARKNESS INSIDE THEIR MOUTHS.
AND COURAGE AND COMPASSION LEACH AWAY IN A MOMENT.
I JUST RUN.
THERE ISN'T ANYTHING ELSE TO DO.
THIS WAY! THROUGH THE REALMS.
WE'LL TRY TO LOSE THEM.
AAH!
TRY TO KEEP YOUR FOOTING.
IF YOU FALL THEY'LL EAT YOU ALIVE.

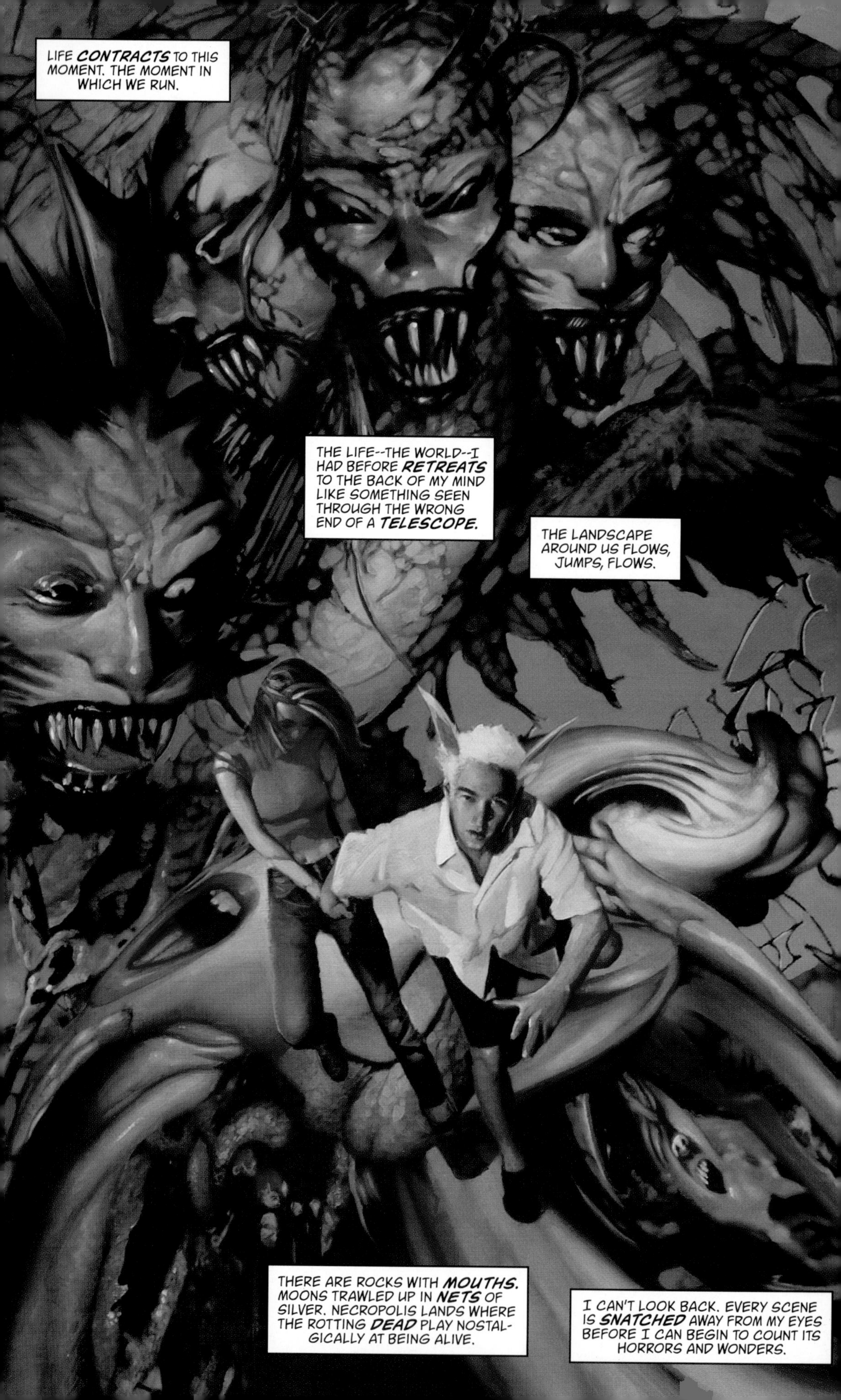
LIFE CONTRACTS TO THIS MOMENT. THE MOMENT IN WHICH WE RUN.
THE LIFE--THE WORLD--I HAD BEFORE RETREATS TO THE BACK OF MY MIND LIKE SOMETHING SEEN THROUGH THE WRONG END OF A TELESCOPE.
THE LANDSCAPE AROUND US FLOWS, JUMPS, FLOWS.
THERE ARE ROCKS WITH MOUTHS. MOONS TRAWLED UP IN NETS OF SILVER. NECROPOLIS LANDS WHERE THE ROTTING DEAD PLAY NOSTAL-GICALLY AT BEING ALIVE.
I CAN'T LOOK BACK. EVERY SCENE IS SNATCHED AWAY FROM MY EYES BEFORE I CAN BEGIN TO COUNT ITS HORRORS AND WONDERS.

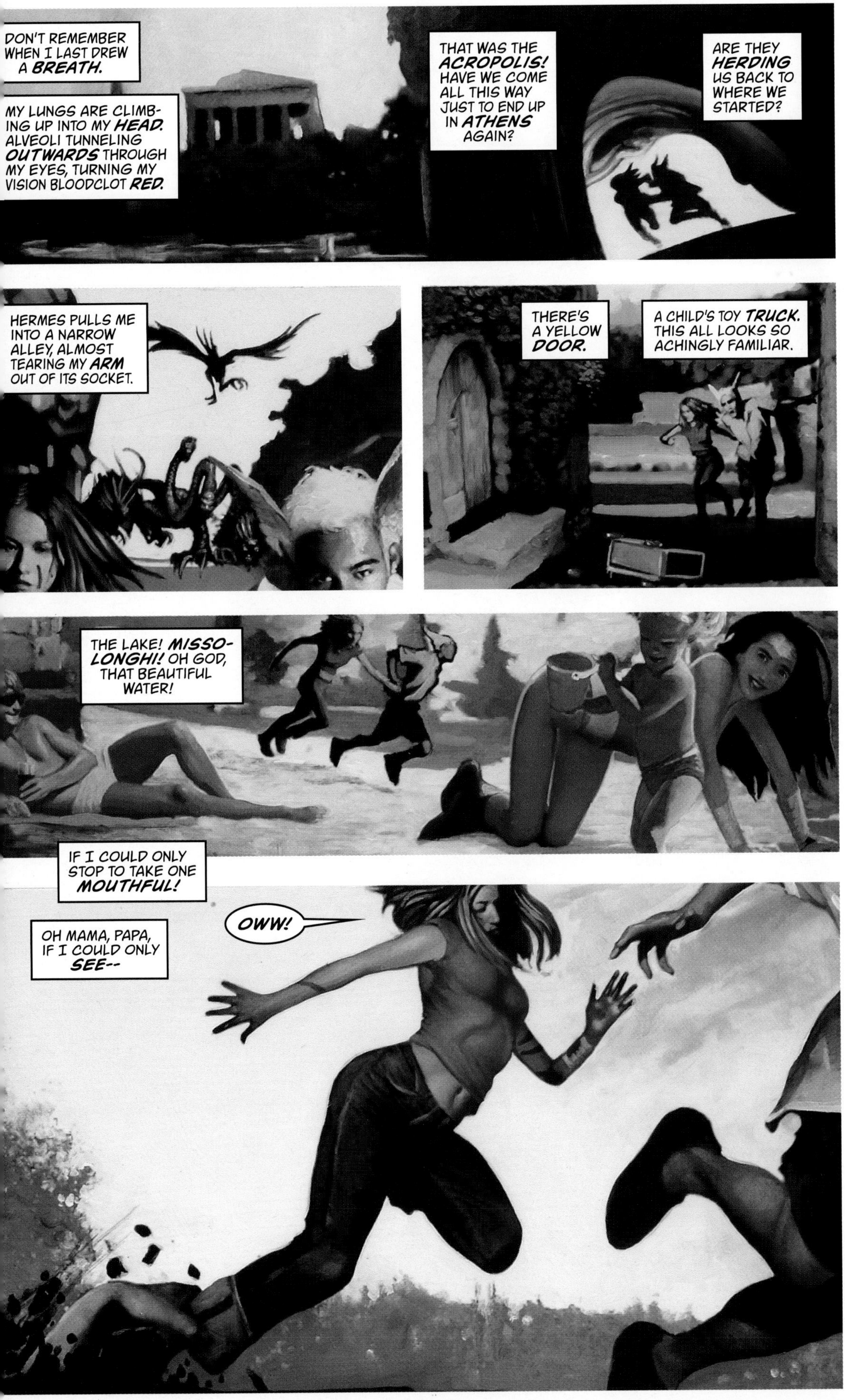
DON'T REMEMBER WHEN I LAST DREW A BREATH.
MY LUNGS ARE CLIMB-ING UP INTO MY HEAD. ALVEOLI TUNNELING OUTWARDS THROUGH MY EYES, TURNING MY VISION BLOODCLOT RED.
THAT WAS THE ACROPOLIS! HAVE WE COME ALL THIS WAY JUST TO END UP IN ATHENS AGAIN?
ARE THEY HERDING US BACK TO WHERE WE STARTED?
HERMES PULLS ME INTO A NARROW ALLEY, ALMOST TEARING MY ARM OUT OF ITS SOCKET.
THERE'S A YELLOW DOOR.
A CHILD'S TOY TRUCK. THIS ALL LOOKS SO ACHINGLY FAMILIAR.
THE LAKE! MISSO-LONGHI! OH GOD, THAT BEAUTIFUL WATER!
IF I COULD ONLY STOP TO TAKE ONE MOUTHFUL!
OH MAMA, PAPA, IF I COULD ONLY SEE--
OWW!

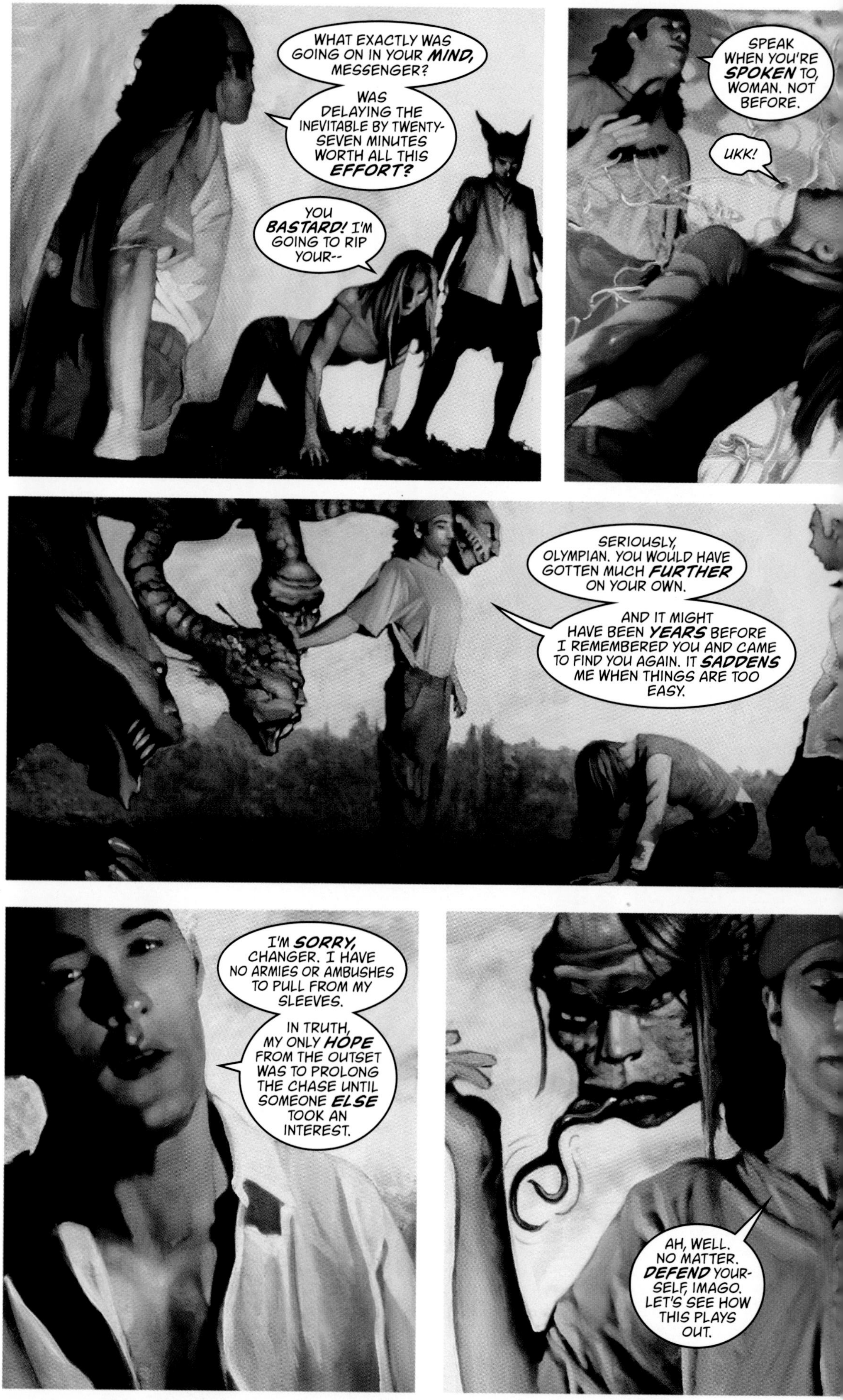
WHAT EXACTLY WAS GOING ON IN YOUR MIND, MESSENGER?
WAS DELAYING THE INEVITABLE BY TWENTY-SEVEN MINUTES WORTH ALL THIS EFFORT?
YOU BASTARD! I'M GOING TO RIP YOUR--
SPEAK WHEN YOU'RE SPOKEN TO, WOMAN. NOT BEFORE.
UKK!
SERIOUSLY, OLYMPIAN. YOU WOULD HAVE GOTTEN MUCH FURTHER ON YOUR OWN.
AND IT MIGHT HAVE BEEN YEARS BEFORE I REMEMBERED YOU AND CAME TO FIND YOU AGAIN. IT SADDENS ME WHEN THINGS ARE TOO EASY.
I'M SORRY, CHANGER. I HAVE NO ARMIES OR AMBUSHES TO PULL FROM MY SLEEVES.
IN TRUTH, MY ONLY HOPE FROM THE OUTSET WAS TO PROLONG THE CHASE UNTIL SOMEONE ELSE TOOK AN INTEREST.
AH, WELL. NO MATTER. DEFEND YOURSELF, IMAGO. LET'S SEE HOW THIS PLAYS OUT.

THEY'RE ON ME LIKE A HOT, SOUR-SMELLING **WAVE** THAT RISES UP IN MY FACE.

I BRACE MYSELF TO **MEET** IT.

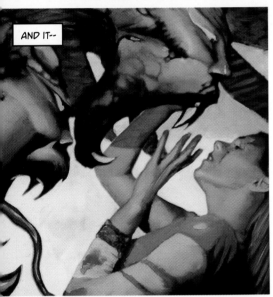

AND IT--

--STOPS.

WHO **DARES?**

WHO DARES COME BETWEEN THE CHANGER AND HIS **WRATH?**

I do.

And who is it that dares ASK?

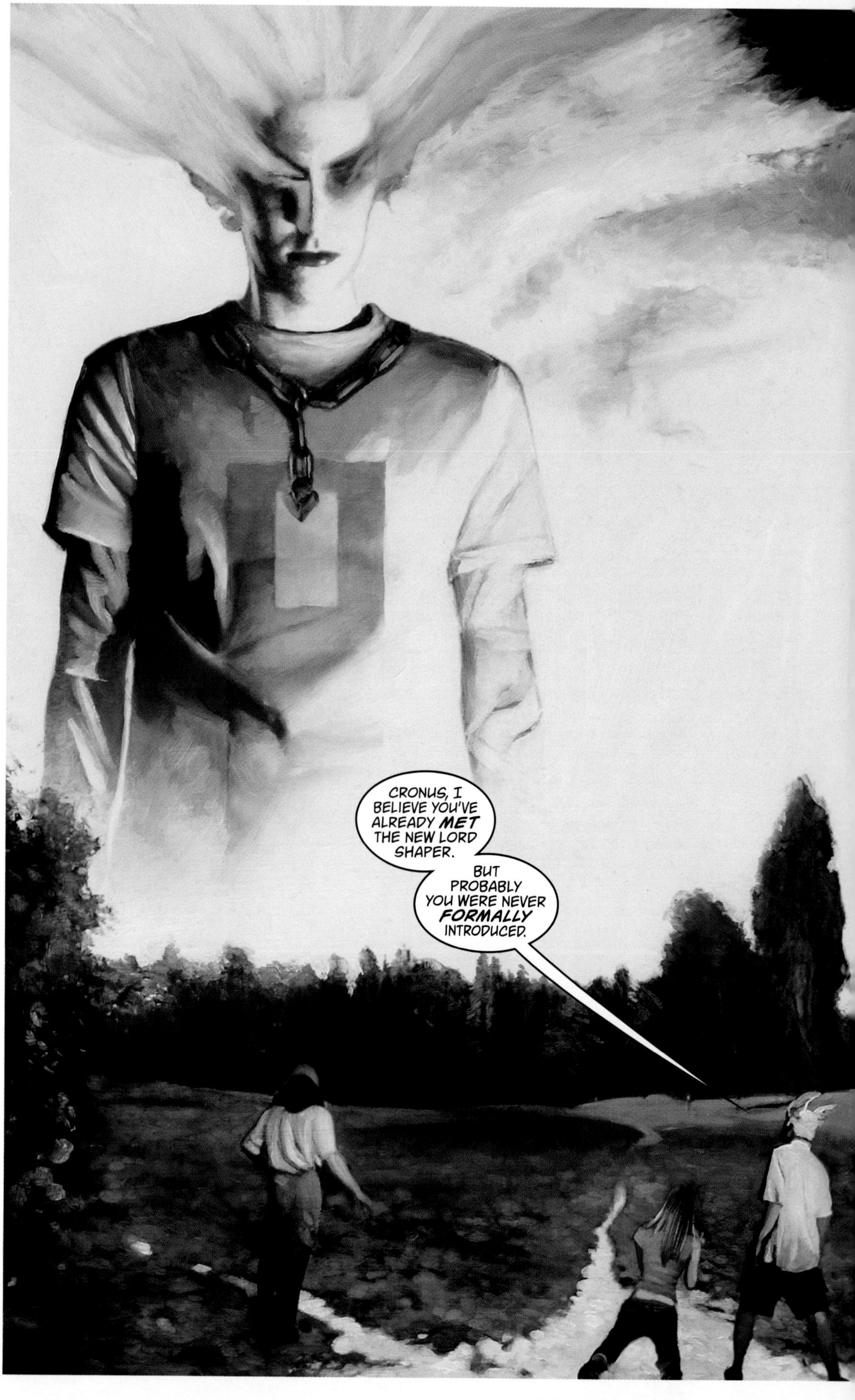
CRONUS, I BELIEVE YOU'VE ALREADY *MET* THE NEW LORD SHAPER.
BUT PROBABLY YOU WERE NEVER *FORMALLY* INTRODUCED.

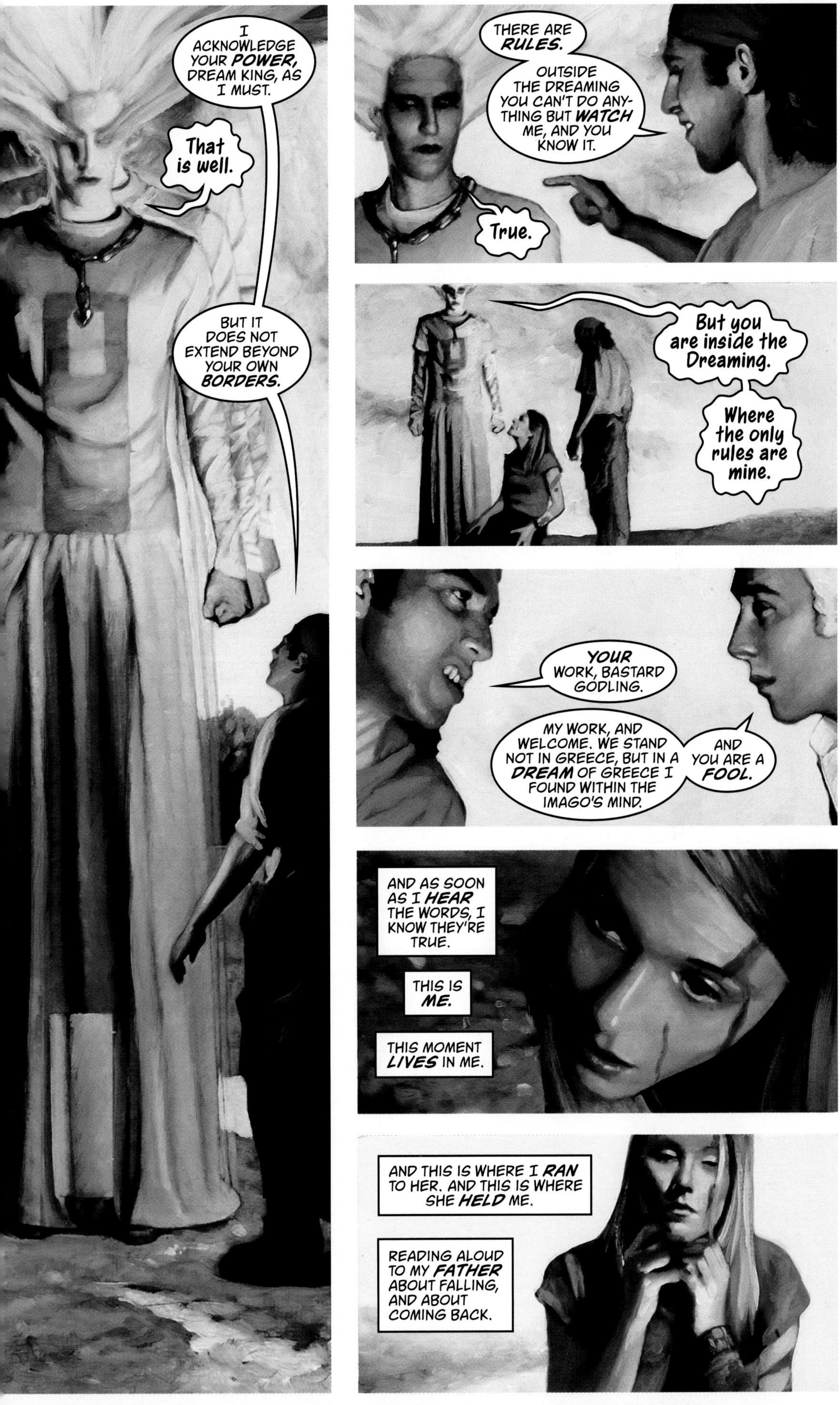

I ACKNOWLEDGE YOUR POWER, DREAM KING, AS I MUST.
That is well.
BUT IT DOES NOT EXTEND BEYOND YOUR OWN BORDERS.
THERE ARE RULES.
OUTSIDE THE DREAMING YOU CAN'T DO ANY-THING BUT WATCH ME, AND YOU KNOW IT.
True.
But you are inside the Dreaming.
Where the only rules are mine.
YOUR WORK, BASTARD GODLING.
MY WORK, AND WELCOME. WE STAND NOT IN GREECE, BUT IN A DREAM OF GREECE I FOUND WITHIN THE IMAGO'S MIND.
AND YOU ARE A FOOL.
AND AS SOON AS I HEAR THE WORDS, I KNOW THEY'RE TRUE.
THIS IS ME.
THIS MOMENT LIVES IN ME.
AND THIS IS WHERE I RAN TO HER. AND THIS IS WHERE SHE HELD ME.
READING ALOUD TO MY FATHER ABOUT FALLING, AND ABOUT COMING BACK.

NONE OF THIS MATTERS. SHE SLEW YOUR *PREDECESSOR*, ONEIROS. SHE UNLEASHED THE *FURIES* ON HIM.

LET ME HAVE HER, AND I PROMISE YOU A VENGEANCE THAT WILL ENGULF *THEM*, TOO.

You are mistaken, Titan. How can vengeance turn upon the mothers of vengeance?

That is a snake that swallows its own tail.

RESPECTFULLY, LORD SHAPER, NO. HE *CAN* DO WHAT HE SAYS.

FOR THE SAKE OF THE *BOND* THAT TIES YOU TO THIS WOMAN, I BEG YOU TO *INTERCEDE*--OR HE WILL USURP THE FURIES' PLACE, AND END US ALL.

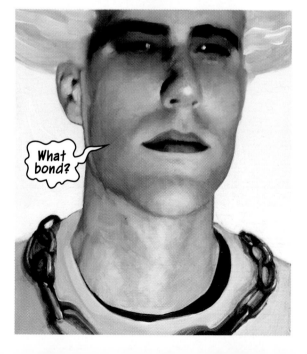

What bond?

I told you once--or perhaps twice--to find your life again, Lyta Hall, and take it up.

DID YOU? I DON'T REMEMBER THAT.

You have not done so. Perhaps, after all, you cannot.

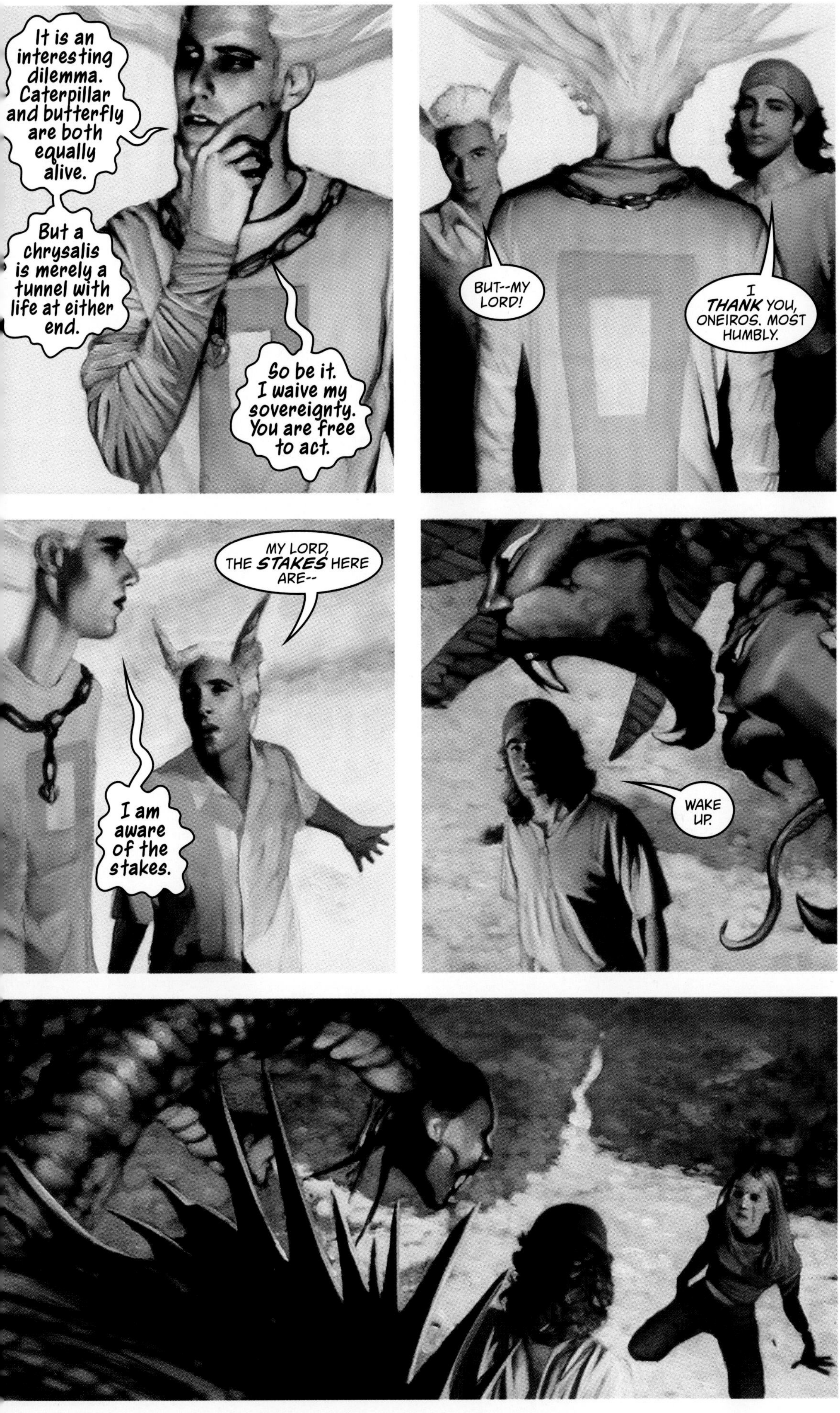
It is an interesting dilemma. Caterpillar and butterfly are both equally alive.
But a chrysalis is merely a tunnel with life at either end.
So be it. I waive my sovereignty. You are free to act.
BUT--MY LORD!
I *THANK* YOU, ONEIROS. MOST HUMBLY.
MY LORD, THE *STAKES* HERE ARE--
I am aware of the stakes.
WAKE UP.

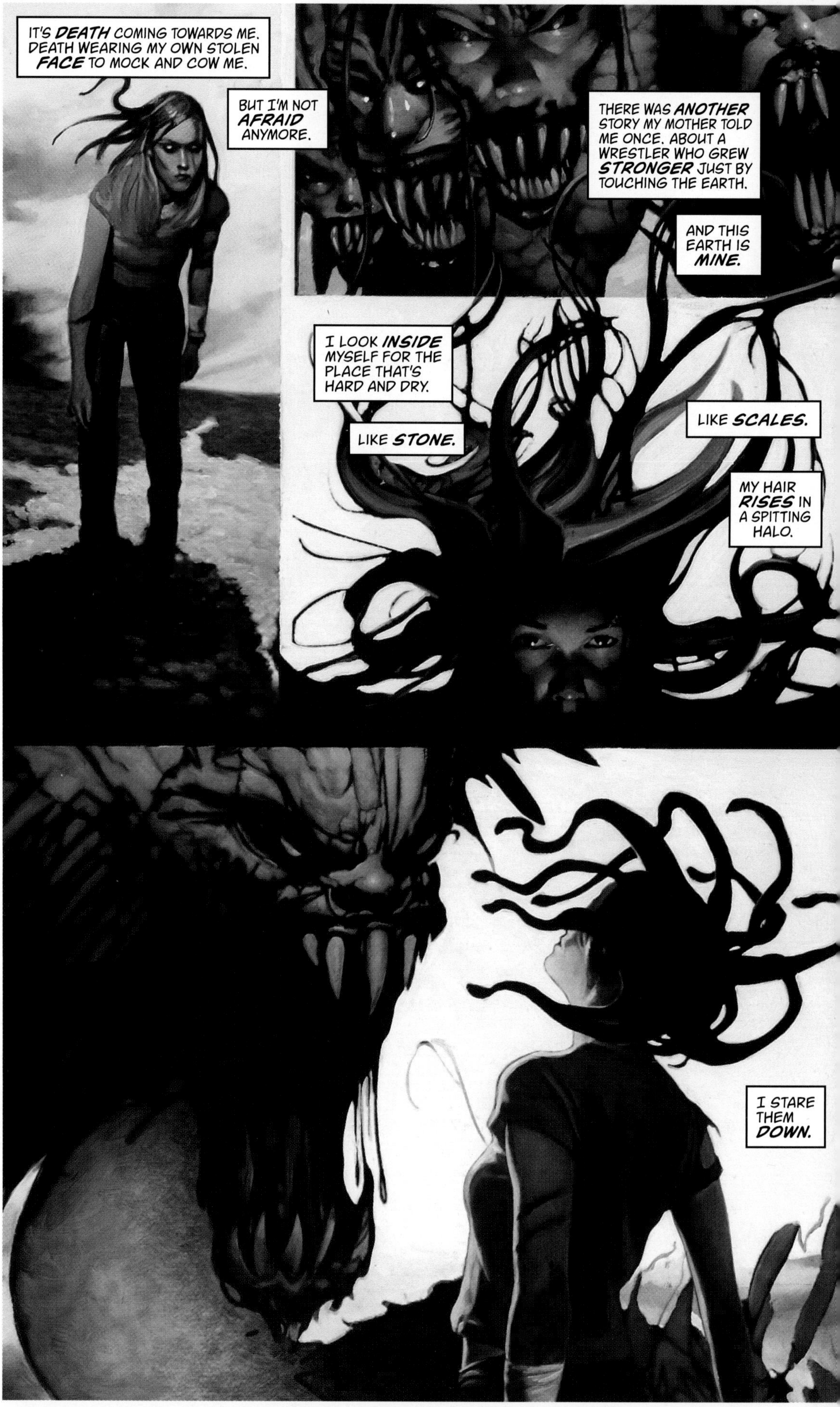
IT'S DEATH COMING TOWARDS ME. DEATH WEARING MY OWN STOLEN FACE TO MOCK AND COW ME.
BUT I'M NOT AFRAID ANYMORE.
THERE WAS ANOTHER STORY MY MOTHER TOLD ME ONCE. ABOUT A WRESTLER WHO GREW STRONGER JUST BY TOUCHING THE EARTH.
AND THIS EARTH IS MINE.
I LOOK INSIDE MYSELF FOR THE PLACE THAT'S HARD AND DRY.
LIKE STONE.
LIKE SCALES.
MY HAIR RISES IN A SPITTING HALO.
I STARE THEM DOWN.

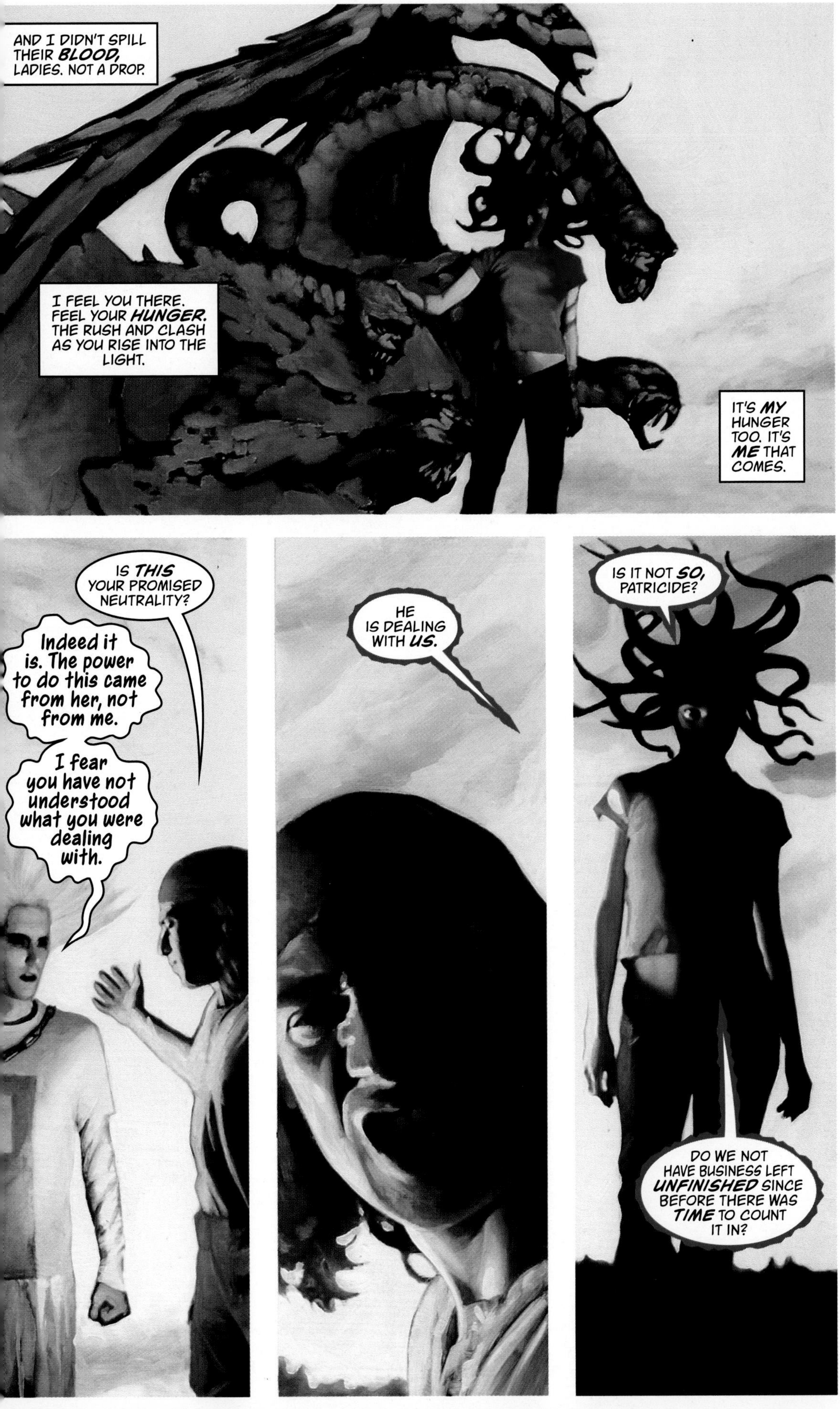
AND I DIDN'T SPILL THEIR BLOOD, LADIES. NOT A DROP.
I FEEL YOU THERE. FEEL YOUR HUNGER. THE RUSH AND CLASH AS YOU RISE INTO THE LIGHT.
IT'S MY HUNGER TOO. IT'S ME THAT COMES.
IS THIS YOUR PROMISED NEUTRALITY?
Indeed it is. The power to do this came from her, not from me.
I fear you have not understood what you were dealing with.
HE IS DEALING WITH US.
IS IT NOT SO, PATRICIDE?
DO WE NOT HAVE BUSINESS LEFT UNFINISHED SINCE BEFORE THERE WAS TIME TO COUNT IT IN?

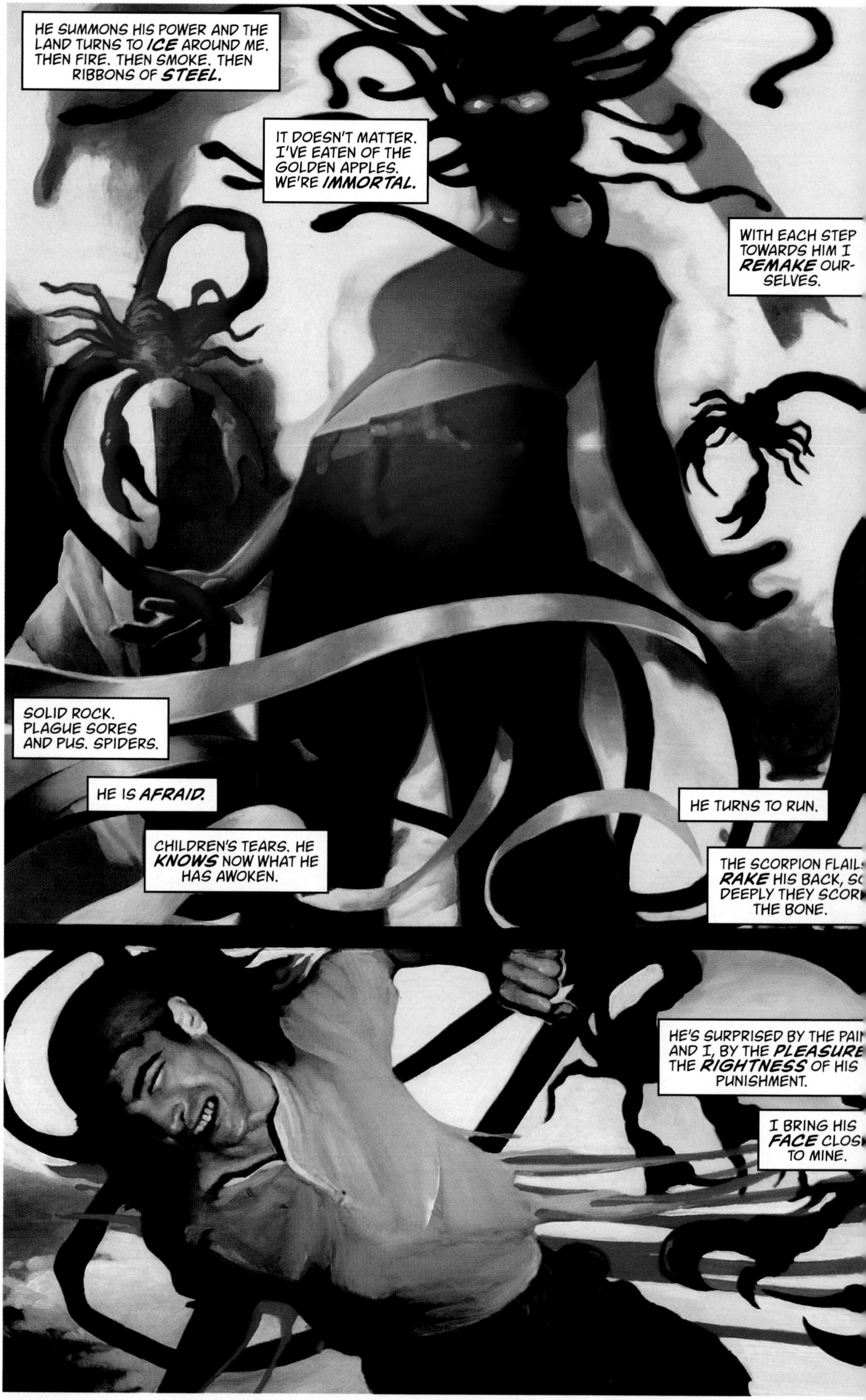
HE SUMMONS HIS POWER AND THE LAND TURNS TO ICE AROUND ME. THEN FIRE. THEN SMOKE. THEN RIBBONS OF STEEL.
IT DOESN'T MATTER. I'VE EATEN OF THE GOLDEN APPLES. WE'RE IMMORTAL.
WITH EACH STEP TOWARDS HIM I REMAKE OURSELVES.
SOLID ROCK. PLAGUE SORES AND PUS. SPIDERS.
HE IS AFRAID.
CHILDREN'S TEARS. HE KNOWS NOW WHAT HE HAS AWOKEN.
HE TURNS TO RUN.
THE SCORPION FLAIL RAKE HIS BACK, S DEEPLY THEY SCOR THE BONE.
HE'S SURPRISED BY THE PAI AND I, BY THE PLEASUR THE RIGHTNESS OF HIS PUNISHMENT.
I BRING HIS FACE CLOS TO MINE.

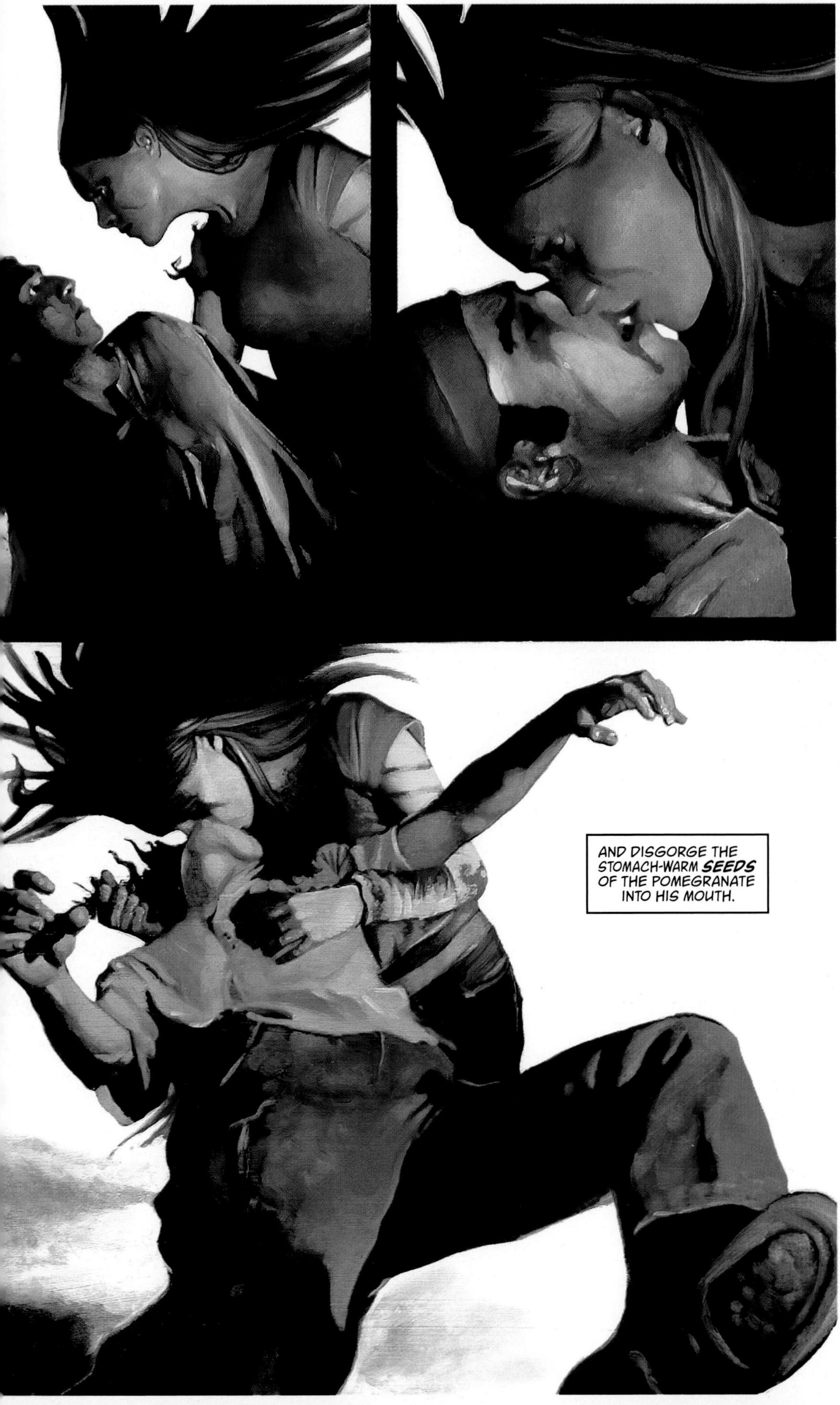
AND DISGORGE THE STOMACH-WARM *SEEDS* OF THE POMEGRANATE INTO HIS MOUTH.

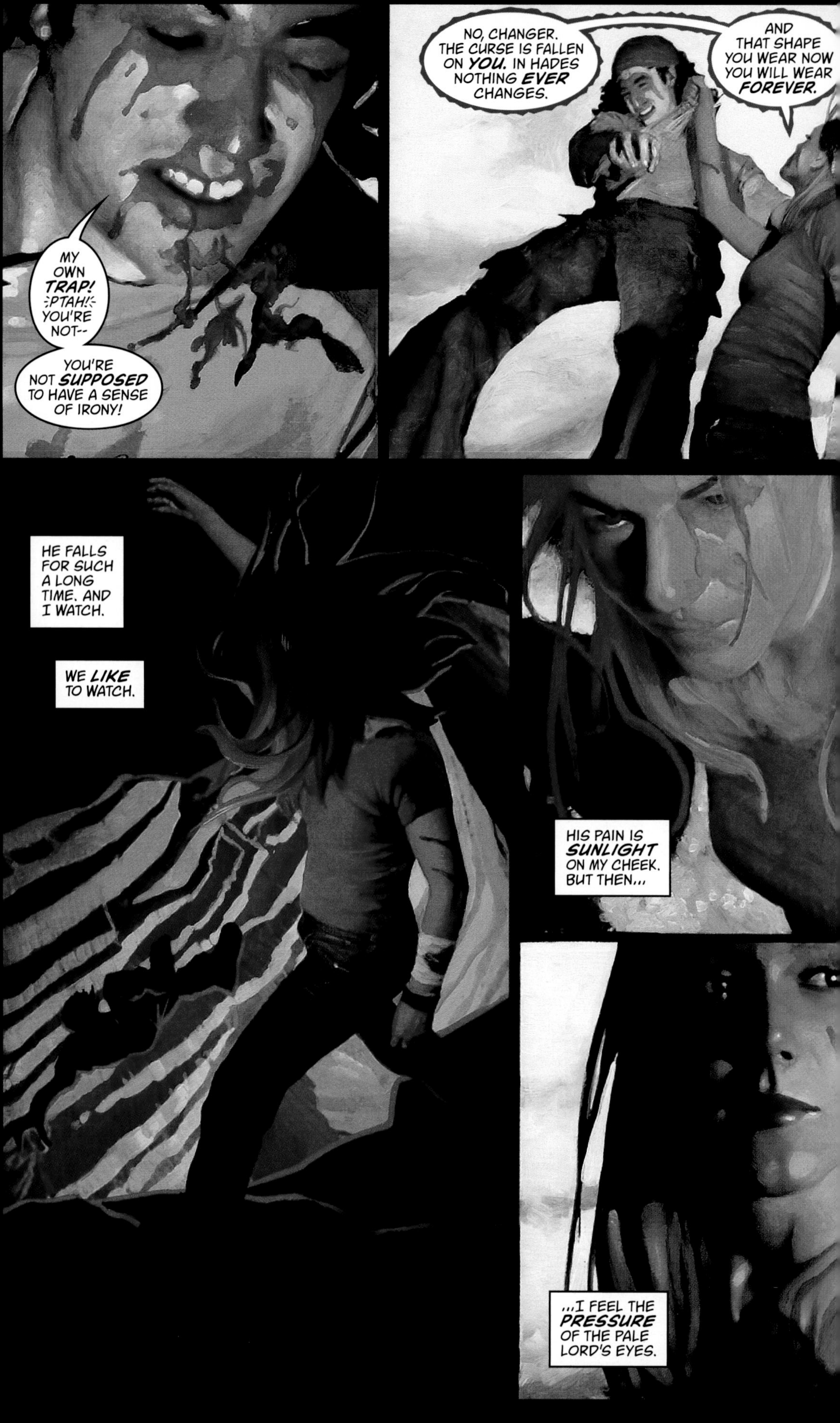
MY OWN TRAP! :PTAH!: YOU'RE NOT--
YOU'RE NOT SUPPOSED TO HAVE A SENSE OF IRONY!
NO, CHANGER. THE CURSE IS FALLEN ON YOU. IN HADES NOTHING EVER CHANGES.
AND THAT SHAPE YOU WEAR NOW YOU WILL WEAR FOREVER.
HE FALLS FOR SUCH A LONG TIME. AND I WATCH.
WE LIKE TO WATCH.
HIS PAIN IS SUNLIGHT ON MY CHEEK. BUT THEN...
...I FEEL THE PRESSURE OF THE PALE LORD'S EYES.

IT WAS NOT *ENTIRELY* SUCCESSFUL, THEN, THE BURNING.

FOR THAT WHICH IS *HUMAN* IN ME SEES THAT WHICH IS HUMAN IN *YOU.*

There is nothing human in me.

I was curious to see what might emerge from the chrysalis.

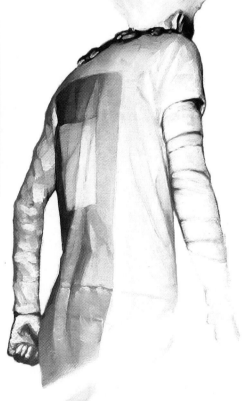

But now I believe our business is concluded.

YES. IT IS CONCLUDED.

ΤΕ *ΦΙΛΩ,* 'ΤΙΕ. ΕΡΡΩΣΩ.

I ALSO BEG YOUR *LEAVE* TO DEPART, KIND-HEARTED SISTERS. TRUSTING TO YOUR FORBEARANCE TO *FORGET* MY SOMEWHAT--

IT'S JUST *ME,* HERMES.

GIVE ME A LIFT HOME AND I'LL CALL US *EVEN.*

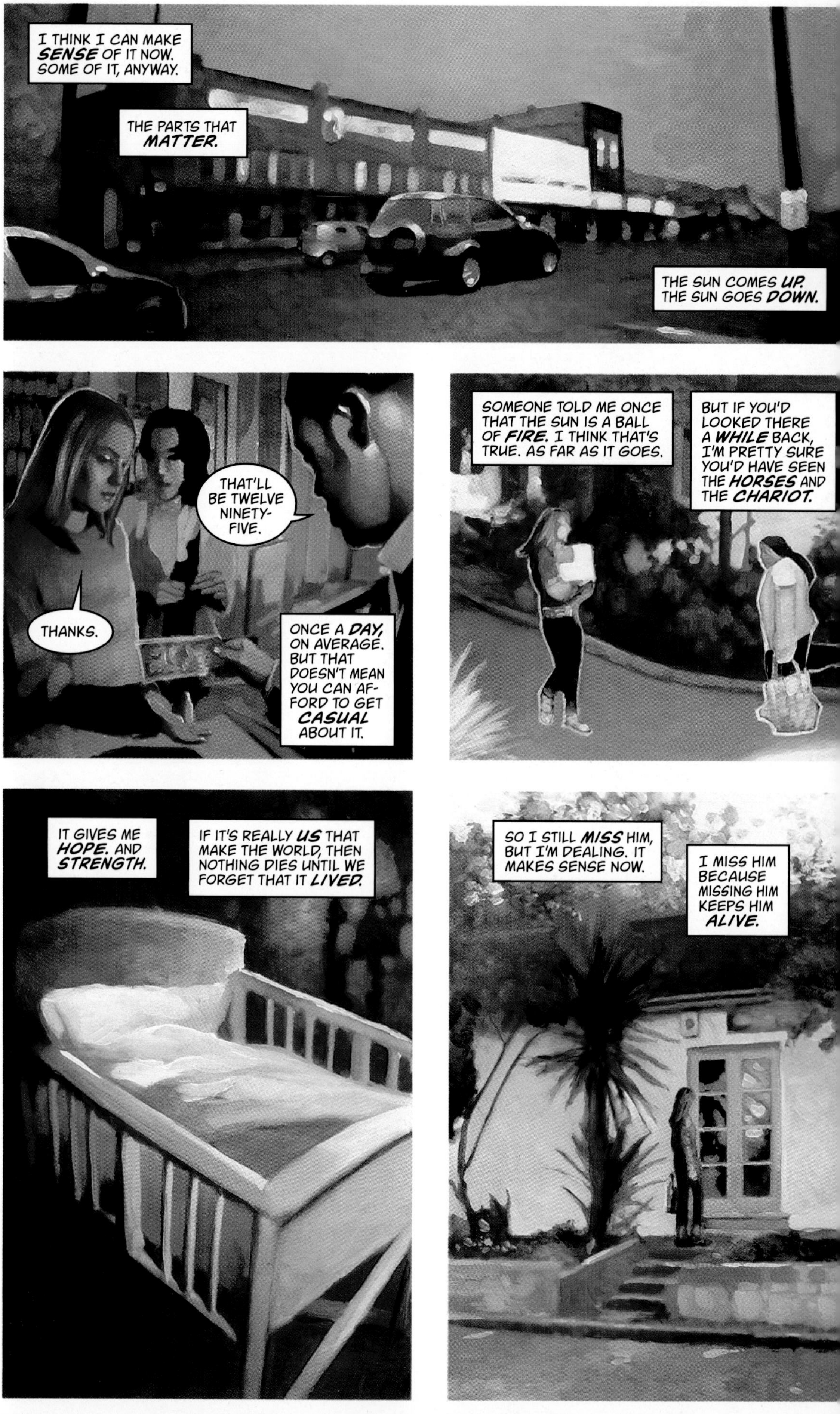
I THINK I CAN MAKE SENSE OF IT NOW. SOME OF IT, ANYWAY.
THE PARTS THAT MATTER.
THE SUN COMES UP. THE SUN GOES DOWN.
THAT'LL BE TWELVE NINETY-FIVE.
THANKS.
ONCE A DAY, ON AVERAGE. BUT THAT DOESN'T MEAN YOU CAN AFFORD TO GET CASUAL ABOUT IT.
SOMEONE TOLD ME ONCE THAT THE SUN IS A BALL OF FIRE. I THINK THAT'S TRUE. AS FAR AS IT GOES.
BUT IF YOU'D LOOKED THERE A WHILE BACK, I'M PRETTY SURE YOU'D HAVE SEEN THE HORSES AND THE CHARIOT.
IT GIVES ME HOPE. AND STRENGTH.
IF IT'S REALLY US THAT MAKE THE WORLD, THEN NOTHING DIES UNTIL WE FORGET THAT IT LIVED.
SO I STILL MISS HIM, BUT I'M DEALING. IT MAKES SENSE NOW.
I MISS HIM BECAUSE MISSING HIM KEEPS HIM ALIVE.

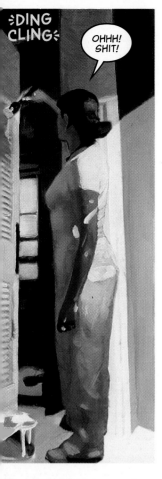

DING CLING

OHHH! SHIT!

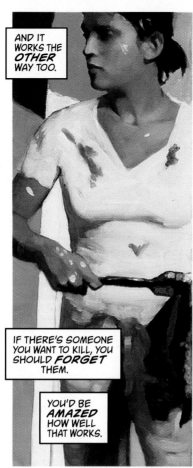

AND IT WORKS THE *OTHER* WAY TOO.

IF THERE'S SOMEONE YOU WANT TO KILL, YOU SHOULD *FORGET* THEM.

YOU'D BE *AMAZED* HOW WELL THAT WORKS.

LYTA!

HI.

YOU'RE OKAY!

OH MY GOD, YOU'RE *OKAY!*

UH...YOU WANT TO COME IN? I WAS JUST PAINTING THE DOOR FRAMES, BUT I COULD FIX US SOME *LUNCH.*

NO. NO, THANKS. I'M FINE.

ACTUALLY, I WAS WONDERING IF YOU'D LIKE TO HAVE A *COOK-OUT.*

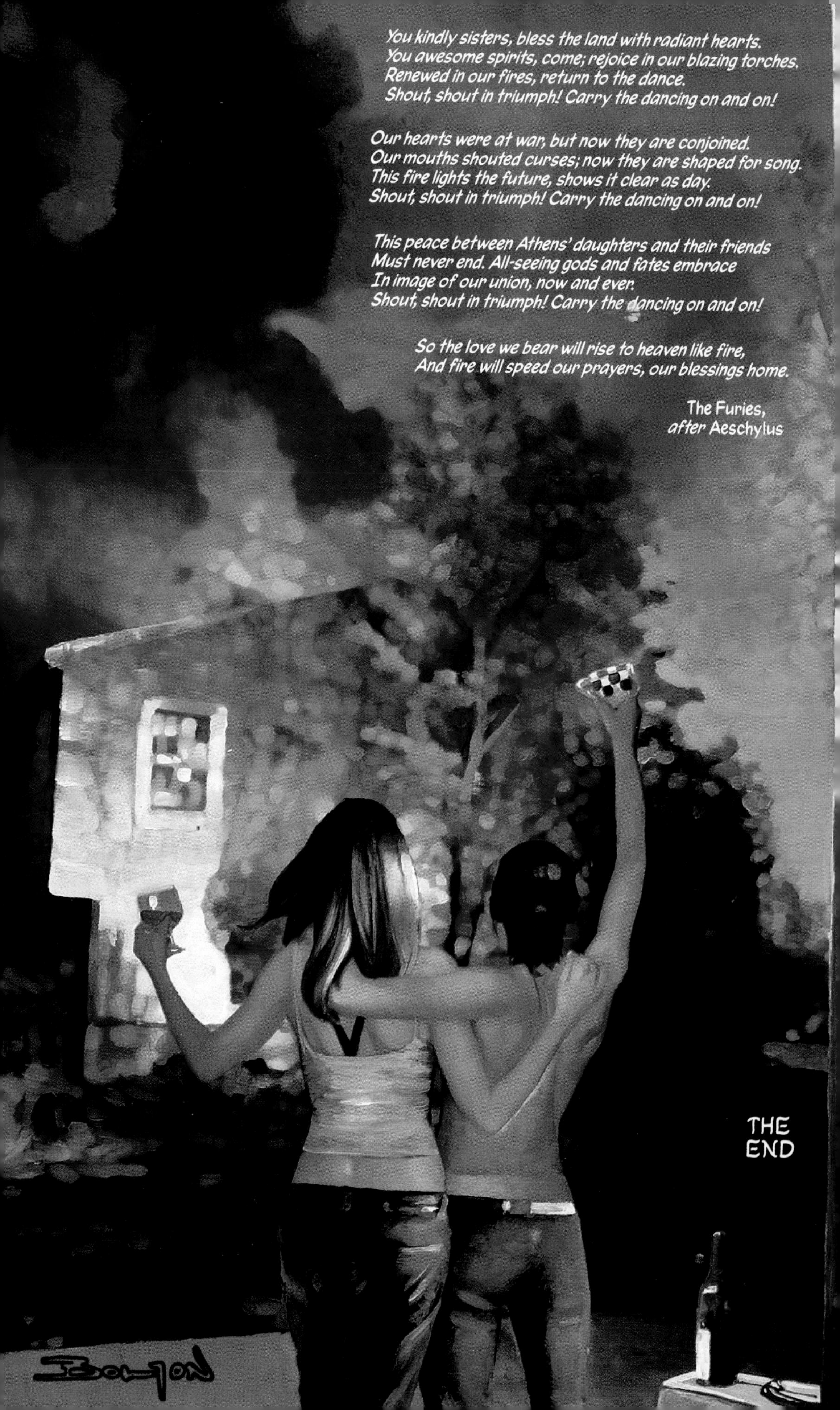
You kindly sisters, bless the land with radiant hearts.
You awesome spirits, come; rejoice in our blazing torches.
Renewed in our fires, return to the dance.
Shout, shout in triumph! Carry the dancing on and on!
Our hearts were at war, but now they are conjoined.
Our mouths shouted curses; now they are shaped for song.
This fire lights the future, shows it clear as day.
Shout, shout in triumph! Carry the dancing on and on!
This peace between Athens' daughters and their friends
Must never end. All-seeing gods and fates embrace
In image of our union, now and ever.
Shout, shout in triumph! Carry the dancing on and on!
So the love we bear will rise to heaven like fire,
And fire will speed our prayers, our blessings home.
The Furies,
after Aeschylus
THE END